# SOMETIMES BONE

Clayton Lindemuth

Hardgrave Enterprises
SAINT CHARLES, MISSOURI

Clayton Lindemuth/Hardgrave Enterprises
218 Keith Drive
Saint Charles, MO 63301
www.claytonlindemuth.com

Publisher's Note: This is a work of fiction. Names, characters, places, and incidents are a product of the author's imagination. Locales and public names are sometimes used for atmospheric purposes. Any resemblance to actual people, living or dead, or to businesses, companies, events, institutions, or locales is completely coincidental.

SOMETIMES BONE / Clayton Lindemuth — 1st ed.
ISBN 9781973572978

FOR CHET, ONE OF THE GOOD GUYS.

I WILL ALSO SEND WILD BEASTS AMONG YOU, WHICH SHALL ROB YOU OF YOUR CHILDREN, AND DESTROY YOUR CATTLE, AND MAKE YOU FEW IN NUMBER; AND YOUR HIGHWAYS SHALL BE DESOLATE.

—LEVITICUS 26:22

# Chapter One

I brace against the ground with my left hand and drag my right arm across my mouth. Spit bile from the back of my throat to the pool of vomit below my face. My knees press into wet dirt. The sun burns my neck, my back, and the sweet humidity from yesterday's thunderstorm mingles with the stench of the rotted child a few feet from my hands. I spit again, swallow bile. Stand and turn to the body of my runt son.

Henry.

I regard the gravity of it: the completeness of a corpse.

My lungs barely fill with each breath; still, I pull a carved cherry pipe from my breast pocket, rap it to my boot, and fill the bowl with leaf. I strike a match and hold the flame to the bowl, mindful of Sheriff Brooks' eyes upon me.

"Not a damn track," Brooks says, "save these dog prints."

I study Henry's face, mostly shredded by fangs. The dog was here after rain softened the ground. Tracks lead across the field and of the thousand possible places he could have come from, the trail suggests that after dining on my frailest son, the dog loped toward the Hardgrave place.

Tobacco smoke and stomach acid burn my throat. The bite is harsh but the tobacco fortifies. I know my mind. I stare at Henry resting on his back, flies circling the oval that used to bear his countenance.

The surrounding dirt is pocked with a jagged mess of paw prints. I stare toward Hardgrave's until Sheriff Brooks looks that way.

"You need anything else?"

"No, Mister McClellan. Plain enough he was beat to death. There's nothing left on the ground to study. I'll have Doc look the body over, just same."

Holding my breath, I slip my arms beneath Henry's back and shoulders and lift him. His head falls back where his neck was cut. Air escapes. I clench my teeth and twist back.

"I'm truly sorry," Brooks says.

"Get the hell out of here."

Long past rigor, Henry is limp. I carry him across the field toward my house and marvel that in all the searching, neither I nor the others crossed the field between my house and Hardgrave's. Everyone agreed the boy had wandered off with mischief in mind, and my foreman Eddie suspected Henry had run off for real, as I did fifty years ago to join the Union.

But Henry never had that kind of grit.

No one searched until he was gone two days, and it took two more to locate him—half way to Hardgrave's house.

I keep my face pointed toward the lake breeze and try to outpace stink that seems to have a lead on me. Carrying my youngest is brutal work.

I arrive at my house. Brooks has already driven the team around.

••

"Mister McClellan, I got to take him into Walnut."

"He deserved to come home first."

I land Henry on the wagon bed. Study the boy's sunken sockets; take in his torn flesh. Behold his crushed cheek, battered brow, sliced throat. I suck in the stench of my dead flesh and blood one last time.

"Who would do this?"

"You'll find him, Mister McClellan," Brooks says. "You'll find him."

"When I do—"

"Best you don't say no more. Best you don't."

Brooks circles to the front and climbs to the seat. "Hiyah!"

I watch my son judder on the wagon until dust and distance cloud him. Enter the house and sit at a writing desk.

Listen to the silence.

Maybe I'll bring in a woman. Maybe one from the house in Dubois—have a hen clucking around. I slump into the chair, surprised by sentiment. Bring a woman and set her to work cleaning and doing laundry. A woman's good for three things, maybe four, but lately I only get use of the primary.

No. I'll pursue to the course I set.

Mame Gainer, from Pittsburgh—a madam of considerable skill who has proven too wily for ordinary negotiations. She demands a contract, total control over all my cat houses, and a salary— regardless of the fruit of her efforts—of twenty thousand per annum. Now that the situation with Henry is resolved will make an alternate proposal.

Henry's odor saturates my sleeves, my chest. I gag at the wash basin. Nothing comes. Gargle water and rinse my mouth, strip my shirt, dump pipe and tobacco on the table and keep the matches. Outside at the porch edge I light my shirt sleeve. Toss it to the

••

grass and watch flames lick the cloth. Gray smoke drifts close to the ground. I remove my undershirt and cast it to the fire.

Upstairs, I dress in a suit. I've spent two days in farm clothes; the time has arrived to get about business.

I have the houses to run. A madam to woo. Grain to purchase. Big plans in Oil City.

And I must assign blame.



I drive a Saxon Six, a smoke-farting touring car with a six-cylinder engine. The newspaper advertisement claimed the manufacturer achieved twenty-five point nine miles per gallon of gasoline over a seventy-thousand-mile test. Further, the motor car averaged a hundred and seventy-five miles per quart of oil.

My experience has been different, but I have arranged for Eddie's brother to serve as my car man. Meanwhile I make do. Normally the drive to Walnut is pleasant; today thoughts claw their presence into my mind.

I arrive in Dubois late in the afternoon. Like my other houses, I leave this one cracked and peeling. It is located beyond the bars in a neighborhood populated with business proprietors who cater to men's baser desires. I pay a stipend, usually tail but sometimes cash, to each police chief in whose jurisdiction I operate. My cat houses draw little unwelcome attention and are seldom visited by evangelists or worse, progressives, except in the anonymity of night when they arrive not to rail against whoredom, but to purchase it.

I sit in the Saxon with the engine running and the clutch disengaged, my foot on the brake. Upstairs a curtain moves—Ursula—a pendulum-busted and ambitious whore who speaks her second language English better than most of the men she uses it

··

upon. I think of my dead son and her powdered skin and perfumed hair and my stomach hesitates on the edge of violence.

My younger son is dead. I've one left, globe-trotting Mitch.

Bernadine meets me at the door. "Word on Henry?"

I pass her, turn left at the parlor and enter the anteroom she uses as an office. Ursula perches at the top of the stairwell then jiggles to the lower floor, flesh lopping against her corset like waves on a steep bank. She joins Bernadine at the door.

I study the ledger.

"Anything on Henry's whereabouts?" Ursula says.

"I'm here to collect."

Bernadine enters the office and kneels at a floor safe. "I don't see why you don't use the local bank." She aligns numbers on the knob. "Just as good as the one in Walnut." She passes to me a thin handful of paper money.

"Light for two nights," I say.

"That's every bit of it."

I count fifteen dollars and compare the revenue to the names and services recorded on the ledger—an operational necessity I learned from an early conversation with Mame Gainer.

"You ever wonder what them boys would do if they knew you kept track of their likes?" Bernadine says.

Ursula, standing behind Bernadine, fetches my eye. Bernadine turns as well and Ursula smiles as if she had nothing to say to begin with.

"What's with McCoy only coming in for a gum rooting?" I flip pages deeper into history. "Each Tuesday... nothing but a slob. With you, Ursula."

"It's his mother. She's with Christian Temperence."

"She services his other wants?"

"He feels guilt."

I study the wall while I collect my thoughts.

**

"It's the truth," Bernadine says. "The boy's saving himself."

"Ursula. Run upstairs."

The corner of her mouth twitches.

I close the door. Bernadine retreats. I fan the fifteen paper dollars and place them on the desk, then eye Bernadine until she looks away. Clench my right hand. Relax it. I press fingers to the bridge of my nose, yet lack the clarity I desire. I stack the bills, tuck them to my wallet.

"Don't leave." I open the door.

"Yeah, well I ain't going nowhere. And before you dip your wick—the roof's leaking again. And Harvey's no roofer."

I close the door on her.


Ursula reclines against a stack of pillows, legs apart, fingers woven across her midsection. Several undone buttons leave the top corners of her blouse folded open, revealing mounds of blue-veined flesh behind a corset straining mightily to withstand the bounty.

I sit at the edge of the bed. Inhale a measure of air and at the right moment, release it.

She sits upright. "What is it?"

"Found Henry."

I extract my pipe and fill it. Inhale smoke and lean forward, one hand on my knee. She's silent, her face painted with dread. "There in a field," I say. "His head beat in."

Ursula spins her legs over the mattress edge and shifts beside me. "God's mercy."

"I only said so because you asked. I come up here..."

"Anything you need, Mister McClellan." She rests her hand on my shoulder.

I remove it. "You had something on your mind, downstairs."

••

Ursula crawls behind me and her fingers work the stiffness in my shoulders. "There's something—this isn't an appropriate time, but I'd never forgive myself for keeping quiet."

I observe her reflection in the dresser mirror.

"The book you checked is not complete."

"I know. How many?"

"Six I'm aware of, from Friday. Then I counted every man who entered the house on Saturday and there were twenty-two. The book says fourteen."

"Why'd you think to count?"

"Bernadine asked me to mind the parlor on Friday. She stepped out."

"Where to?"

"An errand, she said."

"Say who she was seeing?"

Ursula shakes her head. "I found Billy Kroh wasn't in the book, though he was with Linda an hour before. I thought of telling Bernadine, but thought again. I read all the names and discovered another five not on the list."

"Why'd Bernie pick you?"

"Aunt Flo."

I release a long blast of smoke and look at Ursula's reflection.

"But she's gone... Aunt Flo."

"Don't you girls usually polish knobs when your aunt visits?"

"There's only so many need polishing, and none take more than a few minutes."

"Uh huh." I glance over Ursula's belongings. A few European baubles on doilies, maybe frilly things in the closet and bureau. I stand. "Gather your things—"

"I—"

I raise my hand. "Hours' time Bernie's room will be empty. I'll give you the same terms I gave her."

∙∙

"You're giving her an hour?"

I consider. "You're right."

In the parlor Bernadine sits at the desk with a deck of cards arranged in a game of solitaire.

"Local bank where you keep what you skim from me?"

"That's a lie," she says. "I been honest by you."

I head down the hall toward her room.

"What are you doing?" Bernadine shuffles behind, tugs my elbow and I belt her. She's on the floor looking up, hand on her jaw, insolence snarled up in her nose and eyes.

I try the knob at the last door. "Unlock it."

"You got no right going through my effects."

"Open it."

"No."

I clasp her by the neck and pin her to the wall. Fish between trussed mounds and come out with a key. I snap the necklace chain and release her. Bernadine sinks like I ripped out her spine.

"I got six cathouses, Bernie. You have more girls than any the rest and there's more screwing going on here than anywhere. Give me fifteen dollars and I'm fucked too. But I don't get fucked, Bernadine."

"I turn over every cent to you."

I unlock the door and enter. Lift an ostrich-plumed hat, step to the hall and spin it to her. "Put it on." Empty each drawer of a maple bureau; open the closet and cast articles to the floor. Strip the bed and flip the mattress.

"What's this, Bernie?" On the side of the mattress that had been pressed to the wall is a two-finger slit. I withdraw a fold of bills.

"What's this? Two, three hundred?"

Bernadine sits with crossed legs, face salty and shiny.

••

"Leave now and don't come back."

A shoeshine boy snaps his cloth and watches my legs as I exit the Saxon. I'm parked in front of Miller's, the barber, in the legitimate business district. The boy is Marshall Brady, a chap with moxie and presented intelligence. Under my instruction he could become somebody.

"That's a lot of scuffs, Mister McClellan. C'mon here for twenty-cent you'll be strutting like a game cock."

"I am a game cock, Marshall. Maybe you'd ought to learn another line."

"You got better, tell it."

"Tell it? I'm a businessman. I'll sell it."

"What for?"

"Free shine."

The boy squints. "I dunno. My line works 'most every time."

"Because it arouses pity. My line will make a man truly desire what you sell, an infinite improvement. It's a business deal, see? I sell you the line, you increase your business and cover the cost of purchasing the line. The rest is profit."

"But my line fetches any man needs a shine as it is."

"You know why?"

"Cause quinny likes shiny boots and men like quinny. But I don't need your line as much as I need the twenty cents I'd give up to get it."

"I see. But what if my line would allow you to charge twenty-five, even thirty cents?"

"Give me the line and I'll decide if it's worth a shine."

I grasp the boy's shoulder and kneel until he is eye-level. "Here's what I'm thinking, boy. You got a sharp mind, and good instincts. I'll give you the line free of charge. Maybe one day when I have an

**⁑**

errand, you'll be interested in taking your business to a higher plane of profitability?"

"Yes sir, Mister McClellan. Yes sir."

I sit on the bench outside the barbershop window.

"What's the line, Mister McClellan?"

I place my hands on my knees and lean. Look left and right—and notice farther down the road, a gleaming Willys Knight sedan parked at the curb. Unless some new dandy's rolled into town, banker Thurston Leicester is in the vicinity. I twist, spot him in the barber shop. Miller brushes Thurston's suit jacket as the banker retrieves a note from his billfold.

"The line, Mister McClellan?"

I give Marshall twenty cents. "You do the best shine you can, and we'll see if it lives up to the line."

Marshall sighs. With his brush he raps my sole—harder than usual—and sets about cleaning dirt from the heel.

"How's your schoolwork holding up?"

Marshall shrugs.

"Your pap don't mind you playing hooky all the time?"

"He set me up with this shine kit."

"Whole family business-minded."

Thurston Leicester stands at the step. "If it isn't Jonah McClellan."

Marshall finishes his brushwork, dabs his bare fingers in polish and massages the wax into shoe leather.

"I been after that girl of yours up the house," Leicester says. "Struck me the other day I work with every businessman in town. Pay top interest, charge the least. But I've never sat across a desk of paper with the great Jonah McClellan."

I hold Thurston's look as I reach to Marshall, touch his shoulder. "Marshall, listen. If I took a bushel of corn to the granary and they gave me a receipt, that'd be as good as money. I'd be able

••

to give it to the barber if a haircut cost a bushel of corn, wouldn't I?"

"Suppose so, yes sir."

Thurston looks at the boy, then me.

"Marshall, son, what do you think would happen if the folks at the granary said, 'People pass our notes like money. Why don't we write up a bunch of extra receipts, and lend them out at interest?"

"You mean without having the corn?"

"That's right," I say.

Thurston checks his pocket watch.

"That'd be wrong," Marshall says.

"Why, son?"

"It's just like musical chairs, 'cept the last man wouldn't get no corn."

"That's good thinking, Marshall. I might give you another line. What do you think, Thurston? Got any ideas on that?"

"Talk like that causes bank runs."

I stand. "Marshall, here's lesson number two. Never put your money in a bank, or trust a man who makes his living from numbers alone. They're thieves. I'd call them lazy, but some are damn industrious. Anything you want to add, Thurston?"

Thurston Leicester steps closer. "There's two ways of putting down a bank run, McClellan. One involves bringing in more money. The other, guns. You think you suck first tit, got Sheriff Brooks and your man, Eddie. You got the town sewed up." Thurston shakes his head and steps backward. He turns toward his car. "You keep thinking. Good day."

I sit. "That lesson make sense, son?"

"Yes sir." Marshall snaps his rag one last time. "Lookit that. That shine's worth three lines."

I squeeze his shoulder. "Indeed. But I only brought the one. You ready?"

••

Marshall tips closer.

I whisper.

Marshall's mouth draws into a wide smile. His eyes gleam sunlight. He mouths the words and I follow each one on his lips. Marshall finds his voice. "Make your boots shine like snot on a glass doorknob." Marshall beams. "Like snot dripping on a glass doorknob. A glass doorknob covered in snot."

"Endless possibilities, that glass and snot."

"Yes sir!"

"Use that line right, you can charge any price you want."


Five hired men quarter in a bunkhouse fifty yards from the main house. Currently I employ six at the farm, including my jack-of-all-trades foreman, Eddie Bonter, a man whose time at the Pittsburgh state penitentiary, and subsequent reputation with Pittsburgh law enforcement, keeps him at the fringes. Capable of physical work and quiet work, he has proven discretion and flat nerves.

Today I will test him.

I stand at the bunk house entry. Eddie sits at a table at the far end with Jerome, a young fellow who has eschewed education in favor of permanently tilling another man's fields, harvesting another man's corn.

The world needs such men.

Eddie looks at me and breaks off his sentence. He slaps Jerome on the shoulder and the younger man exits through the back door, his head low with a sidelong glance.

I note the thud of my heels on the sodden floor planks. The rot. Pause and look outside at Jerome, barely discernible through dirt-filmed glass.

"I'm amazed that men can live in conditions like this—free men—and not want to look out clean windows."

••

Eddie doesn't live with the men he oversees, but often spends his final minutes of the day chatting with them. He stands as I arrive at the table.

"Ain't a whole lotta ambition left for cleaning glass after a twelver in the fields."

"Much as you nanny after these boy-men, you might share with them that a man can bootstrap himself out of poor straights only by expecting more of himself, and that starts with cleaning the fucking windows."

Eddie exhales. "Sure, Mister McClellan. I'll get after it. You come about the windows?"

"You look like a beat dog."

"I am a beat dog."

"Well, I'm going to Pittsburgh tomorrow. Back the day after."

Eddie nods. "Running two sites tomorrow. Expect twenty gallon. That's what you wanted, right?"

"Twenty is fine. Don't let Donovan skip the doubler. If I get less than twenty, I'll charge more."

Eddie thumps the table with his thumb.

At the door I pause. "Bernadine's leaving town."

"What?"

"What I said."

Eddie stands. "Where—another your houses?"

"Not one of my houses."

"She gone yet?"

"I give her an hour—two hours ago."

"You give her? You run her off?"

"She's a thief, Eddie. Shake her hand you got to count your fingers. Your pecker if you poke her."

Eddie wipes his brow. He faces the wall and sits on the chair like it's a raft adrift.

••

"I left her with her face and her wits. Twenty years ago I'd have left her dead." I turn part way out the door. "You was soft on her and I wanted you to know I did right by her, though she didn't do right by me. And there's plenty of whores to get soft on. Plenty better'n Bernadine."

Eddie faces me.

I say, "Two weeks back you said something about your brother?"

"He'll be along tomorrow's train."

"Skilled with motorcars?"

"He'll be ready to work."

"Younger brother?"

A nod.

"What's got him running up here, so far from the action?"

"I don't know, Mister McClellan."

I open the door, step to the landing, swat a moth that alights with the noise.

Eddie calls after me. "Brubaker found another fire pit."

"I'll be interested to see it."

"Like any other. Ground's falling in all over the place."

"A strange geologic phenomenon."

I pass the charred remains of my shirt along the way toward my house. Standing on the porch, I look to the left through a neck of hemlock bordering my lawn and Hardgrave's wheat fields. Almost invisible through the trees stands the Hardgrave house.

Inside I select a .500 Weatherby from the cabinet in the main room.

••

# Chapter Two

"Not with my girls outside." Grace stood at the register and watched the man's eyes lift from her breast to her face. He stared at her bruised eye. "Not with my girls watching us haggle."

After his proposition, she'd spent five minutes wandering the store, assembling her words, though she knew what they would be the moment he made clear his meaning. The baking goods smelled sweet and as she passed row after row of jarred corn and potatoes and fruits, her empty stomach clenched.

Two hours before she'd asked the clerk, a middle-aged man with leather skin and pomade-slick hair, if she could have work. "We ain't hiring." But he judged the purple-gold ring around her eye and said, "Maybe there's something else you could do."

"What do you mean?"

His smile broadened; his brow dropped.

"For money?"

"Food."

"You mark it up double."

"Money, then. I don't care what you spend it on."

She'd flushed—but his suggestion hadn't been her first contact with the thought.

She'd gone outside and smelled autumn, and thought she was hungry enough to eat leaves. At home the cupboards were empty. Forrest had stolen her last pennies and beaten her when she had no more.

Leaving her daughters on the sidewalk bench, she'd walked to the next store, a five-and-dime that offered a little of everything, most of it cheap but with some kitschy and overpriced items interspersed, like that lamp... essentially a sculpture of a naked man and woman embracing around a street light post... The tag said three dollars... this in a store that had coils of hemp rope three feet from a stack of denim trousers.

"Work?"

The attendant had glanced at Grace's clothes and face, and shook her head.

On the sidewalk again, she'd looked back at Elizabeth and Hannah. She entered the next store, a fabric and sewing place called The Nimble Thimble. She passed table after table of sturdy cloth wound around flat cardboard tubes, each perfectly arranged to exhibit a bolt of color. The walls displayed sewing supplies, threads, needles, yarns, buttons. Brand new Singers aligned on the back wall, shiny and elegant.

"Do you have work?" she said at the register, and the blue-haired woman gazed over reading glasses, moved her face sideways, once.

Then the next and the next. Grace had spent an hour canvassing the street, stopping at each entrance, looking over her shoulder to her girls before entering. Each rejection seemed a harsher judge than the last. Her strength waned. The last two days, she'd divvied up the remaining food between Elizabeth and Hannah, foregoing her own sparrow's portion.

●●

She reached the last "no" and looked to her daughters like a condemned woman about to cross a threshold. She stared into the picture window beyond, and the middle-aged man with light brown skin and greasy hair. If she hadn't already asked every shop master on the street and been rejected, she might have raised an indignant defense of her virtue—but what was virtue, if not feeding her girls?

She'd entered the grocery and found a sack of flour and a bottle of molasses, all she could afford, and standing at the register looked beyond the man, through the window. Elizabeth, her oldest girl, draped her arms over Hannah, and returned Grace's stare.

Grace dug coins from her pocket. "Not while my girls are outside. You'll be here a while?"

The man placed her items in a paper bag. Grace met his yellow eyes.

"A while."

His smile revealed a chasm where his front teeth should have been. His features suggested his ancestry included peoples of every continent.

He was ugly, but she tingled.

"Come on back." He took her coins. "It's slow 'til three."


New York had been nothing but misery. If her brother in Pennsylvania didn't welcome her she'd create her welcome elsewhere, but at least she would know her surroundings. She would create her welcome—for her girls.

Grace crossed the exit threshold with her brown grocery bag in the crook of her arm.

"Mommy!" Elizabeth cried.

"Come," Grace said. "I'll make you pancakes."

They walked and Grace considered her past, how so many events seemed inevitable, and suffering the only possible

\*\*

conclusion. Her problems today sprouted from seeds planted in Walnut, Pennsylvania.

Her rooms were on the third level; she followed Hannah and Elizabeth up rickety stairs.

Grace unlocked the door, steeled herself against the smell of cigarette smoke and feet, and entered.

Forrest stretched across a battered French sofa, his upper body curled into the rounded end, an empty whiskey bottle stuffed between his thighs. He snored, his elbow supported on the sloping armrest, his arm hanging in a delicate, feminine arc.

Grace turned to her girls. Holding her finger over her lip, she ushered the girls to their room and sat them on their bed.

"Mommy has to go back to the store. I want you to be very quiet, and keep the door locked until I come home."

Hannah registered her mother's look and reflected wrinkled brows back to her.

"Very quiet," Grace said. "Lock the door."

Hannah nodded. Grace backed from the room. Forrest choked on a snore. She froze until his breathing resumed, then glided to the door. As she hurried down the steps defiance welled within her. He hadn't done anything to spare her this desperate act. He hadn't stopped at every shop in a square mile, asking for work. No— because he had skills and a sheepskin diploma, and if he asked for work he'd get it. But he'd rather play cards.

Grace retraced the footsteps she'd taken a few minutes before with her daughters. Her feet now carried her toward repugnance and evil. To feed her daughters. To circle back and confront her miseries at their headwaters. Home.

She considered how the clerk's legs would feel against hers. She pondered the likelihood of him being a clean man, given his stubble and the way his breath reached across the cash register to slug her in the face. At the landing she stopped, looked outside.

\*\*

She reached to the bottom of her handbag and felt the reassuring checker grip of a twenty-two-caliber pistol.

Her stomach constricted. Sweat dampened her side. She lowered her eyes and followed the sidewalk.

The clerk stood behind the counter, unmoved since she'd departed with food for her girls. One corner of his mouth lifted.

"Just this one time," Grace said.

"Bully." The merchant hustled around the counter, closed the door and flipped the sign. He clutched her wrist and towed her toward a room lit only by a tired yellow bulb. Grace scuffed her heels, thumped the scarred plank floor but that only increased his urgency. He closed the door behind them and she gathered in her surroundings, a cot along an unfinished brick wall, a wooden desk with a split side panel and mold darkening the base.

She swallowed. "Money first."

He extracted a billfold and placed it on the desktop. "Money when you earn it."

"Show me. That you have any at all."

He split the leather folds and stroked the crisp edges of a stack of bills. "More'n enough to prod your skinny ass."

"Five dollars. Pull out five dollars."

He snapped five singles out one by one and stacked them. "Good luck earning all five."

"My price is five. It's up to you whether you enjoy it."

He looked at the ceiling, twelve feet above. "Just keep the noise down."

He led her by the wrist to the cot and pushed her shoulders downward. She buckled, sat at the edge. His hand cupped her chin and she looked up at his face, his wide nostrils, his pocked complexion harshened by the bulb overhead. He'd positioned her here, below the light, on purpose. His other hand worked his trousers.

∙∙

"That's right. You know what to do with that."

"Wait," she said. "What's your name?"

"Turk."

She closed her eyes.

The stench was like entering a closed room with a hundred unwashed travelers, or a barn with stalls that had never been cleaned. Urine. Turk's flaccid form pressed against her clamped mouth, back and forth, growing firmer with each pass. He made guttural noises. "Open up, take it."

Grace squeezed her eyelids until colors tinged her field of vision. She saw Hannah, standing on her knees on the bench, smiling. Elizabeth, precocious, watching over her. Grace's eyes swam. Turk grabbed the back of her head and plunged himself deep against her throat. She gagged, breathed through her nose, tickled with foul hair. Turk jerked her hair—

Rapping sounded on the shop door out front.

"Shit!"

The window pane rattled. Again, harder than before.

Turk covered her ears with his hands and smashed his stomach to her face. She gasped with each retraction and heard only her own gags. She retched with each strike. He groaned and slammed her head to his convulsing belly.

He tossed her away.

A fist pounded the store entrance door with a harsh drumbeat that grew more frenetic with each second.

Grace coughed and spat on the plank floor.

"In the closet!" Turk pointed to a door partly obstructed by crates and a folded tarp.

Grace passed the desk and stepped around the crates. She pushed aside a pair of broom handles and entered the closet. The door couldn't possibly close.

••

"Hunker down," Turk whispered. "Not a peep!" He buttoned his trousers, left his shirt untucked. "Or I'll beat you."

Turk turned off the light and left the back room.

Darkness swallowed Grace. Her stomach turned. She inhaled deep the musty moldy air and wiped the side of her mouth. Her stomach rolled like she'd eaten rotten worms. She needed to clear her throat but didn't want to invite Turk's return. She bowed her head. Five dollars would purchase food or fare. She'd beg the rest. She'd get home.

"Coming, I'm coming," Turk said. His boots made a gritty sound on the plank floor. He'd left the door cracked open and a plane of light cut the room.

His billfold...

Too busy wiping tears from her eyes, she hadn't seen him take his wallet from the desktop. He could have swiped it when he turned to the door. She hadn't looked when he'd hurried her to the closet.

The rapping continued. Outside the storage room, Turk yelled, "A minute!"

Grace grabbed the jamb, tapped along the floor for the crate and when her toe came against it, eased around to the desk. She dragged fingertips across the top until they touched leather, then opened the fold and secreted the wad of bills into her wraps. The worn paper felt like silk against her breast. How could a clerk have so much money?

Grace turned in a circle and halted facing the door.

Turk's footsteps ceased. The rapping died. The main door screeched open.

"You sleeping again! I said—I remember the day—I said I catch you sleeping you'd be gone!"

"Is this a sleeping face?"

••

Grace returned to the desk and raked the top for the five dollars Turk had left outside his billfold. She slipped it into her pocket.

"You wasn't my own brother's son I'd throw your ass in the dirt."

How to escape?

Grace turned and in the darkness discerned a thin outline of light around another door—on an outside wall.

She eased around the crates and pressed her hand against the door. Traced the outline with her fingertips and finding the handle, twisted. The knob was frozen. She pushed and the door gave as if the wood was dry-rotted and weary. Shouldering it would give her away, but she'd be in the back alley, within steps of escape.

She returned to the cot and grabbed her handbag.

Voices came from the shop. The owner's tenor grew pitched as he approached the back office.

Grace stopped breathing.

Turk would be insane to confess she was a whore. He'd call her a thief; he'd say she must have slipped into the office while he stocked shelves. He'd lie—

She threw her shoulder against the door. The sound was like a flour sack dropped on an oak table.

The voices stilled.

Grace heaved. The door rejected her.

Shouts. Footsteps.

Light burst upon her. Grace covered her eyes and faced the men, the ogre whose seed was in her stomach, and the man who employed him.

She trembled.

What would become of her daughters with her in prison?

Grace reached into her handbag.

\*\*

# Chapter Three

Hal Hardgrave kneaded his hip with his knuckles and worked around, best he could, to the small of his back.

Rose ladled corn beside a stack of mashed potatoes and a slab of roast. Hal lifted his gaze from her axe-handle ass to the apron straps bow-tied at her back.

Also at the table sat Ian and Angus. Dorothy, his eighteen-year-old visiting niece, examined her fingernails beside the sink.

"Sheriff stopped by while you was in the barn," Rose said. "Found the McClellan boy."

"Where?"

"Field." She nodded in the direction of the McClellan farm.

"Imagine they stomped it, then."

"Imagine."

Rose placed Hal's plate on the table and lifted Ian's, their oldest son's. "Dot, you want to fix a plate for Angus?"

Dorothy pushed from the counter and slid her soles. She lifted Angus's plate and joined Rose by the stove.

Elbows on the table, Hal scratched his crown and blinked exhaustion from his eyes.

"Owww!"

"You—!"

Ian and Angus tangled and pinched. Angus shoved Ian's shoulders, swiped his head.

"Stop!"

Hal twisted to the ruckus and his back seized. He slammed his elbow to the table, held his weight with one arm. Pain froze his lower half.

"Settle your ass!"

Hal swung, knocked Angus and his chair over backward leaving Angus on his back, feet in the air. He rolled and stood. Righted his chair and glared at Hal eye to eye.

Hal pushed hand over hand along the edge of the table until he sat upright.

Ian grinned. Angus punched him.

Rose centered Ian's plate on the plank table. Dorothy reached across and dropped Angus's in place.

"What you boys know about that McClellan affair?" Hal said.

"Nothing," Ian said.

Hal studied Angus. Ian was ten, Angus nine, but the younger had corralled every ounce of Hardgrave troublesomeness and mischievousness in the bloodline—and then some.

"Angus?"

"Nothing."

"You didn't see anything, couple days back?"

"No."

"Angus?"

"No."

Rose placed her plate on the table and sat while Dorothy picked over the food at the oven.

••

"Everyone's food's getting cold, Dot," Rose said.

"You didn't give her but a minute," Hal said. He looked at Dorothy, maybe a hatchet-handle wide. "She needs an extra minute, she wants to add any meat to them bones."

Dorothy sat at the table. Rose lowered her head, peeked from under her brow. "Angus, bow your head for grace. Angus—okay. Lord, we thank you for this bounty. In Jesus' name, Amen."

Hal observed the portions on each plate. "Suspect I'll shoot a deer in the morning. You boys can skin it."

Rose clattered silver. "How'll you drag a buck out the woods, you can't even walk?"

"Leave me worry 'bout it. You hear, Ian? Angus?"

"Yessir," Ian said. "Where'll you go?"

"'Long the lake, below McClellan's. See what's in them woods since he's been taking a mule team so often."

Rose stopped her fork midway to her mouth. "You'll be shot and you know it."

"What you think he's doing, Pap?" Ian said.

Hal shoved potatoes into his mouth. "It ain't what I think. I know damn well. I just thought he had sense to keep it away from here."

"What'll you do?"

Outside, the dog barked.

Hal looked to the window. Late afternoon shadows stretched across the lawn toward the orchard and lake.

A rifle blast shook the windows.

Hal jumped, raked his thighs against the table. "You boys stay put!" He clawed from his seat and followed the wall to the other room, one hand pressed to his back. At the gun cabinet he grabbed a lever-action 30-30. Quick to point, quick to cycle.

"It's Jonah McClellan!" Rose said from the window. "He shot Woodrow Wilson."

∗∗

"Woody!" Angus yelled. His chair barked on the floor.

"I'll shoot him," Hal said. He cracked the lever, eyed brass. Hand on the wall, he arrived at the front door and footed it open.

Across the lot, with his back to Hal and the house, stood the unmistakable seven-foot Jonah McClellan. At his boot lay a crumpled mass of black and brown named Woodrow Wilson.

Hal tucked the stock to his shoulder and steadied the rifle barrel against the porch post. He aligned the sights between Jonah's shoulders and pulled back the hammer.

Jonah turned. Stepped toward the house.

Hal pressed his brow to his arm.

"Your dog ate my son's face," McClellan said. "I can't have that."

Hardgrave touched the trigger. Jonah stepped closer, his rifle loose in one hand, barrel to the ground.

"But there's more to it 'n that," Jonah said. "I think it was your boys left Henry in the field."

"You just stop where you're at. I'll put a hole through you, I swear."

"Men like you swear a lot, Hoot. Maybe if you give the rifle to Angus, he'd have the nerve. Not you." Jonah stopped a dozen paces away.

Hal exhaled, rested more of his weight against the rifle, buttressed by the post.

Jonah stared.

"You can't go around killing—" Hal said. "That was my... property. You can't."

Jonah regarded him. Waved him off and turned.

Hal kept the bead centered on Jonah's upper back. He ground his teeth and brought pressure to his finger.

He pulled the barrel and fired over Jonah's head.

••

Jonah walked another step then turned. He met Hal's eye over the gun sights for a long moment, then resumed toward his house.

"Woody!" Angus threw open the door behind Hal, banged into his leg by the post and sprinted to the fallen dog. He plunged to his knees and took Woodrow Wilson's muzzle in his hands.

Feet shuffled inside the house behind Hal. He felt Rose, Dot, and Ian's judging eyes on his back.

Angus jumped, raced in front of the giant Jonah, forcing him to stop. Angus kicked dirt to his feet.

Jonah batted Angus aside but the boy bounced from the ground and leaped back in front of him. He lashed with his arms. Jonah swung his rifle barrel and clubbed Angus at the neck. The boy fell and Jonah turned toward Hal. He lined the barrel to Angus's face and the two of them glared and Hal shook his head at the mystery of his son.

Jonah waited a moment, swung the rifle barrel away, over his shoulder, and walked the long lane to the road.

Hal placed the rifle stock on the porch, leaned forward. The pressure in his back eased.

"What'd he say?" Rose said. "Did he say anything else?"

"Go fetch Angus back to the house."

"He's getting up."

Hal lurched to the door jamb, turned the corner and sat on a thinly upholstered chair. "Bring my plate."

"You need a hand?" Ian said.

"Can't move. Locked up again."

"You want me to walk on your back?"

"Just reach me my damn plate!"

Rose arrived with the plate and Hal rested it on his lap.

Angus's footsteps sounded on the porch. He stood in the entry with blood on his pants and hands, a long wash of it below his nose and across his mouth. Angus stared at Hal.

\*\*

"Why'd he call you Hoot?"

Hal clenched his fist. "Go clean off that blood."

Hal watched Angus enter the kitchen. Where the boy got his moxie, he didn't know, but it guaranteed life would one day kick the shit out of him. Yessir, and that'd be a fight worth watching because Angus would probably give as much as he got. Hal scratched the back of his neck.

Gumption like that showing up in Angus was like Holstein coming out a pair of Jerseys.

••

# Chapter Four

Grace shouldered against the door and the men advanced. Hand still inside her bag, she released the pistol.

Turk seized her arm as he might take a thin branch he'd break over his knee. His uncle stood with crossed arms and smugness oozing under knit brows.

Turk's eyes narrowed. His jaw was set. Grace had expected it—he would lie.

"I know you like it with other men, Turk, but not the both of you at one time," Grace said. "It'll cost double for both of you."

"Lying bitch!" Turk said. "She's a crazy thief."

Turk's uncle chewed an unlit cigar sideways like a cow works cud. He studied the rumpled cot.

"You want evidence?" Grace said. She pulled at the cloth at her breast, marked with dribble.

Turk wrenched her arm.

His uncle said, "Let her go."

Turk eased, but didn't release his grip. Grace yanked away. She pressed backward against the door and flattened her dress. She forced herself not to look at Turk's empty wallet. "Our business is done," she said, and stepped past Turk.

"Hold it," his uncle said. "Turk—get out of here."

"But—"

"Out."

Turk pushed Grace aside and left the door open.

"What's your name?"

Grace studied the store owner's face, the ruddy blush of skin recently scraped by a razor. The perfectly balanced fold of his bow tie suggested he was patient to a single point and not beyond. His face reddened as he studied her dress, and lingered several seconds on her ankles.

"He mount you back here?"

"Just my face." Grace held his gaze. "I had to feed my girls."

His expression gave away nothing. "Did you earn enough from him to fulfill your purpose?"

"My girls will eat."

"You don't come here no more."

She shuffled past. The store owner closed the door and followed her between aisles of food. She raised her hand to touch the clump of paper money in her wraps—but dropped her arm to her side.

Turk watched from behind the counter. His eyes flashed to the back office.

Grace palmed the door open. An inbound man and woman parted; Grace cut between them. She strode over the sidewalk. In moments Turk would discover his empty wallet. She stopped at an alley—a shortcut she rarely used. Tall buildings blocked the sun. The air was damp. Beggars and drunks lurked in the narrow recess. She thought of the pistol in her bag.

"Hey!"

She whirled. Turk barreled out the shop door and slipped. Regaining his feet, he snarled and labored after her.

••

Grace ran down the alley. Each step carried her deeper into shadows and closer to the edge of the corner building, where another alley intersected at a right angle.

She turned the corner and flattened a man with a bottle.

"Wha—"

Glass shattered.

"That man—help!" She rolled away and leaped toward the light at the end of the alley, then stopped. "I'm sorry. Help me—there's a man after me."

The gray-whiskered man held her look.

Turk's boots slapped the alley bricks with a steady, rapid rhythm.

"Thief!" Turk cried, already at the corner.

So close! Grace turned and Turk lunged—where was the old man?

Turk flew forward as if launched; arms cast wide, feet kicking. He landed in broken glass and shrieked.

Grace rushed to the end of the alley and stopped short of the sidewalk. She looked to her right and the storeowner was nowhere in the oncoming faces. Turk's curses chased her from the alley.

Grace joined the sidewalk traffic. She felt the groping eyes of passing men as if the bulge of money was a third breast. She cradled her handbag at her bosom. Adopting the gait of a late-afternoon stroller, she turned into the first store that presented, circled around the entry and watched the street through the glass. Her stomach was queasy; the sudden stillness left her with vertigo.

"Hmm. Can I... Lost, miss?"

A monocled man with white hair, stripped of his suit jacket down to his vest and tie, waited beside her. Behind him—tuxedos, tall hats, hoop skirts. Grace studied the merchant, focused on a pocket watch left partly exposed in its tiny compartment; her eyes followed the swoop of the silver chain to a button hole.

••

She searched his face. "I was faint." She averted her eyes. "I needed a moment out of the heat..."

"Sun's almost down. What heat?"

"I'm a little faint. I'll just be a moment."

The man glanced beyond her. "Shift over a little?" Without touching her, he guided her against a wall where dinner jackets obscured her view of the street—and the street's view of her. "Thank you. Just a moment," she said, and fell onto a chair that would hide her from any customers who wandered inside.

"Please sit until you feel refreshed." He backed away.

Grace inhaled. Released. She pressed her hand to the mound at her breast and shifted it lower.

She'd crossed the line. Two lines. Prostitution, thievery. The same threat had encouraged both acts—she had no alternative. She could starve for the sake of principles, but she couldn't watch her girls starve for them. She would go home to Walnut and start setting things right. She pressed her hands to her eyes. Her precious girls were locked safely in their room.

The monocled man returned, his face anxious to show even a wretched whore kindness. But he stood with his small hands perched like wary birds on his hips, and after leaning close to study her, leaned back and widened his chest.

"Are you quite well?"

"Better, now." Grace looked at his polished shoes.

He noted her stare and dropped his chin, shifted sideways and kicked out each foot in turn. "What?" He lifted his pant leg. "What do you see?"

"I was admiring your shoes."

"Oh, yes. Of course." He smiled, tilted his head. Straightened it. "Nevertheless."

"Nevertheless," she said. "Of course nevertheless. I was just feeling refreshed. I'll be on my way."

••

"Do come again."

Grace crossed the threshold and stood on the last step, six inches higher than the pedestrians. She looked right and left for Turk or his uncle, then turned to the monocled man. "Thank you for your kindness."

He smiled and closed his eyes.

She hurried down the sidewalk and after a hundred paces, shuffled around a corner, peered behind her again, and stepped into a narrow entrance. Grace climbed the steps on her tiptoes and slowed as she reached her landing. With luck Forrest would still be asleep.

Grace carefully inserted the key and eased open the door.

Hannah sat on the sofa where Forrest had been asleep. She sat with her hands locked between her knees, shoulders drawn tight to her neck. Eyes bright like gaslights, silent mouth pursed.

Grace entered. A chill passed from her neck to her back.

Hannah looked at the bedroom door.

Grace crashed through it.


Grace clenched the pistol. Her ears pulsed with her heartbeat and memories swirled with the image before her. Forrest scrambled back on the bed and when he reached the wall and could flee no farther, his eyes locked to hers.

Elizabeth sat on the edge of the bed, clothed, staring at the baseboard.

"Come, Elizabeth." Grace held out her left hand and kept the pistol pointed at Forrest with her right.

"It ain't like it looks," he said.

"Shut up."

"She said some things, though."

"I don't want to hear it. I want you to leave."

••

"I bet you do."

Forrest shifted to the side of the bed. He held his hands aloft and Grace recalled seeing him trick a dog by holding one hand high and then clubbing it with his other. Forrest had the same sheen to his eye, the same hesitant poise.

She pointed at his head and he moved his hands as if the pair of them might stop a bullet.

"Go to the other room, Elizabeth."

Elizabeth backed away and stood in the doorway with Hannah.

"You can't do it," he said. His eyes moved to her breast and remained there a moment.

She wanted to cover the lump of money.

Forrest nodded. "Elizabeth said you had a long talk with the clerk down at the grocery. That be Turk?"

"I don't answer to you, Forrest. Now leave, this minute! Girls, get out of the doorway. Let him pass."

"I guess you was down there whoring yourself."

Her finger tightened on the trigger. She'd never fired the gun before and didn't know the force the mechanism would withstand before firing. Was she close?

Forrest stood from the bed.

Grace glanced at the door. Elizabeth and Hannah peered inside. "Girls, listen to me. Go into the other room."

"You out selling your soul and come back to get uppity on me?" He turned and pleaded to the wall. "Woman got no shame."

Grace jerked the trigger and the gun fired. Forrest jumped; dust popped from the wall.

Forrest looked at the hole, put his finger to it. He approached and stood before her with his chest wide. The smell of his sweat mingled with burnt gunpowder. She pointed the pistol at his breastbone.

"What's shame to a mother?" she said.

**

Forrest studied the gun. Her eyes. He sidestepped and swung his hand, jarring the pistol and wrenching her trigger finger. The gun clattered to the floor.

Forrest swung his fist, connected knuckle to chin. Grace felt her neck elongate as she lost her balance backward. She landed on her behind. She tasted warm salty blood and the wetness of a drop ready to roll over her lip. She blinked. Blinked again.

Forrest stooped to her and pressed his fingers to her collarbone, wriggled to get through her collar and below her wraps. He stank like all day sweat and all-night parties. Grace squirmed sideways.

She lashed with arms and legs; she cursed. Still Forrest stooped to her, his hand wriggling toward the folded paper money.

Grace swung her arm. It was the gun. She clasped it. Pulled back from Forrest and shoved the barrel nose to Forrest's stomach.

"Get off me."

His hand froze and she knew he could feel her thudding heart.

He stared. She stabbed the barrel into him and he eased upward. Grinned. She waited for the barest twitch, any indication that a clubbing would ensue.

"You still haven't figured it out." He extracted his empty hand from her wraps and lifted himself from her. Held his arms high, rocked back on his haunches, and stood. "You may as well turn that gun around and shoot yourself."

Forrest stepped to the two doe-eyed girls at the edge of the room and stopped to touch Elizabeth's chin with his fingertips. Grace rose from the floor, holding the pistol steady.

At the front door Forrest stopped and regarded her with his mouth open. A taunt.

Grace held the pistol with both hands. She tried not to shake.

He opened the door and was gone.

Grace closed the front door. Elizabeth sat on the sofa. Grace met her stare and Elizabeth turned away.

••

"We have to hurry. We're going on a trip."

••

# Chapter Five

Light cloud cover promises a warm night with no rain. I park at Eddie's shack and watch the door while filling my pipe.

Eddie constructed his dwelling from barn boards collected after a twister took down the younger Schucker's joint, down Smithtown road. Hauled a wagon of dry-rotted boards back before the noontime meal, had his place up by night. It's sized like an outhouse and smells the same. He stuffs rags in knotholes come winter, but in summer leaves them open.

I strike a match, hold it to pipe bowl, and after several drags the cherry glows. I consider Henry, the Hardgraves, my plans, reminding myself of the framework I've set and the commitments I've made. I know my mind.

I set toward Eddie's door. Raise my fist.

Eddie plows through, bounces from my chest before looking up and seeing his way is blocked. A small pot-bellied stove sits next to the wall. A bunk, a chair, and a dirt floor. Table with a bottle on it.

"Where you headed?"

"What are you doing here? —going to town."

"You should've known better than to get soft on a whore."

Eddie closes the door behind him. "That's between a man and his conscience."

"You don't have one. That's why you work for me. Now I want you to work for me tonight."

Eddie drops his hand into his pocket. "Tonight?"

"I got a problem, goes beyond the usual—this goes on down the road a ways. You hearing me? A considerable ways down the road."

Eddie nods.

"Course, there's something in it for you."

"What?"

"Before we get to that, this infatuation with Bernadine don't sit right. Irritates me."

"Irritates me, too."

"What you know about her thieving?"

"Naw. Hell. She never stole from you. Not I knew of."

I watch Eddie in the half-light and Eddie stares back. I nod. "You keep yourself on the right side of things."

"That what you come here for?" Eddie looks to want to leave.

"Henry's been murdered, and I know who did it."

"Who?"

"Hardgrave and his boys. It was them all right."

"They fess to it?"

"Nah. I know it from the dog."

Eddie looks at the table. "And this has something to do with you being here, now?"

"I want it to look like an act of God."

*

**

Eddie Bonter watched Jonah putt away in his Saxon Six. Proud son of a bitch—proud of his fancy suits, silver tipped walking stick, shiny boots. Proud of the money he hid all over the place. Proud of grinding other men under foot, proud of floating above the law.

The Saxon veered around a turn down the road like a deer bounded around a stump. Eddie hoped for a moment McClellan had seized up with a heart attack, but the motor's noise droned on, leaving him with the thought that Jonah had survived Eddie's last curse like he survived everything else, and would end up thriving from it. It was his nature.

Eddie checked his holstered piece, hurried around the back of his shack to the crude stable he'd added with boards stolen by night from a local coal company that didn't have the sense to post a guard. He mounted his horse and set off to Walnut.

At the cathouse he tied off his horse at a post in back and slipped to the side of the house. The gap between the cathouse and the neighbor was narrow, but the path well-established. From his earliest escapades Eddie had learned to pay attention to the headboards knocking the walls as he passed outside, to discern which girls were available and thus time his entry.

He'd taken it as a sign of true love when his favorite, Bernadine, continued trysting with him after Jonah put her in charge of the house. She'd let him talk afterwards, and he'd empty his mind and his troubles.

Eddie pressed his back to the sideboards, his ear adjacent the window. Feet shuffled inside. Muted voices mingled like enraged animals heard through a hundred yards of fog. A door slammed. Eddie stepped away from the wall and turned, but couldn't construct a vision from the shadows operating behind a thin stretch of lace curtain. The upstairs walls drummed with the scattered rhythms of thrusting men.

••

Hooves approached. Eddie hurried along, climbed the steps out front and paused, already certain he'd missed Bernadine. He tossed open the door.

Ursula—the German beast of burden favored by Jonah—barked at a fellow Eddie understood in the past to enjoy a special arrangement at the house.

"You'll settle for the last three times or you won't be back." Ursula stood and leaned forward, bosoms flushed and angry, and though the man was of comparable height, he fished bills from his pocket.

Ursula collected, nodded, and the man climbed the stairs.

Ursula faced Eddie. She glanced at an ungainly reed of a girl with a prominent mole, then looked back at Eddie. "You want her?"

Eddie glared.

Ursula stepped into the office and Eddie followed. "Where's Bernie?"

"You missed her by four hours, more, maybe."

Eddie swallowed. "Where'd she go?"

"I don't know."

"Why'd she go?"

"You got the same master I do. Favor one day, famine the next."

"McClellan said she was a thief."

"I don't know." Ursula sat, folded her arms on her lap. "I don't know where he got his ideas, but he came in like a tornado, and Bernadine was packed up and gone inside of five minutes."

"She didn't say where she was headed? Back to the city? Another house in town?"

"Not this town."

Eddie closed his eyes a long moment. He opened them and his voice was taut. "You certain of that?"

..

She stepped back. Shook her head. "Who'd cross Jonah McClellan twice?"

Ursula started a record on the phonograph. The sound was a brush on leather and a man began wailing to a piano backdrop about going home after the ball, and Eddie crumpled his hat and tossed it to a chair.

"Where is she?" He stepped closer. "Where?"

"You know where she went." Ursula held his eyes, her face flat. "Stokes."

"Stokes."

She swung around him and hit the phonograph with her hip. The record skipped.

"Where's Stokes live?"

"Find him yourself." She tossed Eddie his hat. Opened the door.

Eddie stared outside at pale lights between tree limbs and houses. Sheriff Brooks' man Stokes? That little barrel-chested bastard, always strutting chest high like his ass was made of lead?

Of course she had other men—she was a whore. But she'd said there was a line. She'd sweet talk with him afterwards... walking her fingers over his chest... and she said there was a goddamn line between doing it for work and doing it with a man that made her feel clean and good, the way Eddie made her feel. There was a line. Eddie swallowed hard.

Leaving his horse tethered behind the cathouse, Eddie stomped three blocks to Fifth Avenue.

A pair of lanterns glowed outside the Tavern door. Stokes was a fiercely sober deputy. He sometimes sat in the Tavern like he was a regular fellow while he listened to hushed men and made calculations.

Eddie located the barman, George, and shouldered forward. "Where's Stokes?"

**

"Sat right there smoking a cigar and eating pickled eggs 'til a whore come led 'im outside, and 'e ain't been back since."

"Where's he live?"

"Sheep Hill."

"Where on Sheep Hill?"

"After the fork. Don't ask how I know. Right side—number thirty-two."

"I won't."

"I know 'cause he's crooked, Eddie, and by your face I know you're going after him. You watch. He'll throw dirt in your eye."

Eddie left the tavern. His chest was tight. His eyes were narrow and his stride long. He loped back to the cathouse for his horse. Sheep Hill was a mile into the country, a settlement on the west side of Walnut on a rocky hill formerly occupied by sheep, but now home to a burgeoning class of men who held reliable positions with reliable pay, and spent it on respectable clothes and houses. Eddie's horse ambled. Eddie jabbed heels to ribs.

Sheep Hill. The street branched at the bottom; the low road circled wide to the left and then steeply lifted to the summit, swinging over and straight down, completing the circuit at the right branch.

Eddie headed rightward. Studied dim houses. Although an infrequent visitor to this part of town, he had an idea where to find Stokes—a house with an arrogant majesty that had stuck in Eddie's mind since he first saw it.

The edifice loomed robust and threatening. Black spires punched into the night sky. The lower floor was illuminated; the upper dark. A passing cloud freed the moon and in a bolt of silvery light Eddie read "32" on the right porch post.

Was Bernadine inside? Stokes worked the night shift. Why else would the house be lighted?

••

Eddie rode by. To the left of the road, houses. But on the right, to avoid obstructing the hillside views, Sheep Hill was mostly bare. Scrub around a creek and an occasional maple survived. Eddie dismounted, tied off on a tree, and crept back up the hill.

He stood at the front steps of the two-story house. The window was open.

He heard a woman's voice—sorrowful and plaintive.

Eddie crept to the first step and then looked down the row of houses. The settlement was still. From somewhere farther along drifted the merriment of a phonograph. Bright windows dotted the dome of the hill.

Eddie touched his holster, slipped his hand to the butt of his revolver. He listened. The woman's voice came from within... low but mild, seductive like a cat.

Bernadine.

Stokes answered with a sticky, heavy voice.

Eddie crept ahead. From within—laughter... Or passion? Eddie hurried up the stone steps to the porch, crossed on the sides of his heels and soles until he stood at the side of the window.

The heavy drapes granted a slim aperture inside. Eddie leaned to the glass, smelled the scent of Bernadine's powder from the open gap below. He took in the fireplace mantle, the painting of a business titan on the wall. He saw chairs, an end table, and finally, below the window, not eighteen-inches from his eye, a pink rump and a flesh- piston thrusting into it. Eddie looked away. Bernie moaned and Stokes moaned and Eddie's head bumped the glass.

Stokes increased his urgency and Eddie wondered if that was how Bernie liked it, since he was always slow and easy, face to face. She wailed Oh give me that monster cock and Eddie turned away and sat on the porch edge with his back to the wall. He dropped his head against a column and his pistol hand to the floor and heard their mutual triumphs.

●●

*

I hope to arrive in Pittsburgh by midnight. I've completed the trip in daylight a half dozen times, slowing for horse or mule-drawn wagons in the farm country. Nocturnal travel is superior. Only a rare oncoming vehicle—they arrive with blazing speed and palpable disregard for other travelers.

Many are in my employ.

Towns pass, bringing the scent of trees, exhaust, manure.

"Hardgrave and his sons murdered Henry." I say.

Henry wasn't like Mitch, my vagabond son who, if not over there cowering before the Hun, would be stowed on a train rattling across some desolate stretch of nowhere. I promised everything to Mitch. Sent him to a New York university and he telegrammed for money. Upon receiving it he disappeared. Six months later he wanders home bedraggled and worn, toes showing through boot leather. Out of sorts because a friend of his had been shot as a vagrant and he needed a place to meditate on society's ills.

I dragged him to the military recruitment station and gifted him to the government. May as well get something out of the war, if I'm going to pay for it with debauched currency.

I saw it all a decade ago. When Mitch was ten years of age I anticipated his ultimate worth and swore no man of such trifling merit—blood or no—would inherit an Indian-head penny from me.

Mitch took after his mother and to eliminate her contribution, I straddled the neighbor's daughter and produced an heir to take Mitch's place.

••

I intended Henry to be special—the only of my children who resulted from deliberate procreation. But as a boy Henry hadn't an ounce of man in him.

"Hardgrave and his sons killed Henry."

The Saxon chugs over the crest of a final hill that reveals the moonlit Pittsburgh river valley. The gods of industry are in love. Stacks billow coal smoke, black against a black sky. Buildings stand so tall they appear level to my eye. Iron bridges cross the Monongahela and even in the dead of night, the atmosphere is fraught, a cautious repose between bouts of industry. The city is a giant animal spread across three rivers, consuming, belching, producing. The bustle is contagious. I tramp the gas and roar downhill.

Other motorcars' headlamps flash and weave haphazard lines. A man curses me as he veers from my path. I glimpse his face and the Saxon's front tire strikes a rut that rattles the frame and bounces me from my seat. I brake and peer into the narrow band of road. All about are potholes and wheel-cut grooves.

Mame Gainer's current employ is a quarter mile from the railroad yard in a row house distinguished by a dozen lanterns glowing along the pickets, left by yardmen to indicate their whereabouts to their workmates. A line of men follows the fence, their faces orange in the dim light.

I park along the road. I've seen the house in daylight, and have heard stories that would labor the credulity of the greenest businessman. Mame Gainer earns fifty thousand dollars per annum, it is said, but as with all women of her occupation, fact and fairy tale often merge.

Elbows on my knees, I study the line of men and the offer I am prepared to make seems less generous than when I formulated it in Walnut, Pennsylvania.

••

A patrol officer, probably assigned by the stationmaster across the road to keep order, jokes with the men in line. A whore exits the house and presents the officer a steaming mug. He bows slightly at her approach and places one hand behind his back as he accepts the mug with his other.

The men in line stare, each of them already in his mind splaying, thrusting, enjoying her privately. I am aware of the absurdity of the place, yet it does not dampen my desire to participate in the delusion.

Other cathouses exist in the same draw that shoots back from the river and the rail yard, but none attract standing lines.

I study the men's dim faces.

Men everywhere know Mame Gainer keeps a healthy stable. She fusses over her girls. Sailors, soldiers, railroad men—rare is the man who has experienced a Gainer Gal who doesn't reserve a special regard for her. During my investigations I learned these attachments are often deeper than those the men feel for their wives. Work life is misery, time is short, and when a man calls on a woman in Mame Gainer's employ, her uncluttered availability is certain.

Some fellows, I understand, enjoy a woman equally for her company.

I have an additional hypothesis. Gainer's success reflects her belief that a man doesn't want to feel as if he is walking into a whorehouse to participate in a social evil. Even the stockiest railroad brakeman prefers to take a cooing woman in a respectable environment, as if she desires the long transaction—a life as his woman—and not the short transaction—an hour as his woman. Mame Gainer gives men whose sole existence is grime and labor and downcast eyes the respect they seek but do not find in their domestic situations. She creates illusions.

∗∗

And yet, if it was only that I would train Ursula to mimic her. Mame Gainer is more.

I slip over the seat edge, land square on packed mud and approach the line from the front. A steep slope prevents angling across the lawn; I follow the sidewalk into the face of the throng, and cut toward the house at the corner.

"You there!"

"We got a line, fella!"

A hand lands on my elbow.

"Hey bud. The boys got a line. Even a gentleman's got to wait his turn."

I face the man—the dick—balancing coffee in his hand and awkwardly resting his other palm on the end of hip-holstered billy stick.

"My business is with the lady of the house. I'm not here for a whore."

My voice carries and hearing my nomenclature, the men are interested. The dick says, "No disrespecting the ladies."

"You might remove your hand from my arm, before you find yourself shitting it."

The dick steps back, tosses coffee to the ground. "You want a scrap or you want to head for the back of the line?"

"Back of the line, Jack," another calls.

I study the patrolman's stance. It would be a quick move, twisting his arm behind his back and shoving his ass up the stairs, knocking the door with his forehead. I have him by a foot in height and probably a hundred pounds.

But I have found that violence yields its best results in private.

"Mame Gainer's expecting me. Try the door." I stretch my arm to the porch step and step toward the patrolman.

The door opens from inside.

••

Mame Gainer stands in the aperture, framed by silky orange light that obscures her features. I fill them in from memory as a ripple of exhalations and sighs changes the tenor of the men to my rear. Hers is a feline face: a narrow button nose, oval eyes, high cheeks, and a sleek depth to it; her nose and mouth are lifted from the plane of her face almost like a cat's. But not to the point of deformity. No, Mame Gainer's features cease their efforts squarely on the bridge to exotic.

She is even better framed in orange and shadows. She is a creature of night and standing in scant light seems more at home than when I met her a few months ago at a tony restaurant for lunch.

"You kept me waiting, dear," Gainer says. "He's all right, Paul," she says to the copper.

I study her face, now closer on the step, and from her look of expectation I realize she has addressed me. "I had delays."

"I'd love to hear what delays a man from my house."

"My son was murdered."

She crosses the porch and clasps my hand. "Come inside."

I follow, cussing myself for having spoken of Henry too soon, but confused by her beauty and even more confounded by her touch. In seventy years of taking from women what I want, Gainer is the only as capable at wielding her advantages as I am mine.

The room smells of talc and perfume and is dim with yellow light. In one of my houses, the girls would be waiting on a sofa along the wall, or a bench. Here, there are no spare girls. There is no bench, just a carpeted stairwell with a glowing walnut banister.

"How old are you, Miss Gainer?"

She releases my hand, steps backward and closes the door. "I don't think—"

"Woman's got to let her partner lead the dance."

··

"Forgive me, Mister McClellan, but are we dancing? Last you said, you were looking for a manager. I said 'no'. You said you'd come back with something that would knock my knickers off, and I said a hundred dollars would do that—for an hour."

"Your memory is impeccable." I follow her into the office. "That doesn't sound like a two-step to you?"

"What happened to your boy?"

"I didn't come to talk about him."

"I see. My sympathy aroused, we move on."

I speak through closed teeth. "I shouldn't have said anything. I'm here to ask you to marry me."

Gainer appears as if I've struck her with closed hand. Her mouth falls open and her eyes betray a flicker of wild confusion before narrowing. She fills her gaping mouth with speech.

"You're barking mad."

"Hear me out."

"I'm past the age of foolishness. You wanted to make an offer that could top this place, I listened. But marriage is foolishness. There's men in line outside I'd rather share a home with."

"I'm not talking about love."

"I'm not having any of it."

"I have something you want. Every day you work your tail flat to line another man's billfold. I'm giving you the billfold."

Mame Gainer slumps against the wall. After a long hesitation: "How thick a fold is it?"

"Six houses. Thirty-two girls."

"That tells me nothing. Are they clean? You buy them gifts? Take them to the doctor? Teach them to make each man be the love of her life? Without that, they're chattel and I won't work in a barn."

"That's why I want you."

••

"Mister McClellan, you strike me as a blunt man so that's what I'll give you. Why? If it's a false marriage and I get—"

"During my life we'll share the income like any man and wife. After I depart you'll take the houses and my remaining son will get my other interests. I've other businesses on my mind, and I'm running short on time to do them. Meanwhile I'm vexed by the whore business and you have a gift for it."

Gainer hesitates. "Of course I'd need to see the houses."

"I didn't come here to haggle. This is a marriage proposal and you'll be a married woman. Traditional responsibilities and all the rest. You'll have amenities and power, helpmates if you want. But we sleep in the same room, or not all, and never with another. There's nothing to discuss."

"And just how old are you, Mister McClellan?"

"Seventy. Thereabouts."

"Six houses. Thirty girls?"

"Thirty-two, each a looker."

"With so many houses you should have sixty."

"Population won't support sixty girls."

"Bah. Sixty men would, you knew what you were doing."

"You'll be at liberty to expand."

"I've been here ten years. These are my girls. My boys."

"We've got boys in Walnut. Brockwayville. Brookville. Reynoldsville. Clarion. Dubois. We've got boys—"

"This is very flattering." She turns. "I can't. I'm under contract."

"Contracted to avoid marriage?"

"To run this house."

"Another girl'll take your place. There's three angling for it now, if I know cathouses."

She smiles thinly. "I'm accustomed to my own schedule. I'll need time to consider if I'm even going to consider."

＊＊

She takes my hands, stands on her toes. I lean and she kisses my cheek.

"My motorcar is out front. I'll wait outside."

••

# Chapter Six

Hal Hardgrave saw owls. He lay on his back leaning toward Rose. One day he'd add timber to the bed frame, but now he thought about owls and more owls, hooting.

He'd been only ten, but the moniker had stuck like a thrown knife. It was spiteful.

Hoot.

As in, ain't it a hoot that an owl scared the shit out of Hal? His cousins had spread the rumor it was just an owl, but they'd never returned at night.

Hal knew what lived inside the walnut, and why the Indians had passed the name to the first white settlers. The tree stood on a tiny isthmus that probed Lake Oniasont called Devil's Elbow.

He was with a pair of cousins, Joseph and Abel, from the other side of Lake Oniasont. They were at the water at dusk, fishing lines in, nothing biting. They'd long since forsaken hope of catching anything, but left their lines in the water on principle.

An old walnut tree stood thirty yards from the water's edge, and in the growing darkness the tree's crown was a black border to a bruised Pennsylvania sky.

The walnut had existed long before the first McClellans and Hardgraves had seen Devil's Elbow. It stood fifty feet tall. Its crown dominated the entire isthmus, held up by a pair of massive limbs that split from a trunk more than fifteen feet in circumference. The center was rotted, but each massive limb grew straight and almost independent of the other, and the giant hollow in the center neither weakened the tree nor lessened its grandeur. If anything, it seemed the tree would live forever. Sometimes the boys would pitch rocks from twenty or thirty paces, making a game of getting them to fall into the hollow. Once, Abel climbed the tree and fell into the center, and when they finally dragged him out, he said it was big enough he could have moved his whole bedroom, and then didn't speak again the remainder of the day.

Small ripples lapped against the eroded bank. The boys dangled their feet. Hal enjoyed the warmth of the lake breeze, the smell. After a day of farm chores wearing oversized boots, nothing was quite as satisfying as plunging his feet through warm water into the cool mud.

His cousins sat a few yards away. They talked of the coming winter. Abel said, "I like the cold almost as much as the warm," and the three laughed at that. Hal leaned back and stretched his back on the grass, with his feet still in the water. He watched blackness overtake the sky. A firefly glowed at the edge of the dome, and he rolled his eyes back to see more of it.

"Shhh!"

The brothers grew silent.

"What is it, Hal?" Abel said.

"Shhh."

••

Hal lay awash in adrenaline acuity. Senses alert to the whine of a mosquito, goose pimples above his knees. He searched the noises, minded different directions for telltale sounds. He searched his consciousness for the origin of the knowledge that something was watching them.

He was secure, on the grass, between tufts, cloaked from the sides. But the thing that watched was above. Hal tilted his head and took in the black walnut, a giant black form whose leaves whispered but were unintelligible under noisome lapping water.

"What is it, Hal?" Joseph said. "Quit playing games."

"Someone's watching us. Shhh!"

Hal rolled to his belly and slithered farther up the bank until his muddy toes found purchase in grass.

"Where?" Abel said.

"In that walnut."

"I don't see nothing," Abel said.

"Accourse not. It ain't a person. You can tell when it's a person."

"You'd hear a bear." Joseph said.

"You'd smell a bear," Abel said.

"It ain't a bear."

"What is it?"

Hal remembered the story of the butchered Indians on Devil's Elbow, and shivered.


Hal opened his eyes. He'd been asleep. His neck and the back of his head were soaked. The pillow was cold. Rose snored. From outside, the shrieks of alarmed cattle had roused him.

Rattling bellows became panicked cries.

In his mind's eye Hal saw Jonah McClellan standing over the dead Woodrow Wilson.

••

Hal rolled from bed, took a single step. His heels tingled and he collapsed, his back locked tight. The pain crippled him. He righted himself to all fours and reaching to his leg with his hand, dragged it forward. He rested on his elbow and pulled the other leg forward with the other arm.

Rose snored.

Hal banged the side of his fist to the floor. "Rose! Rose, dammit! Wake up!"

"What are—where are you?"

"On the damn floor. You got to see about the milkers. Something's spooked 'em. Get up, Rose!"

Hal inched forward until he reached the wall. Rose clambered from bed, lit a candle, wrapped herself in a shawl. "I don't hear nothing."

"Something got 'em riled."

"You got to do something 'bout your back. See Doc Whistler, or something. Take to drink."

A cow bellowed, a long, drawn-out call that ended in a death sigh.

"Shit," Rose said.

"Get Ian out there with a rifle."

Rose whipped open the door, thudded down the hall. "Eee-n!"

Hal crawled to the rifle cabinet on the wall, braced on the lower shelf and hand over hand, walked himself erect up the side of the cabinet. Inside was an array of deer rifles, carbines, a flintlock that family lore claimed had taken the lives of a dozen Redcoat during the Revolution. Hal chose the .30-30 he'd brandished upon Jonah McClellan only a few hours before.

Ian entered the hall with white eyes and fear writ on his gaping mouth; Angus tore past him bearing a single-shot twenty-two caliber rifle.

Cattle bellowed and snorted.

**

"Give that gun to Ian!" Rose said, "Ian get out there and shoot whoever's doing that!" But Angus was already leaping down the stairs.

Hal dragged his shoulder against the hallway wall and steadied his balance with the .30-30. Each footstep sent a searing jab through his legs but if he leaned just right the pain lessened and he could shuffle forward. He reached the stairs as the front door slammed after Angus. Ian followed and left it open. The cattle grew more frantic. Hal reached the landing. Angus was a silvery moonlit reflection sprinting across the grass toward the barn. Hal rested against a porch post. Ian and Rose stood behind him.

"You get out there Ian and see about that hullaballoo."

"No! Ian, go inside," Hal said. "Grab a rifle—check the load—and a lantern. Bring 'em back here."

Hal inhaled deep, locked his belly to fortify his back, and shifted down the porch steps, his gaze stretching back and forth from his bare toes to the barn.

Angus stood at the bottom floor barn entrance where the moonlight would frame him to whomever might look from inside. Hal saw, and opened his mouth, but Angus shifted sideways and dropped to the ground.

Angus slithered into the barn bearing the rifle before him, as if he'd spent a former life soldiering.

Hoot smiled. That boy had a mess of hell in him and though he was only nine, closer to fifteen, he'd punch a twenty-two caliber hole through somebody. Yessir.

But the boy's rifle was a single shot; in his haste, Hal doubted Angus had brought a pocketful of shells.

Hunched, Hal hurried forward.

A spasm clenched his back. He dropped. Rolled to his side and gasped.

**

The rifle lay inches from his fingers. His nose and teeth rubbed dirt. He squeezed shut his eyes and ground his temple into the dirt, pressing tiny stones into his skin, delicious sharp pain to accompany the agonizing paralysis radiating from the bottom of his back.

\*

Angus Hardgrave tingled from his fingertips to his toes. He clawed against packed mud at the barn entrance. The rich scent of manure and straw carried a new bite that livened his senses. Blood. He could almost taste its saltiness on the air. Awareness rose within him and he moved without thought, alert and primal with the entirety of his awareness informed by instinct.

His knees scraped; he banged his elbow on the jamb. Inside the barn, cattle shrieked. Their hides thrashed and bounced against board stalls. They kicked.

Angus heard within the din the voice of a man, speaking calmly, soothingly. Angus slithered deeper inside and the blood smell grew alarming. The walls were normally lime white but in the faint moonlight they now dripped black.

Bovine blood pooled on the floor. It stank of life. He slid through it and grew intoxicated. It was black like tar and slick under his fingers, his belly, his thighs.

Angus came to the form of a slaughtered animal. He grabbed the hoof and slid forward and the stench of urine and shit overcame him. He glided through it, excited by his proximity to the quiet-voiced man who had started killing at this end of the barn and had slaughtered his way to the other, where beyond waited pasture and escape.

**

The man stood on the opposite side of the center aisle; Angus heard the hacking of his knife blade and after a horrific, shocked delay, another cow's throaty death bellow. The man was a shadow, a head and elbow thrusting furiously up and down.

Angus slid to the next dead cow and entered the stall. He propped his rifle barrel across her rib cage. With his hand next to his cheek the odor of excrement was dizzying. He blinked. His heart raced. In darkness the rifle sights were invisible. He barely made the shape of the barrel, but pointed at the man's head.

One shot.

The man stopped—his shadow narrowed as if he turned his head, and just at its narrowest he stopped. The man faced Angus.

Angus squeezed the trigger. It was frozen. He exhaled through his nose and rolled the safety mechanism at the back of the bolt. Resumed his aim and the shadow had shifted. The form now moved fluidly to another stall. The bellowing cows had quieted in the last minutes as more faded into death. Only one remained.

Angus pointed his rifle, waited for the shadow to appear beside the animal's neck.

The man entered the stall beside the one housing the last cow. He reached over the wall. A knife glinted and disappeared.

Angus pointed the rifle. The man plunged his blade. The cow loosed a jarring cry that grew higher and more frantic with each pulsing second. Angus blinked. The cow was dying and the smell of a dozen others' blood filled his brain with lust. He pulled the trigger.

A tiny orange flash barked from the muzzle and the bang left the barn silent for a second before the cow resumed her tortured cries.

The man slipped behind the last stall.

\*\*

He'd killed him! Angus had killed him! About to stand and rush to see the dead man, Angus saw a shadow form at the last stall's edge.

Angus pressed low against the dead cow, squeezed his body close to her breast and tucked his left arm into the crevice below her belly. He pressed his face to her udders.

Footsteps approached with a sound like two strips of bacon being pulled apart.

Angus gripped the rifle close to his chest and suppressed a cry. A man-sized devil blotted the scant light above him. Angus saw the man's legs between the cow's knees. The man turned a half circle. Angus held his breath. The half-circle became a full circle.

"Where are you?" the man grumbled. "That all you got, Hoot? Whoo-hooo!" His voice trailed into a laugh. "Whoo-hooo!"

The last cow groaned and thudded against its stall.

Above Angus, the man wheezed one nostril clean and then the second. "Pure fucking yellah," he said, and walked toward the open exit and pasture.

Angus slipped forward, enough to see beyond the cow's rump.

The silhouette man paused and flexed his arm, then pressed his hand to it.

Angus wriggled around the cow's rear legs and glimpsed over her, watched the man become part of the darkness at the edge of the pasture. Silver glinted in his hand—the knife that could have ended Angus's life, a moment before.

Angus watched the exit. His heart raced and his ears were acute. Outside, behind him, came a dragging sound. He imagined it was the man he'd shot, finally fallen from his wound, circling to exact revenge from behind. Angus hunkered beside the cow again, molded his body to hers, pressed his cheek to her udder and suppressed a whimper through gritted anger.

All these animals dead.

..

His dog.

His father, there on the porch, allowing it.

Something squeaked. Angus lifted his head. Yellow light seeped in through the entrance he'd taken, and a moment later Ian stood in the doorway, with mother's wide gown behind, and Hal braced to her shoulder.

Angus stood. He walked toward them and read their faces, watched them study him from top to bottom. In the light he looked at his hands, arms, chest, legs smeared in a shiny maroon paste of blood and liquid excrement.

"Heard you shoot," Hal said.

"Didn't hear you," Angus said.

They blocked the entrance but backed away as Angus passed through. His father leaned on a .30-30.

"That got bullets?" Angus said.

"He's gone now," Rose said.

"Gimme that gun." Angus reached and Hal braced against the wall while Angus swapped the empty twenty-two.

"Check the load, like I taught."

Angus cracked the lever, observed shiny brass. He looked toward the house, then turned the other direction and hurried around the back of the barn. Heeled around the corner and came abruptly to a barbed wire fence. He dropped to the ground, crawled below, and surveyed the silvery pasture. The tufts of grass. The stumps, behind which a man could easily lurk and prop a gun barrel for support.

Beyond the pasture stood black, impenetrable forest. The darkness would give way to gray, with proximity. The cow-killer might stalk those woods, but he might be on the road, confident it had been Hal Hardgrave that fired upon him. Confident he wouldn't be followed.

••

Angus crept on fours along the barn wall, dragging the rifle by the barrel, bumping the stock with his knee. The grass was dewy and sharp and cold and smelled clean. Above, the thinly clouded sky was gray with the ambience of the moon, with stars shouldering through.

Behind him, lantern light cut through knotty barn boards and the gaps between them. Hal cursed. "The livestock... Slaughtered every blessed goddamn one."

At the barn corner on the side facing the rocky lane, Angus crouched and peered around the side, then stood again.

The moonlight revealed hoof pockets in the mud; maybe he'd find the man's boots and learn his direction. Angus slipped along the wall, stopped at the opening.

"My girls are all gone," Hal said.

Angus gripped the rifle. He considered how his old man, a year before, had instructed that when an animal was in misery you had to put it down. Angus thought about that. He shook his head and stepped into the opening. Peered along the ground and stopped where a moonlit boot print cut through mud. He dropped to his knees and followed the trail until the prints led to the barbed wire fence along the drive toward the main road to Walnut.

He pressed his chest to the ground and slithered under the wire. A barb caught his nightshirt and raked his skin; he pulled through and when the tearing sound ended, climbed to all fours, and then to his feet.

The ground was hard. Pebbles pressed his callused soles and he drifted alongside the pasture until it ended and the black forest began. Angus drew close to the road. A horse's clompy hooves rapped the cobble as a shadow raced away.

The form a silhouette against an almost equally dark skyline. Angus raised the rifle, pointed and pressed the trigger. The rifle barked, jumped in his hands, blasted the stock against his

••

shoulder. He levered a new round into the chamber and lifted the rifle again, barely aiming, and pulled the trigger again.

He ears rang. The shadow disappeared and the echoes of the horse's footfalls died. All that remained was Angus and his ringing ears. The stench of cow shit and blood beginning to dry on his skin.

\*\*

# Chapter Seven

I sit outside the cathouse in the Saxon and watch the demeanors of men accumulating at the back of the line, their slow progress to the front, and their frivolous gaits as the escort lady—the one who fetched the copper coffee—walks them inside.

Sick men strutting up the aisle to a healing.

Rail men, most of them, interspersed by the occasional businessman's buffed shoe and cuffed pant. Mame Gainer's girls appeal to men of all stripes, rockers and chevrons—the police from the station across the street, as well. Nothing quite so savvy as making a common enterprise between law breaker and law enforcer.

My houses never have law trouble because I operate below visibility in a district found only by those seeking it. Regular folk don't know my houses exist. But if I am to escalate activity to the degree Mame Gainer has achieved, the Women's Christian movement will mobilize and ban my cathouses, just as soon as they finish banning liquor.

The politicians and the Baptists are winning the fight to make alcohol scarce. I cry for temperance right there beside them, give money to all three, the Baptists, the politicians, and the Christian Women's Temperance Union.

The common man who desires a cheap drink has no natural allies. And as soon as the Baptists and the politicians band together to stamp out the blight of paid fornication, this same artificial scarcity will improve the brothel business as well.

Everything hinges on Mame Gainer. I see her shadow on the curtained window. She chooses this form of visibility so the boys know she's there taking care of them, while simultaneously stimulating their moods with her curvaceous outline. Excited men spill fast, easing the wear and tear on her girls, while increasing capacity utilization.

She could run a factory as easily as a brothel, and the more I study Mame Gainer the more I want to put my hand on the back of her neck and own her.

I know her mind. No matter her station, a woman covets the next higher. City women believe nature imposes no limitations. Vote. Own stock. Run a company. Yet her sex holds her one step shy of the pinnacle she seeks. She runs another man's house better than he ever could and receives pay—not equity—for her effort.

Because she has no stake, her authority is always pending a man's imprimatur. Her power is a place keeper and always one man's fancy shy of revocation.

I knew her mind by looking in her eyes. She jousts like a man while sneaking like a woman. I know her, and want her, and understand the attractiveness of my offer rests on my age; the promise that while I am alive she will share my authority and when I die it will vest to her.

Except I will not die.

..

The front door opens. I prepare to be summoned—but it is the girl, Sally—there to escort another man inside. She floats down the steps and over the walk. Her waist is thin and her bosom thick. Her face gay and unblemished.

Her parts appear serviceable and beg the question: what removed her from service?

She links her elbow around the man next in line and glides alongside him toward the house, he moving more urgently than she. The john opens the door for her and she leads him inside. In the orange aperture she follows, her hands on his shoulders, while he converses with Mame, now sideways in the window, her silhouette pert.

I drag on my pipe and brood.

What could she have to consider that requires more time? Have I not offered everything she could want?

I am a crooked, ugly man; I shirk no truth. Brash and successful—appealing enough. My dress, my vehicle, my promise of allowing her to control the enterprise. Own the enterprise. The equation is sound. Any moment Gainer spends beyond a minute in contemplation indicates madness.

I refer to my watch. Has Eddie completed his evening assignment? Or is he lovesick? Drunk in a bar, or galloping after Bernadine to declare his undying love?

Mame stands. Her shadow turns as if facing the window. The curtain moves sideways.

I wave my pipe hand.

Mame motions me forward.

I step from the Saxon. The line is shorter now. I hold my watch carefully to catch the glow of a lantern on the picket fence. Almost three ante meridian.

••

*

Hal Hardgrave felt a wood burr on the barn wall press into his shoulder, a pinprick of feeling that focused his comprehension. "He bled each one."

An hour had passed. He'd studied the milkers-turned-beeves the whole time, sitting on the dirt at the far end where the blood had not pooled. He leaned against the wall with his legs folded and knees high, lessening the strain on his back.

Sometimes—when his thoughts were spare as mountaintop air—he placed his head to his knees.

Rose had been inside the house. She returned. "We got to do something," she said.

"I suspect we got to get Frank Willard out here and take them off our hands. I got no place for fourteen head."

"Good of him to bleed them," Rose said. "At least they bled out."

"I swear to Christ Almighty I'll kill him, McClellan and every one of his crew. I'll castrate the sons a bitches, and string them up by their nuts, and saw their heads off."

"Hal."

"I swear to ever-loving Jesus I will." Hal pressed his face into grimed hands and inhaled the stench. "Jonah McClellan will die as hard as I can make him."

"Hal. We got to end this feud. We got to take whatever money we can get from these milkers and start over. And we got to make sure that while we're putting everything back together, Jonah McClellan don't have reason—"

"You didn't hear me, woman."

"...don't have reason to set us back again. You got to make the peace."

••

"McClellan made war."

"Listen to yourself. Angus is outside."

"Send him to bed."

"He won't go. Tomorrow you got to go over there and tell Jonah he can have the Devil's Elbow. You know that's what this is all about. Why, Ian and Angus didn't kill his boy, but he's using that boy's death as an excuse 'cause he wants to drive us off this land, like he's been trying all these years."

"Jonah can and will go to hell." Hal sniffed. He wiped his elbow to his nose. "Leave me be."

"All these years without peace. Give him the land, is what I say. Before he kills every one of us and takes it anyway."

*

I walk the gravel path to the door and my fingertips tingle. My balls roll around heavy, corded to my ass making my whole frame ache to lay seed. The late hour and chilled air sharpens my nerves.

She'll pack her things and we'll leave the city by dawn.

Load the Saxon and vanish—and let her current master try to fetch her back to Pittsburgh without knowing her whereabouts.

I take the steps two at a time and stand on the porch. Mame Gainer occupies the doorway, her arm lifted across, blocking access.

"Shall I come inside?"

"I don't think that is necessary."

I cannot contain my smile. "Then let me have the good news here."

"I am turning you away, Mister McClellan."

"You can't."

"I've made inquiries into you. Your practices."

••

"Inquiries."

"That's right. And I'm afraid we'd be at sixes and sevens. I run my houses my way."

"And mine would be yours to run."

"Could a man like you stay out of the way of a woman like me?"

I step back. I've seen games. Clever people playing games of wit, hoping for a laugh, or to advance a position. But her face betrays nothing. "You're serious? You are."

"I am. Oh dear. You look heartsick over a business deal."

"No." I right my frame. Stick my pipe in my mouth and inhale until a cloud fills my lungs and the euphoric sweep of the drug elevates my mind. "Good night, Mame Gainer."

●●

# Chapter Eight

Grace rested her head against the seat, her torso twisted sideways. The metronomic thumping of the rails conspired with her shock and self-loathing to make rest impossible and yet unquenchably desirable, if only to escape her failure as a mother.

Still, Hannah and Elizabeth rested now because Grace stood sentry. And her prostitution had paid for their journey toward safety.

Her prostitution and theft.

Her eyes had adjusted to the dim electric lights—something she had never expected to find on a railroad car, of all places. Midway through the ride she had switched places with Elizabeth, locking the girls between herself and the window.

A gaunt-faced man in a seat one row ahead on the opposite side glanced back. He held her gaze. His face was bone hollow, his eyes wide and round. The combination magnified his expressions into a grotesque handsomeness.

He lifted his arm to the seat back and flicked his hand. "How do?"

Grace clamped her jaw and nodded. Turned away. Looked back and he kept her eye longer than she could squint in return.

Hours passed and the man opposite never again looked back. She watched him until she slept, and when she awoke and found her girls safe, her first look was to the stranger.

The sun rose. Sunbeams burst yellow over the horizon, fracturing grayness. The train chugged through a bend, and Grace beheld a small town a few hundred yards away—Reynoldsville, her destination. She recognized the tallest building, a hotel where she'd had a bitter experience after watching brothers who performed on the street with a trained brown bear.

She would have to prepare herself. Memories riddled her past. Her chest tightened at the thought—how many ugly moments stood ready to claw out of their caskets and trouble her at the slightest provocation? She might look at anything and remember one of the thousand events that compelled her away.

The train slowed and an elderly man brushed against her; she watched his progress, jostling travelers with each stride.

Beside her slept Elizabeth and Hannah, cuddled like kittens. Safe and their bellies full of pancakes and molasses. She'd find an eatery and treat them to eggs and sidemeat before finishing the last leg of the journey.

Her brother would not be happy to see her. He'd never approved of the men she ran with, the height of her skirt or the flexibility of her... accessibility. He'd made no bones about telling her, and had ceased corresponding when Hannah, her second, was born.

The train slowed. Grace leaned forward and the motion was so tedious she was certain the train had stopped, then jolted forward when it finally halted.

"Wake up, Elizabeth. Come, let's get off the train, Hannah."

••

CLAYTON LINDEMUTH | 73

Her brother had inherited the farm and though he wouldn't be pleased to see her, neither would he cast her out. Not with young girls. And on a farm there was always enough work to earn a meal.

If she could face her reasons for leaving, she could start over and the girls would be safe.

Grace corralled the girls and followed them to the end of the car, banging her case on the seats and her calves. The man with a face like city architecture lingered at the exit. He pulled his hat brim low and looked up and down the deck before stepping onto it.

He lingered.

Grace descended the steps after her daughters. The man offered his hand to Hannah.

"She doesn't—"

Grace closed her mouth. She looked at the faces on the platform—men, women, decent enough folk, in the open.

Hannah leaped the last step. The man transferred Hannah's hand to Grace. "Need help with your luggage, Miss—?"

"I'm fine without."

"Well enough, Miss—?"

Elizabeth walked off. Hannah tugged. The train engine made a groaning sound. "Can't you see I've got my hands full?"

"That's why I offered."

He smiled, and Grace studied his features. Plain, large. The nose, wider up close. Eyes cut deep into his face—his only remarkable feature. An honest face, maybe, or one belonging to a man unaware of his deceits.

"I got it just fine."

"Good day." He smiled again, though his eyes didn't confirm his warmth. Grace watched him walk away.

"Elizabeth, come here. Stay beside me."

She looked again for the young man, and he was gone.

Grace entered the Allegheny Valley Railroad depot, crossed through the thin crowd and lugged her case through the opposite doors. On the far side of Sandy Lick, a short walk away, waited Reynoldsville. She'd find breakfast for the girls and be on her way home.

She stifled a butterfly in her stomach. Fifty paces ahead walked the man from the train.

Five miles to the farm. Too far to lug a suitcase, even if she took all day.

Grace led Hannah; Elizabeth followed. They descended the steps from the platform and walked. Her grandparents had called it Ohioville, and told stories of the earliest days when it was an Indian village stretched out in a hemlock lowland. The first Main Street was a corduroy bridge, parallel logs topped with a crosswork of smaller poles, a log road laid across mud and water.

Uncle Elmer—she shook at the recollection—made up stories about Indians and war parties, scalped men and horses shot through with arrows. Elmer was the one her mother said don't never go to the barn alone with—and when she was stranded with him in Reynoldsville the day the Bear Men came from Pittsburgh, she'd learned why.

The Bear Men: two traveling European brothers, skinny, bearded, bedraggled, traveling with two European brown bears trained to do silly tricks in the streets for tips and applause. The brothers came every year during her youth, and to the children in the outlying areas their visits were a reason to save pennies.

Elmer worked in the macaroni factory on the west side of town. He'd left the farm to find his way, seemingly at the urging of Grace's mother. Grace remembered the moment her mother warned her: she'd been playing in the rain, aware that Uncle Elmer watched from the open barn bay. He waved to her, motioned her nearer. Grace's mother arrived instead.

··

Grace stopped under a maple tree and rested her case on the sidewalk. She stretched her side. "Hannah, don't wander off. Elizabeth, you need to look after your sister."

Two men approached on horseback. The slighter one she recognized from the train—the man with the gaunt face. He rode with a thick man whose look, even in the distance, seemed cast from bold shadows and stark lines. They rode closer. Grace took Hannah's hand.

"You know which way you're headed?" The larger man said.

They shared the same barren features, eyes set below cliffs so deep they peered out from shadows, over faces as flat and undistinguished as cut limestone. They wore hats that augmented the darkness and the grave line between light and dark.

"I know I'm headed into town, and that's all I need to know for now."

"You got an edge," said the man from the train. "We were being polite."

"Don't let me keep you."

The horses clomped away and Grace released Hannah.

"I'm hungry," Elizabeth said.

"This morning we'll have a breakfast you'll never forget. Remember what I said last night on the train, about how my brother has a farm with animals and crops, and an orchard and a lake. You'll never be hungry again."

"But I'm hungry now."

"I know, and that's why we're going to a restaurant this morning."

Grace lifted the suitcase and they advanced into Reynoldsville. They passed the macaroni factory, set a street back from Main, and stopped short of the hotel where the Bear Men had performed, short of the opposite alleyway.

••

Grace paused at Moore House, stared at its false front, an extra story of bricks to match the height of the neighboring buildings.

She exhaled. Led the girls inside.

The last time she'd been here was with her infant Elizabeth. Grace took in the tables, the lights on the wall, the large mirror. She'd sat unrecognized while travelers regaled her with stories they'd soaked up with a cup of coffee and a plate of pie. Walnut was a strange town; you should stay on the train and never venture near it... They told of the haunted tree and how every town has a big man, and in Walnut it was Jonah McClellan. Said he couldn't hang onto a wife due to his violence and wandering eye.

And Grace examined her cuticles and smiled, for she had been the reason the last Missus McClellan had vanished.

Refreshed from the meal but reminded of every horror that bid her leave in the first place, Grace had accepted her fellow travelers' advice. She took her infant Elizabeth and re-boarded the train.

Now, years later, she braced herself for more stories. Seeing the town, feeling its pulse, she knew her problems had been faithful. They'd waited for her.

But it was a different Grace visiting today. Last night she went to the brink and no decision had ever felt so right. All her life had been coercion, manipulation, exploitation—a continual metamorphosis, blooming from one kind of prey to another and another. Always she had been meek. Never had power nor an idea how to wield it.

Until yesterday. Her words hadn't made him fear her. She'd jammed the pistol to Forrest's ribs, and it did all the work. Next time she wouldn't speak at all.

And next time she would squeeze the trigger.

A thin man in a vest approached. "Will you be taking a room?"

"Just breakfast."

"Staying in town?"

••

"Family."

"That so?"

"Yes."

"Which family?"

"Hardgrave."

The man lifted his gaze from the counter, shot a glance at dining patrons. "Hoot?"

"Hal." Grace looked at the other guests, sitting at tables deeply ensconced in the smells of sausages and eggs and sticky syrup.

He waved his arm. "I don't want trouble. You may as well just go on."

"What do you mean?"

"Now, don't make a fuss. Just turn around and find some other place, or head out to Hoot's directly."

"Hal's. What is going on?"

"If you don't know, it ain't my place to tell you." He stretched his arms and shooed her and the girls like a farmer shoos birds.

Hannah wailed.

"Shhh," Grace said.

She squared herself to the man in the vest and withdrew the pistol partway from her purse. Heat cascaded across her cheeks.

"What am I to you? Shoo me like a goddamn chicken?"

Grace pointed the pistol at the man's face.

Patrons hushed.

The man lifted his hands. Opened his mouth but no words followed.

"Mister, you owe me and my girls an apology."

"I'm sorry?"

"Are you, now?"

"I'm sorry. Truly, Mam. What would you, uh, like us to serve you?"

••

"I've decided to leave this place. But the next time you see me, courtesy."

Grace tucked the pistol into her purse, lifted Hannah in one arm and grabbed her case with her free hand.

Her path to the door was clear.

"Elizabeth, come!"

Across the street at an angle was the Reynolds store, a grocery and what-not collection of goods. She waited—shaking—while a motorcar passed on the bricked Main.

What had changed, that uttering "Hardgrave" was enough to get a mother run out of an inn?

She entered Reynolds' store and smelled pastries at the end of the counter. She took three, paid for them. A young man in a white shirt and Teddy Roosevelt spectacles changed her money and smiled. He regarded her peculiarly.

"Beautiful morning. Not so crisp as yesterday."

"Not at all," she said.

"So you're headed out of town?"

"What do you mean?"

"If you was here yesterday, and you have a bag with you..."

"I see. I'm visiting my brother."

"Your brother?"

Grace backed to the door. "Good day."

The sun had risen rapidly and the morning moistness dissipated. Soon it would be hot. She stood on the stone step and unwrapped her pastry. Having not eaten since the pancake feast, and that her first meal in two days, her belly was tight as a fist and her strength more a factor of her mind than her physical power.

"Hey!" the young man inside called. "Ain't you Hoot Hardgrave's sister?"

She turned, shook her head.

••

"That's it! I knew it! You want a ride out there? That where you're going?"

"What do you mean?"

"Frank's headed back there for another trip."

"Frank?"

"Willard. The Butcher. Hoot slaughtered some animals and Frank's buying 'em, story goes. See him if you don't want to walk."

"Where?"

"East side of Main."

"How do you know me?"

"I'm Gabe." He removed his spectacles and flattened his grin. She'd known him years ago from school.

"Gabe. Thank you."

Grace looked toward the sun, made out the turn at the end of town. A quarter mile up the road was the old meat market.

She dropped her case at the step and rotated her shoulder. Leaned hard and stretched the tightness out of her side.

"You two stay here. Right here on this step. You hear?"

"Yes'm."

Grace slipped inside the store. "Gabe?"

"It's Grace, right?"

"That's right."

"I knew it. Ciphered you the moment you walked inside. Two girls of your own..."

"Listen, do you suppose Frank'll pass by here, on his way?"

"Not likely. He keeps the slaughter truck off'n Main on account of the smell."

"Hmm."

She slumped. Looked to the entrance, where Hannah and Elizabeth watched her through a display pane. "You're sure he's making another trip to Hal's?"

••

"He came by first off this morning. Said it'd take all day, and he'd have to work like a madman to get it all done. He's going back—you can be sure of it."

Grace measured Gabe's face. "All right if I leave my case here while I walk up? It's plenty heavy."

"I'll stow it behind the counter."

She placed her elbow on the wood top. "Why on earth did Hal butcher so many cattle?"

"I don't know. But word's out that the McClellans and Hardgraves are at it again, and I wouldn't be surprised if folks align with McClellan."

"Why do you say that?"

"You're brother's fortunes ain't been good."

"I understand."

"I'll fetch that case for you. You just tell Frank to swing by and grab it on the way. Town can survive the smell of cow blood, one time. Wasn't nobody but the meddlers complaining anyhow."

"I will."

He winked.

Grace backed away, mindful of the paper still tucked against her breast. She felt Gabe's eyes follow her out. He'd been smitten from the first and had a wolf's subtlety.

That was the way with most men. The initial contempt always dissolved into deceit, as if a man's first impulse was to announce his rightful place in the universe, and his second was to discover the lie that would make a woman sweet.

She hauled her case through the door and Gabe took it from her and hefted it behind the counter.

"You should carry it a quarter mile and try to do that," Grace said.

"Would you like me to? I'll close shop and walk with you to Frank's."

••

"Thank you, no."

Grace knelt by Hannah and Elizabeth. "We're going up the street to find a ride. You both stay right beside me."

••

# Chapter Nine

It's after ten a.m. The barn remains cool. I sit in the Saxon with the engine off, jam knuckles to eye sockets and press my back against the top rail of the seat. It aligns with a portion of my spine that's been misbehaving for hours. I've been awake more than a full day.

Exiting the Saxon I steady myself on the hood, burning my hand. In a moment my balance and alertness return; I cross the lawn toward the bunkhouse.

The barrack house is deserted. The coffee percolator, empty. I smell the grounds, place a pinch in my lip like tobacco.

At the house I look across silent fields. This time of day my men are scattered over a hundred acres of corn fields, a half dozen stills in the woods, just as many brothels.

Thinking of Eddie, I scan a patch of hemlocks, the field beyond where Henry's body rested, and still farther, to where the Hardgrave farm appears as a pair of buildings cut by a thousand jagged lines. The homestead is still.

Did Eddie fail? Chase after Bernadine and allow himself to be seduced to a new city?

Inside, I light a fire in the stove. Fill the coffee pot at the well. Without coffee, I might as well abandon the day. But business calls. I am required to speak with the undertaker, and four days have passed since I visited my other cathouses. Though I want rest and clarity—so I might ascertain a new method of achieving the outcome I have so far failed to implement—I will not have it.

Standing at the window, I look back to the barn where I parked the Saxon. Around the corner at the bottom level, a pair of horses grazes next to the entrance. I watch while the coffee percolates, then drink it scalding hot, refill, slap water on my face from the basin, and set for the barn entrance.

Inside, Eddie looks up at me and slaps the man beside him. The young man whirls, snaps-to like a private discovering a general, and at my nod, approaches with outstretched hand. "Hawkins Bonter."

"Hawkins." I take his measure.

"Just picked him up at the station," Eddie says.

"You're the one so good with the motorcars?"

Hawkins smirks. "Any which way. Drive it, fix it, drive it again."

"Can you race on a midnight road without upsetting the cargo?"

He smiles big. "I didn't come here to wash the fucking thing."

"Too bad. You'll be doing that too. I got a Saxon Six in the bay above us. Go look it over."

Hawkins exits.

Eddie says, "He's got a mouth but there ain't a thing about a motor he can't puzzle, if he don't know right off. I'll straighten out his mouth."

I am silent.

"You ride all night back from Pittsburgh?"

"Right. What happened with that special job?"

"It's done."

"All of them?"

••

"That's right. Just one thing."

"Yeah?"

"He saw me." Eddie pulls his sleeve high, winces as he works it over a bandage wrapped around his arm.

"You shot?"

"Uh-huh. Twenty-two, is all"

"Hoot come after you with a twenty-two?"

"I don't know. It was dark and I didn't see."

"If he had the gumption to do something about it, I wouldn't mind. I've half a mind to go tell him it was me. But I got to see about putting Henry in the ground. I'm taking Hawkins with me today. You got your work on the grain and the stills, and I want to poke around your brother's head."

"I vouch for him. He's blood."

"That means more to you than me."

I climb the steps by the feed chute to the upper deck. Hawkins has the Saxon's hood open. He peers inside.

"Fine piece of machinery," Hawkins says.

"I'm going to Walnut in a half hour. You'll drive."

"Yes sir." Hawkins backs from the vehicle, closer to me.

I face the open bay, then stop. "Something on your mind?"

"Well, sir, Eddie said I'd find work here and we ain't said a word about my wage. I'd like to say it wasn't important..."

"The wages of sin is death."

He smiles taut. Laughs.

I don't.


"Turn left." I search back to the right, across the field to the Hardgrave place, and see nothing going on.

"How do you rile a man with no gumption at all?" I say.

Hawkins cuts the wheel and turns on the road toward Walnut. He accelerates and I watch his face.

"You ever kill a man?"

"I have a few souls on my conscience," he says. "I don't know how to answer."

"Eddie's told you about my outfit. I find scarcity and fill it. That's what I do—and the scarcest things are often lawed almost out of existence. You bring those to the people that want them, there's profit. Take this prohibition movement. A godsend for an operator like me. I can 'still hooch cheaper than buy it, what with the tax. Sell it at my cathouses and a handful of local pubs. Make a loss a gain. But I didn't make any money 'til the county went dry."

The wind picks up.

"That's about as fast as I like to ride," I say. I pack a pipe bowl with tobacco and lean close to the dash. Strike a match and the flame vanishes. "Take it at a crawl while I get this lit."

Hawkins down-shifts and the engine whines. I strike another match, light the bowl. Suck the mouthpiece.

"When this prohibition comes all the way, beyond just Walnut County, I'll extend my reach even farther and charge what I want. God bless the Baptists. Now you knew all that—you knew I had two businesses and I'm on the hunt for a man can stay awake from here to Philly, or Chicago, or any place I send him. A man can handle a rough spot." I turn and watch Bonter's profile. "If I tell you to put a bullet in a man's head, I want to know who you fear most. Me or God."

Bonter eases lower into his seat. "Eddie said you needed a car man. I'm a car man. But to take a man's life on another man's orders—" Bonter glances at me. "Job like that ought to pay fairly well."

"There's more money in it than a car man would know what to do with."

••

CLAYTON LINDEMUTH | 87

"That's the case, give the order."

I lean back, close my eyes and open them. Vertigo. Don't feel right having someone else at the wheel. I watch the ditch fly by, the blur of grass.

Eight miles pass.

Hawkins Bonter parks where I indicate in front of Sheriff Brooks' office, taking the space closest the steps. He kills the engine and twists in his seat.

I say, "I expect Eddie'll have you knowing your whereabouts soon enough. But get up and look around, if you want. Stay close."

Bonnie Welch smiles from behind her desk as I head to Brooks' door. "He with somebody?"

"Mayor. Just be a few minutes. You can take a chair and get off your feet."

"Happy to be on them."

"I was terribly sorry about Henry. Such a brutal world, and him such a bright one."

I study her face, trying to isolate what awkwardness renders it compelling. Nose a projectile, jaws like a rock lying beside the road. Eyes that have a heat to them. There isn't an ounce of beauty in her. But her hunger—that compels.

Sheriff Brooks' door bursts open and conversation spills out with Mayor Spenser.

"—expedience, and you better get behind it." Spenser sees me and stomps to the exit.

Brooks stands in the entry to his office. I take in his red face.

"Mister McClellan, I don't have time."

"I'm here about Henry."

"I don't have any news—"

"I'll see you in your office."

Brooks steps back. "I'm pressed for time."

••

"Still, I'll have a minute of it." I nudge Brooks entering his office. "Have a seat, Sheriff."

He remains at the door. "I don't have anything on Henry. Got Stokes on it."

"I said take a goddamn seat."

Sheriff Brooks hesitates. Closes the door and circles the room to his desk chair. Sits.

"Take Stokes off. I know who killed Henry, and I'll handle the justice."

"Jonah—"

"And you'll listen to the mayor. This time."

"Spencer? He said your name one minute before he saw your face. Said to put you out of business."

"Let's get something in the open. You can't put me out of business. You can't dent me."

"I'm only relating—"

"You want to keep that star on your chest, you need to look more'n two feet ahead. I want you to throw everything you got at me. I want you to hit me hard. And if I got to spell it out any more'n that I'll see to it my driver gets elected to fill your seat."

"Hit you hard?"

"The stills, you daft fuck. Mine. Patterson's. Hinckle's. Buzzard's. Wipe us out. Make your mayor happy."

I withdraw my pipe and pack the bowl. Sheriff Brooks rests his hands on his desk. "That's what revenuers are for."

I inhale smoke, exhale gray words. "You need to beat the band for the Women's Temperance. There's a tide coming. Prohibition. You got to do your part—and you got to hit every one of us equal."

"I don't understand."

"Tell me once more and that badge is on my driver. Hit the shiners hard. Take Riggle's best newsman with you, so it's in the papers big. I want to read about tonight's action tomorrow. Clear?"

••

"As mud, Mister McClellan. But if that's what you say."

"You heard me say it."

I leave Brooks without a backward glance. Bonnie watches. I stop at the door, swing back to her desk. Lean until I smell her hair.

She slaps my arm. Blushes at the white scalp part of her hair.

"Might swan by after my rounds tonight."


Hawkins stands at the driver's side. He jumps aboard.

"A literal man. Tell him 'stay close' and he keeps one hand on the vehicle."

"Yes sir."

"I almost made you sheriff."

"I don't know as I'd be the man for that."

"Can't be any worse."

I instruct Bonter. In a quarter hour we bounce over a wooded trail I leave foul to slow unwelcome guests. I study shapes between trees and motion with my hand. "Slow."

We close in on Sandy Lick through dense undergrowth. A half-mile ahead, deep in the woods yet close to the railroad line to Falls Creek, hides one of my still operations.

Former competitor Brubaker runs it. I cut my rates by two-thirds and lived off my cat houses for six months. When Brubaker was eating corn instead of stilling it, I visited him with a jug of shine and a rifle; slapped his shoulder. "If we can't understand one another, I'll kill you."

I hired Brubaker to continue running his still as before, with the promise that once I oversaw all the tri-county producers, I'd raise the price and Brubaker would share the prosperity.

Bonter parks. A fire licks around the bottom of a boiler. I study the flames, crafted from dried hardwood that emits no smoke.

No caretaker present. I sweep side to side, seeking motion.

••

Brush rustles at my window.

Brubaker emerges from a rhododendron thicket, Remington port arms. He wobbles closer, grins lopsided. From a dozen feet his breath affirms he keeps close tabs on the quality of his product.

"Jonah," Brubaker says. "Pull up a log. Who's the prick?"

"New fella. Might have him run some boxes out of here. Get a look at him so you don't shoot him next time. And Eddie said you found another fire pit."

"You passed it on the way in."

"I'd like to see it."

Brubaker looks at the Saxon, then Bonter. "Don't need me to show you. Recall a lightning blasted beech on the left, coming in?"

"Uh-huh."

"You walk to that tree and your nose'll point you to the hole. Down the ravine—I 'spect the miners drifted closer to the surface'n they thought—you'll see it from the top."

"A coal mine fire?" Bonter says.

Brubaker gulps from a jug next to a log. "Got mines burning ten years. There's surveyors say them coal seams go all the way to Falls Crick and past, out by Brockwayville. Hell, it could burn a hundred year."

"Nothing to stop it," I say.

"What keeps it from burning down the whole woods?" Bonter says.

"It's tried," Brubaker says. "Hell, we got three mines on fire, and there's places won't hold snow all winter, the seam's so close to the ground. Sets roots on fire, and next you know, a hundred acres is ash. Happened a couple time."

"But what about this sink hole? Don't the fire get out?"

"Nah, there's dozens of 'em. No worry. Ground caves in, and though it's hotter'n the hubs of Hades deep down, most times the fire don't climb out. No sparks, no flames. Just pure heat at the

••

bottom. Sinkholes is no trouble. It's the root fires that worry a man, but there's no predicting them."

"Let's go," I say. "If you're done, Brubaker."

"Yep. Oh—I'm holding off on the next run. Last batch o' yeast was bum. Slow ferment."

"Been cooler, nights."

"That too."

"Back how far?"

"Three, four days. 'Less you say otherwise."

"I got the stock. Three days." I take my seat in the Saxon. "You getting by?"

Brubaker drinks. "You give me more money, I'll just stick it in the bank. What the hell use is that?"

"You want I should send a woman, instead?"

"Christ. Then I'd need a bath."

"Uh-huh. You see my man here, Hawkins Bonter, don't shoot him, you hear?"

"I try and remember." Brubaker grins and Bonter backs the Saxon to a grassy turnaround.

"Man's a character." Bonter guns the engine and works the clutch.

"Loyal," I say. "You take two boys, each does things his own way. Let them pummel one another and the winner knows his place and the loser gets respect. It ain't how most men see it but that's what happens."

"Yes sir."

"Then you get old and can't afford schoolyard games. A man challenges you, you end him."

The Saxon bounces over ruts. In the dim of the forest Bonter's complexion looks half-breed swarthy. Not like Eddie.

"Here's the beech tree."

∗∗

I dismount, survey a ravine that was invisible from the road. Brubaker was correct—the smell of scorched dirt, burned rocks, baked roots guides me. Like creosote, but not quite. Every time I whiff one of these pits I struggle to pinpoint the mineral odor.

I follow the ravine and stand at the edge. Several feet in diameter, the pit is large enough to entrap an unwary black bear. I ease forward a step at a time, mindful of my weight, and circle until I discern a side with a vertical wall of solid ground, and there I stand.

Heat radiates to my face. The pit bottom wavers luminous orange.

Bonter stands beside me.

The furnace sucks a draft of air over the edge and sends roiling heat up through the center. I stoop, brace hands on knees and bask in the radiation.

Bonter shifts on his heels. "The door to hell."

I let him examine my face. "No, that's not it."


Coffee's worn off and I have a long day ahead. We enter town and I instruct Bonter to pull over.

"I'm going to see the mortician down at that green and white awning on the left. I'll walk. You drive."

I amble, my mind tossing back and forth between the things I want and threats that conspire to keep them from me.

I am buying a different house in Brookville.

Postpone? Now that Mame Gainer has cinched the rope on my balls and is waiting for them to fall off...

Then there is Eddie's fascination with Bernadine.

And Hawkins Bonter. Business is a never-ending mess of poison, and if a man isn't borne to it...

••

I need a new motorcar, sleek and fast. Can I trust Hawkins Bonter to buy it?

And finally, I will destroy Hoot Hardgrave and every contemptible being associated with him.

His cattle?

I'll kill Hardgrave's chickens and poison the lake. I'll burn the barn. Tie his piss-bitter wife to a pole and soak her in honey. Drown the oldest boy in a burlap sack like a bag of cats needs dispatched. And Hoot? The coward that messed himself at the call of an owl? Whose lifetime of groveling has rendered him capable of absorbing any insult? I'll shove him head-first in the rotted crotch of his prize walnut, funnel a gallon of kerosene in his ass and set fire to the whole cursed wood.

I stand on the street opposite the funeral parlor. Looking at it grounds me to the present evil. Of the many at hand, this is the ugliness I will deal with: Henry, swaddled in a tarp and placed in a coffin with the lid sealed to hide the stench.

Henry is over there.

I      spit      to      the      bricks      and      proceed.

••

# Chapter Ten

Grace looked across the truck seat at Frank. She'd waited hours for him to return to the Hardgrave farm, and because he'd been in a closed-off section of the slaughterhouse, she hadn't been able to ask questions.

Frank stared off into a cornfield and the truck drifted off the rounded edge. He pulled it back in. Said, "Roll down your window and shift the mirror in a bit."

Grace rolled and Frank checked the other side mirror, then hunkered into the seat as they neared a wood row, and twisted his eyeballs to gander at the tree tops. He checked Grace's side mirror and said, "That's good. That's good." Then again checked his own mirror.

Why had Hal killed his cattle? The only possibilities were so drastic Grace couldn't follow them to their conclusion.

"Awful kind of you to let us tag along."

Frank dipped his head.

"Hal slaughtered the animals last night?"

"Mmm."

"Why would he do that?"

Frank down-shifted and turned on the Hardgrave lane. He shrugged, cut his eyes back to the road.

Grace hadn't seen the farm in eight years. She studied it now: the bright red barn, white house, and a pair of ten-foot spruce trees at the corners of the front porch—those were new.

Beyond, the orchard her father had planted shortly before she'd left, and as the truck approached the barn, the distant edge of Lake Oniasont appeared beyond the house.

She looked to the floor of the truck. Closed her mouth and swallowed over a dry throat.

Hannah and Elizabeth had never seen a farm. Never felt a Holstein's wet nose, nor heard a night so quiet the only sound was crickets and an occasional frog hopping into the lake.

Where was Hal? The family?

The truck bounced. Frank cut the wheel hard and braked. "You want to get out now? I'll have room to back up to the barn."

"What? Here at the lower deck?"

"That's right."

"He slaughtered them in the lower deck?"

"In their stalls." Frank held her look, then glanced at the door latch.

Grace pulled the handle and dropped out of the truck with Hannah in her arms. Elizabeth jumped down. Grace closed the door.

She'd anticipated the smell of death but it manifested more powerfully than she expected, and combined with the stillness, the lack of reception and the blankness of the sky, Grace felt as if she stood on a battlefield moments after the last moan failed.

Frank revved the engine and the truck inched backward. The barbed wire fence separating pasture from drive had been cut and the wire lay coiled on the side. The truck followed a set of tracks.

••

A shadow appeared in the barn's bottom deck entrance, hidden in a shadow cast by the side of a giant door that hung from a rusted metal track.

The shadow figure drew closer to the light but before Grace discerned the angular face and tall Hardgrave brow, she recognized Hal from his bent stance. He walked with his hand braced to the wall and didn't retreat until the truck was at the edge of running him over.

Though Hal had been stooped for years he seemed worse than she remembered. A skeleton wrapped in skin.

"Hello?"

Grace spun.

It was Rose, even more fleshy than Grace remembered. She squinted, her brow wrinkled, her jaw set as if to ward off surprise. Her eyes were red and her cheeks flush as if tears had been a recent consolation.

"I'm Grace."

"Grace?"

"Hal's sister..."

"Grace."

"I..."

Rose studied Elizabeth, then Hannah.

"I... wanted to say hello to my brother."

Rose nodded to the barn. "They got half 'em loaded and gone."

"I don't want to put you out. I'll find my way back to town and call again."

"You look like a reed in the wind," Rose said.

"We've had breakfast."

"I'm hungry," Hannah said. Elizabeth nodded.

"We have beef," Rose said. "Lots of beef." Her cheeks rose and her brow lowered and her eyes pressed tears. The giant woman shook, and Grace embraced her.

**

"I don't know what'll become of us," Rose said.

The girls sat at the lake's edge soaking their feet. Swatting bugs.

Grace knew she had been foolish to anticipate a warm greeting. In the past, Rose had barely stifled her contempt, and it seemed Grace's arrival had worsened an atmosphere already pregnant with despair.

She didn't remember the country as a place where people gave up hope... They submitted to forces beyond their control, but they toiled on in hope.

Hal hadn't returned from the barn and the butcher had taken away the last of the animals.

"He slaughtered them all last night?"

"That's right."

"That doesn't make sense."

Rose lifted her gaze. Her eyes flickered up and down as if to remind her what Grace wore. Or remind Grace. "It ain't for you to question your brother."

"Why hasn't he come out of the barn?"

Rose snorted. "Probably laying on his side with his hand on his back. And now you're here. Can't feed your kids but expect Hal to. Well, he's got plenty of beef now."

"I don't expect anything."

"You may as well go see him. Might be hours 'fore he comes inside."

Grace opened the front screen, looked back at Rose through the mesh. "I only brought the girls by to visit. I have a little bit of money, if..."

Rose shook her head. "It ain't a lack of money that has it in for us."

••

At the porch steps Grace looked to the lake. She made out Hannah's gaping mouth and wide eyes, and a few yards beyond, the object of her fascination: Angus Hardgrave skipping rocks.

Hannah—gleeful as a cloud.

Not so with her older daughter, Elizabeth.

Grace had made mistakes that left the girl headstrong. Motherhood came with effort. Grace had taken years to accept the responsibility. Not the day-to-day responsibility of seeing to a child's welfare, but the long term power over whether she delivered a good person to the world or a bad one. It had dawned on her one night as she lay under a man. She'd thought of a stray cat that had taken lodging at the Hardgrave barn while she was eight or nine years old. The stray grew fat, dropped a litter and disappeared. She'd asked and her mother said some animals just don't understand being mothers. The words never made sense until she remembered them under a thrusting man and realized Elizabeth was in the other room like an abandoned kitten.

Taking the first step down from the porch, Grace looked at the barn and remembered Uncle Elmer.

Dead Uncle Elmer.

Being home called up all kinds of ugliness.

Grace crossed the dusty yard again sensing a pregnant stillness to the farm. The acre that held the barn and house and chickens had never in a hundred years been so quiet. With the chickens quiet and the cattle dead, the hogs rooting in the woods, the air was desolate.

She approached the barn and stood where the butcher had backed his truck to the lower entrance.

A muffled sound issued to her; she stepped inside. Closer. It came from the back. She stepped inside the shadows, into air clammy with blood. The stench of death came up like a knee to her stomach. Grace covered her mouth. Again she heard the sound—

••

making her think of a child in trouble. Her feet stuck to the floor like she walked in honey.

Hal lay on his side, huddled against the stone foundation of the last stall.

"What?" he said.

Grace rushed the last steps and knelt in the blood and effluent. "Hal... I came to show you my girls. To see you."

"Grace?"

"Let me help you."

"Grace?" He coughed. "That you? What you here for? My back's locked up." He coughed again. "Stones are cool. The blood's cool."

"I didn't think about whether I'd find you at a good time. I just had to get away from the city."

"My back's locked up. You're going to have to walk on it, like you used to."

"Can't we get you out of this?"

"Eight, ten years, Grace. And you come see me in shit." He laughed. Sniffed.

"I'll help you."

"God help me."

"I'll help."

Grace clasped his shoulder and rolled him. Held Hal's feet and tugged him straight. He yelped at each pull, clenched his fists and cursed, "Ah Christ a fuckin mighty. Okay, do it again. Ah fuck." She heaved until he was straight and on his belly.

"On my ass and tail." He slapped his side. "Not in the small. I swear you'll kill me if you hit the small."

Grace reached to each side of the stall and balanced against the top, slightly lifting her weight. First one foot—she tapped the wall and a clump fell—then the other. She eased more weight to Hal's back. Felt vertebra pop through her soles.

∙∙

"Aughhh!!"

"How long, Hal? Eight years since I did this?"

"Rose was too fat even then. God that's nice. Shit, right there. Hit that one harder."

Grace was silent. Her arms tired and all her weight rested on his back.

"Knead a little with the heels."

She ground her feet into her brother's back and as her eyes adjusted to the poor light, Grace let her gaze drift along the horror of the stalls painted red, the effluent splotched and sprayed, the curdling fetor.

"We have to get you out of here and cleaned up," she said. "If you have even a single cut, it'll get infected. I swear. Then we have to scrub this place down."

"Take a thousand buckets from the lake."

"We have to do it before all this dries."

"Not if I burn it."

"You haven't seen me in ten years and you want to lay that on me? No sir. That's not Hal Hardgrave." She stepped to the cement and rolled him. He pushed away her hand. "Can you get to your knees?"

Hal brought one leg up and pushed with his arms. "Give me your hand."

She stooped and clasped his, slick with grime, and it was like old times—shit coming between them. She was ten years old. She'd wanted to see the traveling brothers from Europe with their two brown bears. They came every summer and her mother and father said she was too young to go alone so they told Hal to take her to Reynoldsville. Mother gave Hal money for a few yards of cloth to bring back. But Hal had been having trouble with a few of the boys in town and didn't want to go. It was a rowdy place. Men wore pistols and spat on the planks, and Hal had shot off his mouth to a

●●

few boys who'd called him Hoot and had run when they tried to beat him.

Hal didn't want to go and when, approaching Sandy Lick, they happened across Uncle Elmer, her brother and uncle found rapid agreement.

Grace remembered being in shock, pressing money to the counter for a few yards of the ugliest cloth she could find.

The day after being stranded with Uncle Elmer, she'd marched into the woods saying she'd run away, and Hal had begged her not to go. She'd be better in the woods on her own. Ten years old, fending off wolves and wild cats. The prospect of their midnight howls and screeches held no more terror than Elmer's grunts and the pain of being ripped open. Hal had taken her hand and tugged, him bracing toward the farm, her leaning toward the forest, strengthened by a desperate need to abandon trust and embrace self-reliance.

Grace blinked until the memories went away, and she was again kneeling in an inch of gelled blood and manure.

Hal climbed her. Grace braced under his weight. Hal clutched the stall.

"That's better," he said. "At least I ain't locked up."

"How've you been getting along?"

"It's getting worse. When you was still here, it was once every year. Now it's every God-cussed day. One time soon I won't get up at all."

They reached the muddy pasture. "This isn't what I imagined," she said.

"Why'd you come? What'd you expect?"

"I don't know. Home."

He was quiet. At the pasture exit he said, "I'm wiped out."

"Why'd you slaughter every one? It's madness."

••

"I didn't." He leaned against the rough barn wall. "You know that story Pap used to tell about Grandpap—the story about the wolves?"

She nodded.

"That's me. That's where I'm at. I got Rose backed up against the tree and I got a tomahawk and that's it. Them fuckers is coming through the trees—a whole goddamn slew of em, and I got to cut em down or die."

"Oh Hal."

"'Cept I ain't Grandpap, and I can't even muster the strength to lift a damn hatchet. You come upon us in bad times."

As he spoke his eyes seemed to focus on the swath of trees between Hardgrave and McClellan land.

It was her barn too, in a way. Not that the deed would ever bear her name at the courthouse. Though the part of her mired in her past leapt when Hal said he'd burn the barn, another part of her thought if anything in her was to be redeemed, the barn must be cleaned and filled with living things again.

Rose didn't want her around, but she'd deal with Rose later. For now she sat on the porch with Hal, smelling pan-fried beefsteaks and onions through the window.

She'd stained her dress in dung-smelling magenta helping Hal get off the barn floor. Both she and Hal had washed up and changed clothes, but a deeper filth troubled Grace. The stolen money pressed against her flesh seemed hot, at times, like a brand that would scar the side of her breast with a dollar sign.

"Who's that girl helping Rose?"

"Dot. Your niece."

"Louie's girl?"

Hal nodded.

••

"He was so old."

"Yeah, well he's in jail, now. Dot showed up like you."

"I'll move on soon enough. I suppose. Leave you to manage your happiness alone."

Hal snickered.

"I remember the story," she said. "Grandpap sat to supper complaining about a hound that run off, and soon as he put a fork of venison in his mouth the dog starts baying."

Hal twisted as if trying to reach his left foot. "Stuck in one of Grandpap's own traps."

"He grabs a tomahawk he stripped off an Indian when he was a young man and heads with Grandmum to the woods."

"And the wolves started howling," Hal said.

"How's that like what's going on now? What happened to the cows, Hal?"

"Jonah McClellan happened. And she—" he jerked his head toward the kitchen "—says I got to make nice. Says give him the land. He's a wolf, him and his boys."

"So do what Grandpap did. Back everything you love against a wall and cut the wolves down as they come."

Hal nodded. "If I could walk right, it might be different."

"You could lean a barrel against that last porch post and shoot him through his kitchen window, through trees and all."

"In the winter, maybe. Without leaves on the trees."

"I'll let you think on it. I'm going to take the girls and after supper, start hauling buckets from the lake to the barn. Think your boys will help?"

"They will."

Grace stood at the steps. "I haven't been to the lake."

"Supper in a minute or two. We'll holler."

Grace walked the slope to Lake Oniasont and studied the bank where her girls had soaked their toes—sitting on the same rock

••

Grace had used at their age. Behind her, the tree line was the same except the walnut seemed bigger and darker.

Being close to Devil's Elbow had always set her on edge. It was all superstition, of course—but she'd believed Hal. It wasn't an owl that spooked him.

Hal had bucked up when she'd told him to shoot Jonah McClellan from the porch. He could, if he had the guts. Grace imagined him again, face down with excrement smeared into his clothes and hair, streaked across his face, him whimpering. The pain was real; she'd never doubted his pain. But Hal was more capable than any man alive of lying there and taking it.

Grace faced the walnut tree and felt as if she stared into another face. Hal had never said what exactly lured him close. But Grace had been there when it happened.

She'd seen Hal come screaming from the tree, blood drawn from his                                    face.

# Chapter Eleven

I grit my teeth, fatigued. Bare of my cuffs and shirtsleeves, I wash in the basin, dry with a hand towel, and sit naked on the edge of my bed, reviewing my frame. At seventy my chest is full and my thighs and back could hoist a mule over a mountain. My best years are ahead. I am more than flesh.

I thump my manhood, a slumbering emperor. "You ready?"

Dressed in a suit I roll the shirt I wore to the funeral parlor. Outside the front porch, I light the collar and toss the shirt to the blackened grass and watch until the flames wilt and embers gray.

The dusk air is crisp. The sun has retreated. The cloudless sky holds no heat and the breeze that rises from the lake is damp.

One more shirt and the whole affair will be over.

A whiff of perfume arrives with a breeze from the lake. I detect a woman's silhouette against the water's gloom.

Hand at my eye, I wander. Ease away low branches of scrub oak and birch. Hold my nose high and trace the feminine sweetness until I stand under a walnut canopy, enclosed in a darkness that extends to the soul. I know it the way a priest might know his cathedral by the echo of his footsteps. My grandfather—the first white man in this territory—fought Seneca Indians here. They'd been traders when he arrived but after he built a cabin above the lake a mêlée ensued. He met them in the field of battle with a studded targe and a claymore sword, long as he was tall. He hung their corpses with straps of horse hide from the walnut, one piece at a time.

I can't stand under this tree and a chill doesn't pass through me in remembrance of ancestral greatness. We buried him at the foot of the walnut, only a couple feet down, roots were so tangled and thick.

I feel the chill now but don't know if the specters loiter or if I'm just whiffing pussy at water's edge. I step closer and unbidden the memory crosses my mind: a young woman bathing here, knowing I watched.

But not this girl.

This girl is thin. Hair dark and long so the top of her head bells out into her shoulders, hips, the swoop of her dress. She bends to a clump of weeds and plucks a flower with a teenage girl's commitment to elegance. Like she trusts it.

I pad closer like a wildcat until she is within reach.

"Evening."

She doesn't turn. "Beautiful night," she says, voice high. I've heard enough warble-pitched girls trill to know her intimately before I ask her name.

"You're Jonah," she says.

I step beside her and the lake breeze shifts her perfume like smoke follows when you move around a fire. She tosses the blade of grass to the water.

"You killed Hoot's dog. His cattle."

"What's your name?"

"Dorothy. I'm eighteen."

••

"Plenty old to go your own way. Sitting on a gold mine and don't know it."

"I know what I sit on, Mister McClellan. You call it a gold mine, and that's what one would expect from a vulgar man. There's other ways to say a thing, if it must be said."

"Well, there's the mine shaft. But we don't know if there's gold until we go looking. You a virgin?"

A nod.

I take her chin in hand and hold her face so I can see what she writes on it, now she knows she don't control a single goddamn thing in the whole world. "You a virgin?"

Her head moves sideways.

I release her. "I thought. You love slinging that thing around, don't you?"

"There's... nothing for me here."

"You know I represent certain opportunities to women in your situation?"

"I know."

"You've considered this path?" I take her hand, feel the contour of her wrist, the swell of her forearm. I study the silvery scallop above her collar bone, watch her eyes dance away. She turns, pulls her arm. I rest a hand on her hip, slide it behind.

"I've thought about a great many things I'll never do," she says—but her voice lacks the steadiness of her words.

I take her wrist with my other hand.

"I'll shout!"

"Who'll come running? Hoot? Or my boys?"

"Loose me, Mister McClellan."

"I think you're the sort of talent I need in my Clarion house. I think you'll be comfortable there."

"I'll run."

"And when you come back you'll find a barn in ashes and Hoot's bones inside. You can stay and be part of it."

Water ripples at the bank.

"Or you can follow that thrill coursing through you right now. You ever been so wet in your whole life?"

She faces the water and folds her arms.

"You got a bunch of thoughts in the back of your head. I've had this conversation before. I know they're there. Let 'em wander up front. You're not the first girl's wanted to kick up her feet and fuck her way to oblivion. You're empty inside and men'll pay money to fill that empty."

"The shame."

"My ass. That hole was made so men could fill it. And you were made so it's all you want. I saw it the moment I saw you. Some women are built for fields. Some for houses. Some factories. A rare few are made for whoredom. You're one."

She whirls and throws a hand like to strike me, but it's open and slow. I catch her wrist, drag her close. She presses her breast to my stomach, bends her leg around my thigh and grinds her pelvis to my leg. I shove a hand down her neckline and under her wraps, but the sweetness comes from elsewhere and I want that sweetness like I'm seventeen and she's rubbing it in my face.

I withdraw my hand, bend and get my arms under her. Carry her upslope to the dark of the walnut canopy, drop her where my grandfather's bones call for remembrance, like tipping a jug on a gravestone.

Her face is feral, daring a smile, afraid, wanting the fear. I clasp her ankle, run my hand along the inside of her calf, her thigh. Beyond.

"I told you. Dripping."

I kneel, bare myself, lean into and take her.

She beats my back. "Hurts."

••

"Sure."

"More."

My neck is cold like touched by ice. The feeling shifts along my back, through my shirt. Stops at my shoulders.

Her hands sweep over my back and stop.

She is still and I might as well auger a log. "C'mon!"

"What is that?" she says. "On your back?"

"Whatever it is, there's only one of us in you now."

Dot screams. I clasp my hand on her mouth.

The air is still and walnut leaves rustle.

The ice claws lower on my back and stops at the small, flat and cold like a rock drawn from an icy stream, with an edge like a serrated blade.

There, parked inside this whore to be, listening to her scream into my shoulder—I think of my grandfather interred in the twisted roots, and of Indians hacked to pieces by a claymore sword, hung by leather thongs. A thigh. A torso, with one arm gone—hung from a different limb. I think of blood that dripped to the earth where my knees dig for purchase, and Dot's ass drips juice.

What do these specters want?

A turn at a whore?

"I intend to break your fucking mind," I say, and finish inside her. "You lay here 'til I say otherwise. Get up and I'll cut you in half."

I stand, turn partly aside, look back. She writhes against the ground, cries, moans. I listen, catch my breath.

The crisp air stokes my mind. There is opportunity here. The tree... the woman...

The specters.

\*

\*\*

Grace sat on an old iron bathtub in the barn, set off in a side room on the ground floor. A half-bushel of corn covered the bottom—feed for cattle that now hung upside down at the butcher's. She sat in the gloom smelling the sticky sweet odor of blood.

"GRA-ACE!" A shout arrived from the porch.

She emerged from the barn and walked toward the kitchen.

Inside, children lined the side of the crowded table. Hal sat at the end and Rose forked steaks onto a large platter. The center of the table was open, waiting the main course.

"Where's Dot?" Hal said.

Rose dropped the tray to the table. Glasses rattled. "I sent her to find Grace fifteen minutes ago."

"She wasn't at the barn," Grace said.

"She's at the lake," Angus said.

"Run and get her," Hal said.

Angus darted out of the kitchen. The door slammed. Hannah and Elizabeth sat with hands clasped prayerfully at table's edge. Hannah's head was bowed; Elizabeth watched everything. Grace sat beside Hal. Rose placed a Dutch oven with mashed potatoes on a hot pad next to the meat. Steam rose and Grace watched with fascination her daughters' restraint. Hal had said they were ruined, but this bounty seemed ordinary to him. There must have been fifteen pounds of beefsteaks piled on the tray—glistening grease and pan-seared blackness.

"She ain't there no more!" Angus called from the porch.

"Then she'll come when she's hungry," Rose said. "She's got her own mind. I think she's warm to one of those McClellan men. She's never here when you look. Time for you to send her off. Especially now."

••

"She got no place to go," Hal said. He hesitated, staring at the door, the window, as if contemplating the difficulty of standing. A moment passed. Hal spiked a steak and dropped it on his plate. Ian and Rose were next; Angus climbed onto his seat and speared a slab. Hannah and Elizabeth watched without unclasping their hands, and Grace nodded. There would be no giving of thanks in the Hardgrave house.

Grace helped her daughters and sat with a plate of mashed potatoes, brown gravy with pepper floating in it, and beef.

It was good to eat.

Grace stationed Angus at the well while Elizabeth and Ian ferried splashing buckets.

Rose was in the house. Dot had not returned.

Hal sat on a milking stool while Grace brushed blood from the white-washed wall. With each new bucket she doused the area she'd scrubbed. Though her strength waxed with the food in her stomach, the long row of stalls promised an endless evening, and her will ebbed.

Especially with able hands idle beside her.

"Don't make sense, she'd wander off," Hal said. "Only been here a week."

"I'm sure she's been out of doors enough to keep her bearings."

"Not at night. Not much."

"Young women get lonely."

Hal grunted.

"You're walking better since I stood on your back. Grab a lantern and look for her."

"Maybe."

"Have you thought of using a walking stick?"

••

Hal snorted. He braced, assumed a half-bent stance. A line of lanterns hung from the rafters; Hal lifted one from its hook and shuffled toward the exit. He stood aside as Ian approached with a sloshing bucket.

"You think she'll be at the lake?" Hal said.

"Where else would she be?"

"Dunno. Rose thinks she's across the field."

Ian rested the bucket at Grace's side. She splashed the remainder of the one she'd been using and gave it to him.

"Thank you, Ian."

He carried away the empty bucket.

Hal said, "Jonah McClellan as much as promised he'd kill every one of us."

Grace dipped her brush. Blood diffused into the fresh water. "Maybe you should do something, if that's what you believe."

"I do what I can."

"Sometimes maybe we have to do what we can't."

Hal tramped away. He turned the corner. Grass rustled and then Grace slumped against the wall. She wiped her brow with her sleeve. "What am I cleaning your stalls for?"

Elizabeth arrived with another bucket and the last was barely used.

"Splash it over there," Grace said. Loosen the blood. It's getting dry."

Elizabeth was still. Pale.

Grace studied her, followed her eyes.

Slow, she turned to face the entrance by the corn tub.

A man stood in shadows, hands limp at his sides, expression hidden by darkness.

Elizabeth dropped the bucket.

Hal was gone—not that he'd be any use.

••

Grace pressed off the wall and squared herself to the man. She glanced along the barn wall to a leather harness, a broken axe handle.

The man stepped into the lantern glow and she recognized him.

Grace heard Ian turn the corner behind her and stop.

"Who are you? What is your name?" she said.

He removed his hat. "Hawkins Bonter, miss. We met on the train."

"What do you want?"

"Called to say hello, make a full introduction. Circumstances on the train was hurried, this morning."

"Called on me?"

"My brother works for your neighbor. Well, I do too, now. I got a bunk and was cut free for the evening and when I saw you I thought I'd say hello."

"When you saw me?"

He stepped back, partly into shadows. "I guess you got an edge today—and that's all right. Maybe we'll hit it off later."

"What do you mean, when you saw me? At the station?"

"No, just now. I was strolling. Nice evening. Thought I'd say hello to whoever was here, and saw it was you."

"You were strolling by the doorway, there, and happened to see me." Grace splashed water to the wall and resumed scrubbing. "I guess you said hello. Anything else? Goodbye?"

"You need a hand? What in hell happened in here, anyway?"

"Your boss."

"Word in town is Hoot did this last night."

"His name is Hal, not Hoot. You shouldn't disrespect a man you don't even know. In fact, I can't think of any further offense you're capable of giving that you haven't, so you might as well go back to your bunk."

⁑

"You can't think of one?" Hawkins Bonter tilted his head. Flashed teeth and shuffled an inch backward.

Grace took in his features. The lantern accented a pink scar at the edge of his eye socket. His hair was shiny and straight, his nose crooked. The shadows made his face harsh and suggested lineage the ordinary light of the train hadn't.

"You part Indian?"

"My grandmother was Seneca." He stepped inside, studied the interior of the adjacent stall, then the watery muck he stood in. Hawkins swatted a fly. "They got features strong enough to stick around. What'd you mean, you said 'my boss'?"

"There's always been bad blood. Now there's more. Jonah McClellan—him or someone working for him—came over here and slaughtered these animals last night. Hal can hardly walk, can't defend himself or his property, and your boss sent a man to kill his livestock. Dumb luck his youngest boy got a shot at him."

"That so?"

"With a twenty-two—didn't do much damage, I suppose. If he hit him at all."

Hawkins nodded. "Word over there is this family had something to do with Jonah's son being murdered, just a few days ago."

Grace stopped scrubbing. "Who?"

"I don't know."

"How old?"

"Nine or ten, I guess."

Grace's paused. Scrubbed.

Bonter said, "Just saying what I heard. That's why feelings are hot over there."

Grace looked at the bloody wall to bring her thoughts fully into the present. "So what are you doing for Jonah McClellan?"

••

"I'm good with these new motor cars. I can tear one down to nuts and bolts and put it back—" Hawkins tilted his head. "You hear that?"

"Didn't hear—"

"Stop with the brush."

Grace was still. A shout arrived from the night outside, distant.

"I got to go," Bonter said. "May I call again?"

Grace opened her mouth. Looked to the rafters.

"I'll call again." He tromped forward with a taut smile, exited where the children brought water, and as he disappeared Grace wondered how long he'd stood at the door behind her before making his presence known.

Had he watched her, alone?

Had he heard Hal?

The murdered boy was nine or ten...

Her belly clamped tight as a fist around a rock.


Grace cleaned three stalls before Hal returned. He winced with each step—though she wasn't sure if his face was drawn over the agony of walking or from worry about Dorothy.

"Didn't find her?"

"Nah."

Hal glanced back the way he'd come. Grace looked as well, through the gate, across the pasture.

"You think she's gone over to McClellan's?"

"She didn't go over there. She was happy here."

"Why was she here, Hal?"

"Her daddy was thrown in jail for armed robbery. She's just past legal age and 'til she gets married, there's no money for rent. Hell, that's why Louie robbed the grocery to begin with."

Grace resumed scrubbing.

∗∗

"She had no place to go and just showed up last week. This whole mess with McClellan's only two days old. I don't know where the hell it come from, I surely don't."

"You think they took her? And not that she wandered off to town? Or that she's out at the edge of the woods, sitting on a stump, reciting poems or something."

"Dot ain't exactly a poetry kind of girl."

"Girls have secrets."

"Nah." He balled a fist. "It's Jonah, taking us one by one." Hal turned. "Where's Angus and Ian?"

"Isn't Angus at the pump?"

"See? That's part of his strategy. That's why he killed the dog first, and all the cows. He knows I'm over here whipped and shaking in my boots. Well I'm about sick of it."

"You feel like you got to, we'll walk over McClellan's and see about Dorothy."

"I feel like I got to."

"Come on." Grace stood from the milking stool. Stretched. "You plan on going over there without a rifle?"

"Hadn't    thought    it    all    the    way    through."

••

# Chapter Twelve

Hawkins drives and I look over my shoulder. Dot's sprawled in the back, fucked out. She'll arrive with the clothes on her back. She giggles. I've seen women deranged on alcohol and some on the opium smoke, but Dot cuts precedent. She speaks to the ghosts even now.

Specters—on this drive I have come to believe—have needs.

The headlamps cut a swath of field in yellow. Hawkins drives too fast but says his eyes are good. My clock calls it ten. No one else is out. We park behind my Clarion house.

"Wait here 'til I tell you to bring her in."

Alberta meets me at the door. Some women wear jewels. Alberta wears fifty years' experience selling flesh. The travail has supplanted curves with angles and too-long solitary hairs. Although a missing tooth drains her speech she is anything but touched. I bought my first house from under her and learned the trade at her side.

While Hawkins parks I think of the fence posts at Mame Gainer's. No line of men waits here, prancing side to side with excitement. No bought-and-paid police keep them straight.

"Alberta, got a girl for you," I wave to Bonter. "Hawkins—carry her up here."

"A girl that needs carried? Bringing me a circus ride?"

I follow Alberta through the open door, breathe in the must, feet, old carpet—again, thinking of Gainer's polished banister and clean floors.

Alberta sits on a bench, peers up from sallow sockets.

"She'll screw anything that'll mount her. Just needs to wake up. You got the take since I come last?"

Alberta extracts a fold of paper money from between her breasts. I strip the outside bill, return it to her, place the fold in my pocket.

"Problems?"

She blinks.

"Girl's name is Dot. She's a natural. Keep a tight leash 'til she feels at home."

Alberta nods.

Hawkins appears in the doorway with Dot in his arms, comfortable, arm thrown back and a careless whiff of sex about her.

I step close and stoop to her ear. "This is your lot, girl. Rise as far as you're able."

Alberta stands, examines Dot's face. Pokes her breast, then squeezes one. "Carry her upstairs, third room on the left. Leave her there."

*

..

Grace braced. Hal took her elbow in his hand and after a couple quick steps, pitched his arm across her shoulder.

"Maybe you ought to let me carry the rifle," Grace said.

Hawkins Bonter had been running loose in her mind like a colt that kicked down the fence and made it out in the open. She'd seen him on the train—couldn't help, the way he looked back at her, sending a thrill down her back. After prostituting herself she thought she'd feel disgust when a man looked at her. But this thrill meant does he like what he sees?

When he showed up at the barn he had seemed perfectly interested.

But a deeper nagging thought, one that kept her from musing about Hawkins Bonter in any romantic fashion, wasn't what he'd repeated three times: that he'd come there looking for her.

She and Hal walked toward the McClellan farm.

It was what he said only once.

McClellan believed Hal had something to do with the murdered boy... Henry.

She'd forced herself to be cold for so many years... Grace clamped her eyes. She'd face her demons one at a time, each when she was ready.

Neither Hal nor Rose had mentioned Henry having been murdered, but they didn't know she'd care.

Could Hal have murdered Henry?

Hal grunted and stopped walking. She lurched under his weight. "Gimme a second," he said, and exhaled a pent-up blast.

"All right," Hal said.

They turned from the driveway to the road. Hal's weight brought the pebbles through her soles.

"Hal, you said Jonah McClellan threatened to kill you and everyone. What's got him so riled?"

"I don't know where he got the idea."

••

"What idea?"

"That me or the boys... hell, maybe he thinks all of us... got together and beat his boy to death."

Grace stopped. Hal groaned. She stared dumbly ahead at darkness and realized Hal was studying her. She said, "How did it happen? What happened?"

"Don't know, Grace."

She peered at him.

"I didn't kill him. Shit. That what you think of me?"

Grace blinked several times and wiped away her eyes. "I don't remember Henry."

"He was only a babe when you left."

They walked. She wanted to cast Hal off her shoulder so she could expand her chest, breath deep and release the anxiety in her breast.

"Little Henry?" she said. "I remember he fell in that tar slick and came out bawling and half blind."

"I didn't remember the tar. Well, I didn't do it, and the boys sure as hell ain't old enough to kill nobody. Even if it was an accident, just having fun."

"As boys will have fun."

The McClellan farm was a dim outline against dimmer trees. The barn she'd known from her earliest memories was part of a vast shadow blocking the particulars of the black forest beyond it. Light shone from the bunkhouse where workmen stayed, but the farmhouse was unlit and invisible.

"You don't think McClellan's bedded down, do you?" she said.

"I don't keep up with his habits."

"Seems early."

"I'll wake his ass if he is."

"Maybe one of the men at the bunkhouse would know."

●●

"The bunkhouse? He's got nothing but snakes working for him. They won't be no help."

"Still, we ought to see... if you want to find Dot."

"My situation's with McClellan."

"If Dot took after a man, you think he'd live in the house or the bunkhouse?"

"Fine."

The McClellan farm was situated with the barn to the right of the house, set back fifty yards. Beyond, and barely on the wooded crest of the hill that rolled to the lake, sat the bunkhouse. Lantern light glowed from inside and a lazy harmonica tune drifted over calm air.

"Coming from the bunkhouse," Hal said. "You'd think if Dot was down there and didn't want to be, we'd be hearing more than that."

"It won't do any harm to ask."

Hal suddenly stopped, squeezed her close for support. "Maybe I ought to stay back with the rifle. I can't take another step. I'm all locked up."

"You can't make it to that tree there, where you'd have some cover?"

"Maybe. Christ, my back."

"I believe you, Hal. I'll talk to these boys, but if it looks like they're about to drag me inside, you start shooting. Can you do that?"

"Oh, I'm ready to shoot. You bet."

They moved toward a wide tree outlined by the glowing bunkhouse. Hal hitched, dragged a foot, gasped with each step. Growling, Hal reached to the tree and removed his weight from her shoulder.

Grace watched her brother.

"Let me get situated, before you go," Hal said.

＊＊

She heard his hands on the bark and his feet in the dirt, but her gaze was on the lodge.

The harmonica became more drawn out between notes. More lonesome. Tucked against her breast, sweaty from her labor in the barn, was the fold of money she'd stolen. The .22 pistol was in her pocket.

Hal's pant legs rubbed, then stopped, and then the only sound came from the bunkhouse.

"I'll take that rifle now," Hal said.

She passed it to him and bringing back her hand felt the pistol secured in her dress. She walked toward the bunkhouse entrance.

"Hey," Hal said.

"What?"

"Don't get them excited if you don't have to. Just ask if she's been over this way."

"Thanks, Hal."

Grace strode across packed dirt to the entrance. The harmonica stilled and from inside came the rumble of gruff men. She paused before the step and observed the long sagging bow of the porch slats, smelled the must of decaying wood.

Would her slight footfall cause the sodden wood to groan? Might the sound carry inside and make the men fear an interloper? Or would they believe it was the wind confirming their solitude?

She paused.

Henry.

Grace rolled her foot to the porch and grasped a post. She balanced and brought her full weight. The harmonica moaned a low, abbreviated note. Someone chuckled.

A different set of smells came to her now: sweat, alcohol, oil— they hit her like a flurry of blows, utterly repugnant like a filthy man named Forrest. She stepped forward, cast a backward glance.

••

The darkness beyond the yellow lamp's glow had blotted Hal and the tree.

A porch plank croaked.

The bunkhouse sounds ceased. Footsteps approached from inside. Grace rapped the door. "Hello?" She stepped to the screen. She dug into her pocket and clasped the pistol.

"Hunh?" A man arrived at the door, brow wrinkled, eyes confused. His breath came through the screen, whiskey and bad teeth.

"I'm looking for a friend of mine. I'm Grace, from the Hardgraves' across the field. I'm looking for a woman who might have passed by here a couple hours ago..."

"What?"

"I said—"

"I know. I uh. Hey boys—" he turned to a cluster of men arrayed around an upended crate, functioning as a card table, in the center aisle between bunks. "Any you seen a woman tonight?"

"Shit," one said.

"Well, there's one here looking for another. You seen any or not, goddammit?"

"No."

The men shifted for a better vantage through the screen.

"No one seen a woman. What'd she look like?"

"Only one of them answered," Grace said. "Ask again."

He held her gaze and a look she interpreted as mirth molded his face. "What she look like?"

"A woman. You have so many stopping by, you need a description?"

"We been inside last half hour. Was at the barn before that. So unless she came about the farm looking for us, we wouldn't a knowed anyhow."

"We ain't seen nobody," said one of the men inside.

••

"Thank you." Grace stepped back.

The man opened the screen.

He stepped into the aperture and then he was on the porch beside her. She stood in Hal's line of sight—could almost feel the rifle bead resting on her shoulder. She stepped to her right.

"Pleasant evening," the man said.

"Good night, and thank you for your help."

"Maybe I ought to go out looking with you."

"I'd appreciate if you'd just keep the lookout here, and let us know if she happens by."

He stepped closer. She retreated into the waning reaches of the lantern glow. "You should know that a man with a rifle is in the trees over there. He's got a clear line from his barrel to your head. His mood is bad but his aim is good."

Grace stepped back again.

"Maybe if he made a sound, I'd trust he was there."

"I don't know whether the sound would reach you first or the bullet."

"Ain't seen your woman, miss." He retreated to the door. "But we'll keep an eye peeled."

She backed away slowly, hoping the man would reenter the bunkhouse, but he halted. She turned, looked for Hal, didn't see him in the dark.

From behind her came the clonk of the man's feet on the bowed boards. A steady, direct step. He was coming. His heels scuffed dirt.

She squeezed the pistol grip and lifted it to the top of her pocket.

Get it close to a man's head, her father had said when he gave it to her. Put it right to his temple and pull the trigger, and that bullet will roll around inside like a marble in a milk jar. No warning. Don't tell him you've got a gun or what you're going to do with it. Just make it happen.

••

"Stop right there," Hal called.

The man stopped.

"Less you want your head busted in pieces," Hal said.

"Who's there?"

"I ought to shoot you right now, on account of my beeves."

"Hardgrave?" The man resumed toward Grace. "I know something about you, Hardgrave. So long as it's not your boy with the gun, no one's getting shot tonight."

"Stop where you're at," Hal said.

The man arrived. Grace was still, her hand submerged in the fold of her pocket. His breath smelled of alcohol—more than she'd realized. He seized her left arm. Another man was at the door, and another behind him.

"I swear I'll shoot you now!" Hal called.

"Keep swearing, Hoot."

The man pulled her toward the bunkhouse.

"I—" she said.

"What?"

"Not everyone at once," she said. "One at a time."

He grumbled and she failed to parse his words. She jerked the pistol from her pocket toward his head, pressed the metal to his neck. She used the way he held her arm for leverage and jammed the barrel tight.

"That's a gun barrel, mister, and Hal doesn't have a thing to do with whether a bullet comes out of it."

The man released her arm. His form was mushy like she pushed the barrel into heavy cream. He retreated a quick step and she lurched. He brushed sideways; the lantern caught her eyes. Blackness—his form—something moved in a flash, connected with her arm and knocked it sideways. The pistol flipped from her hand. The man's other arm swung to her head. She dropped and he lumbered above her.

●●

The man grunted. "How 'bout that, Hoot?" He stooped, swiped at her foot.

Grace kicked and pushed away and saw in her mind Forrest from a day and a half ago. She remembered how his fear had dissipated as he righted his capsized authority. Grace kicked again. She saw the glow of a barrel reflecting lantern light. The man swung for her foot again.

"Shoot him, Hoot!"

There was no sound save the man's labored grunts. Grace rolled and kicked. She reached for the pistol. He yanked her. Stood erect. The pistol was at her fingertips, but he dragged her back.

"Shoot him!" she screamed.

A rifle exploded. Orange flashed. The man ceased; she watched his profile, saw apoplexy take hold of his mouth and brow. He released her foot, patted his chest, arms.

"You missed. He missed," the man said, and laughed. "Twenty feet and he missed."

Grace rose to her knees and lunged. Flat, stretched, she grabbed the pistol, swung it around, pointed into the man's belly.

"Back!" she cried. "Step back or it's over right now."

He raised his hands. Stepped back.

"Go along back inside your barracks there."

Another step.

"Turn around."

He remained facing her.

Keeping her pistol arm straight and the muzzle aimed at his midsection, Grace stood.

He backed across the porch. Someone inside pulled the screen for him and he disappeared around the jamb. The door slammed and Grace suppressed a shudder that started at the base of her spine.

She backed to the tree.

••

"I'm sorry, Grace," Hal said. "I locked up and couldn't move. I wanted to shoot but I wasn't steady enough to squeeze the trigger. I'd have hit you as likely as him. Finally I just shot in the air."

"Can you stand now?" She stared into the darkness between here and the Hardgrave house.

"I'm trying."

"Try hard, Hal."

She turned to the bunkhouse. "You know, they might have guns inside. We don't have a whole lot of time."

Hal braced against her leg with both hands.

"Hang onto the tree, Hal. Let go of my leg."

He grunted. In a moment he pitched his arm across her shoulders. She steadied herself.

"You want me to hang onto you or stick the rifle muzzle in the dirt?"

"Come on. And don't talk. I want to hear that door, if it opens."

"I'm doing my best, Grace."

Grace                    was                    quiet.

**

# Chapter Thirteen

I wade through thoughts like water; they slide around, resist me, but gradually fade.

Bonter drives in silence.

"Pull over."

Bonter eases to a stop without leaving the lane.

I stand to the side of the headlamps' glow and piss on the nearest clump of grass. My crank burns from my bladder to bit, but it isn't entirely unpleasant. So long as there's no blood.

The route from Clarion leads through whispers of towns, some no more than a couple of stone buildings with nary a lantern, and only a scattering of barking dogs in the hills to argue people live there at all.

Henry rests in a box. Already his blood is solid. Already his body slumps in an eternal wilt; nothing ahead save the slow decay to dirt.

Hoot Hardgrave has no idea what waits.

Dot.

Body firm like cold butter, but a damn aquifer inside. Them specters did a job on her. Left her a puddle, lying there like they'd torn every bone from her body.

I can't help myself.

Any time a man wants something and has something to give, there's a deal to find. Same with specters—especially with one of them family.

I climb in the Saxon. "Go."

Press my back against the upper seat until the pressure in my spine eases. It's been a day and a half since I've slept.

"If you don't mind me asking," Bonter says, "my brother said you need a different kind of driver. You mentioned it yourself."

"That so?"

"Said you was already running product to dry counties."

"You have experience with this other kind of driving?"

"Steeped in it."

I wait.

"You heard of Bahama rum? I ran it all the way from Miami to Chicago, and from there, wherever I was told."

"Rum."

"Sure. This temperance thing ain't new. It's all taxes and tariffs, what I understand. Down in Miami they got it so a pub can't have frosted windows, can't serve a man if his breath smells like hooch. Politicians dug right in. They hired spotters to buy bootleg and turn in the bootlegger. So I was a runner. Miami swam in rum, and once the boats brought it in, I'd run it to Chicago and they'd sell it for a pile less than someone paid taxes at the dock."

"Anybody ever get in your way?"

"Law. Other runners. With the right wheels and guns, there's no trouble. It's all adventure. But that was on my side. The pubs and what not—they had it worst. They were fined for not having the right licenses. For serving on Sunday. Serving Indians. Drunks.

••

For clean windows or frosted windows. People on the street put in jail for being drunk. Miami had a fit of it. At least on the road you can shoot back. Man in society, trying to make a living—he's a sitting duck."

"That's what we got brewing here."

"You don't want to see that, Mister McClellan. They'll flat hound a man, your line of work."

"Let 'em. Good for business. Why'd you leave?"

"Grass is greener. Plus it was getting hot. They got that new federal bureau. Revenue agents. Local sheriffs, constables. And half the population ready to turn a man in. Eddie told me you might have use for a fellow with my aptitudes, and I hopped the first train."

"What sort of trouble were you in?"

"All kinds. None in particular. I won't lie. Hell. Somewhere in the great metropolis of Miami, there's a few rumrunners that would shoot me on sight. A big fella in Chicago—really just a two-bit thief—but I pissed him off good. A body here and there nobody'll ever find. Outside of that, no trouble. You have a use for a fellow with a story?"

"For now I want to get to Walnut before midnight."

\*

Bonnie opens the door as I lift my hand to rap it. I left Hawkins Bonter in the Saxon, having instructed him to drive a block, turn around, and watch for me to emerge in a half hour.

Candle light frames Bonnie in the doorway. The glow makes her skin creamy. The air smells spiced like sassafras and cinnamon.

Lace covers her neck but leaves her arms exposed. Her face is a boxcar run over a cliff but the rest of her appeals.

I can't help but compare her bold calculation to Dorothy's coquetry and deceit—the young pretends her virtue spares her of animal desire; the old promises an appropriate caliber of enthusiasm.

"Coming in?" Bonnie says.

"I'm thinking."

She swings the door and I grab it before it closes. I cross the threshold and take in the shadows. Rainbow colors. Frilly items. I bring my hand to the back of my neck. Tamp hair that stands at attention and stiffen my back against a shiver.

I smell oil.

Something crosses behind her eyes while her smile invites me deeper inside. "It's late," she says. "Close the door."

I look behind the door.

She takes my hand and studies the lines. Pulls my fingers to her lips and places my index finger in her mouth.

The floor is clean. Window curtains open. The sink—two glasses drying upside down. I listen to the brush of her dress as she leads me along the table, the scuff of feet on a floor needs swept.

Shadows enclose the next room.

I take my hand from her and lift the globe on a lantern resting on the upper shelf of a pine hutch, strike a match and hold it to the wick.

"That shoots the mood all to hell," Bonnie says.

"I'll be a minute, 'fore I find the mood."

The lantern casts a beam into the adjacent room. Been ages since I had Bonnie.

I hold aloft the lantern and proceed to the entrance, search the floor for a telltale boot.

"Jonah... What are you doing?"

••

"Quiet."

I step forward; the light reveals a bare wall, makes the shadows hard.

"I guess you came from the cathouse."

"What you say?"

"You're antsy tonight. I can't blame you."

"What?" I turn to her. She stands in front of a door to a second closed bedroom.

"Didn't you just come from one of your houses?"

"Came from Clarion. Just now."

"I thought you knew. Sheriff Brooks is this very minute raiding your operations."

"Of course he is. I told him to when I was in."

"Oh, no, not the stills."

I take her arm. "The cathouse?"

"He didn't say anything to me, but when he called Stokes into his office I overheard. They're closing the house tonight."

I drag her close and study her eyes. Give her a shake and see if any truth falls out. "I'll close him."

"After you left, Mayor Spencer went back in. He must've waited outside because it didn't take him two minutes after you were gone."

"And?"

"Spencer came out, smug, and it wasn't long until Brooks told Stokes he was sick of complaints and pressure from all sides and it was time to shut down your house of ill repute."

"Heard that from your desk?"

"Had my ear to the door."

I release her and lean against the wall. I see faces, Mayor Spencer, Thurston Leicester, Sheriff Brooks. Imagine Stokes at his house pressing Ursula against the wall while the girls look on,

••

surprise writ across their faces—each of them thinking Jonah McClellan ain't the man they thought.

I shove Bonnie.

No one stands against me because I keep stories of the past fresh in the present. And now a new cabal of money and politics and law lash out from nowhere. The day before I bury my son. The day before I wipe out— The day I seize upon the most compelling business insight of my life, that specters crave quif. This day, an attack from friendly ground.

I press my fist to the bridge of my nose. "I'll squash that little fuck."

"Maybe we ought to go into the room first."

Her eyes go to the closed door. Mine follow. "Who's in the room?"

"You're frightening me."

The door opens. Sheriff Brooks stands there, sidearm pointed.

"Little fuck," he says.

I meet eyes with Bonnie. Convey my inner sentiments. "What's on your mind, Brooks?"

"You was too antsy. Bonnie had to make things up as she went. Pat him down."

Bonnie taps my sides, reaches inside my jacket and withdraws a P-.38. Drops to her knees and pats about my boots.

"You like it down there, don't you, old girl?"

"Shut up, McClellan." Brooks waves the pistol. "Outside."

"Where?"

"Where I say. Move."

"You haven't been to the cathouse yet."

"Now. Later. No difference. Outside."

Brooks lifts his revolver. I meet his eye across the top of the barrel.

••

The sheriff has never been a rigid man, never been true. His gift is political; he bends to the prevailing wind. If Brooks has murder in mind, someone is blowing hard.

I open my hands and lift them, ease my right into my jacket and clasp pipe and tobacco. "Join me for a smoke, Brooks?"

"All these years you never offered 'til I put a gun on you."

"Never liked you. But you got the nerves of a jackrabbit and I thought I'd let you know I was going for a pipe."

"Outside."

I pinch tobacco and tamp the bowl. Bonnie shifts to the wall, shrinks her carriage so she seems barely there. "Bonnie, you ever find a man that'll stay with you longer than one night, you got to learn how to pack a pipe. You don't want to push too much tobacco in the bowl, or the air won't circulate and your man'll be lighting it every time he wants to take a puff."

"Shut up." Brooks steps closer. Waives the pistol.

"Use less tobacco, not more. That is, you ever decide to be loyal to one man."

Brooks is five feet away, arm outstretched. One step away. The muzzle is within lunge-reach.

"I know what you're doing, Jonah. If I have to rescue the lady here, I will."

"You talk too much."

I step into the kitchen. Bonnie remains in the other room and Brooks follows me with a level barrel. I hold a match for Brooks to see, strike it against a cast iron skillet hanging from the wall. With the flame to the pipe bowl I suck it into the tobacco.

Brooks thumbs back the hammer. "Let's go. The front door."

He steps backward as I approach and then follows to the door. I pause with my hands aloft and look up the road for a glint of headlamps reflecting the moon's silver glow. The shadows yield nothing. Brooks is at my back.

••

"I imagine you'll be taking down all the cathouses in town, that right? All the stills? This isn't just about you and me."

"This is about you interfering with the proper administration of the law."

"I see. At the behest of whom? A banker?" I cant my head and listen, but don't turn around. Still searching for Hawkins Bonter.

"Law don't need a behest."

"But it got one from Thurston Leicester, didn't it?"

"Keep talking, you'll be dead on the porch."

"How's a man with no net worth pushing you into suicide, Brooks?"

"What?"

"I said the man can't rub two dimes together, 'less he swipes them from some old woman. What'd he promise you?"

"You're talking out your ass."

I hear boot steps. Feel the barrel nuzzle my back. The pressure disappears and reappears between my shoulder blades.

"I'm raising my arms so you can see nothing's going on..." I say. "Nice and easy. No excuses, Brooks. You want to—"

I spin. My elbow connects with metal. The pistol fires and Brooks' face flashes alarm. I follow through. Brooks is on the floor, feet up, arms wide. I kick his pistol arm and the gun flies.

From the other room arrives a plaintive groan.

I drag on my pipe, examine the glowing ember's health. I want smoke for what comes.

I stomp Brooks' face twice and leave him unconscious but gurgling. Hawkins approaches the door at a run. I step to the pistol, bend to it, think better. Instead I kick Brooks in the head again and see about Bonnie in the other room.

Her eyes are marbles. The lips that glowed inviting a half day ago are dried cherries. A rose blossoms on her breast and swells downward as blood pours from her heart.

••

CLAYTON LINDEMUTH | 139

I touch her hair.

Brooks moans. Bonter stands in the doorway holding a pistol on him. "What you want to do, Boss?"

"Grab his feet. Leave his gun and his blood on the floor. Take him out of here."

Brooks spits a tooth to the floor. He begins to sit erect. Hawkins grabs his feet and jerks him toward the door, rapping his shoulders to the boards and whipping his skull.

"That's right. Leave his tooth, too." I inhale pipe smoke and blow a gray cloud to the ceiling.

Bonter drags Brooks. The sheriff's holster and belt catch on the doorstep and Bonter jerks a boot free.

"Leave it. I'll get it." I follow, avoid stepping in the sweep of blood. I palm the sheriff's boot. Bonter pulls Brooks down the steps and I circle.

Brooks wriggles. "You can't do this!"

I stand in front. "Hold up, Bonter."

Bonter stops.

I smash Brooks' boot heel to his skull.

"Go ahead."

Bonter says, "I wish you hadn't done that."

I study him.

"This fucker's heavy. I thought I'd make him walk."

"Get him in the car. I hope you thought on that question I asked earlier."

Bonter drags Brooks across the short lawn. The sheriff's head lifts and falls with the swell and ebb of the terrain. Bonter pulls him over the ledge to the street.

The distance is free of pedestrians or other traffic. "Leave him here. Get the vehicle."

Bonter goes ahead and I kneel to Sheriff Brooks. "I hope you wake up."

••

I draw pipe smoke and remain squatting. Bonter trots ahead. I smoke my pipe and close my eyes. The action is exciting but at this stage of life I prefer when events unfold predictably, like pieces of milled metal coming flush, not the surprising snap of good fortune.

I have built my empire stealthily, one small house in each town within reach, and enough untaxed moonshine to keep the johns as sated at home as they are in my whorehouses. My adherence to basic principles—such as never failing to buy a man of authority when he's for sale—has helped my enterprise to grow.

Jealous men notice, however, and the first principle of running a surreptitious business is that its problems must also be solved surreptitiously.

Hawkins arrives in the Saxon, leaves the vehicle idling and joins me beside Brooks.

Bonter lifts below Brooks' shoulders and I take his feet. We hoist the limp man through the Saxon door, Hawkins entering the back seat and dragging the sheriff behind.

Bonter climbs to the driver seat, settles in with a nervous slap to his thigh and pumps the clutch. I slip into the seat, hold my pipe upside down and, about to rap it against the baseboard, halt.

I spit into the bowl and place the pipe on the floor.

"Go."

Bonter engages and the Saxon rumbles forward. "Where to?"

"Straight."

Bonter drives. I twist in my seat and watch Brooks, then Bonter. "Let me see that pistol."

Bonter fishes it from between his thighs. I get the feel of its weight and shape in the dark. "What is this?"

"Colt."

"Got bullets in it?"

"No use without."

••

I drape my arm over the seat and leave the pistol pointed vaguely at Brooks. "We get where we're going, you might need this."

Bonter smiles quick and looks back to the road.

"Turn here."

We follow a road that parallels Main. Bonter hasn't been around long enough to know the ins and outs of town; I direct him at each turn until we emerge on the other side of Walnut, headed toward Reynoldsville.

"How long since you had any shuteye?"

"Yesterday. No matter," I say.

"Let me tie him up, and you can catch a wink."

I regard the gurgling sheriff. "Keep on to Reynoldsville and turn on the Sykesville road."

Miles pass. Our headlamps sever trees of their crowns. Ruts in the road. The air turns brisk. I watch the moon through the windshield, fragmented by a hundred fleeting branches that pass into and out of view as the vehicle rattles along. Part of the sky is gray, and part of the terrain ahead, and the rest is black.

"Ease up. Watch for a trail on the left."

Hawkins Bonter slows the Saxon to a crawl. Brooks remains un-alert.

"Here. Turn here."

Bonter swings the wheel. "You smell that?"

Ahead, an orange glow filters through the trees as if from a camp fire.

"Who's up there?" Bonter says.

"Pull up and park."

The road is a pair of tracks cut through a barren meadow. The trees are leafless, having died when their roots burned from under them. In daylight, swaths of land cleared by forest fire, cloaked now by saplings and briars, make the terrain a choppy combination

••

of green and brown, life and death. Blackberry briars scrape from the right as Bonter comes too close.

Bonter drives over a small hill. Ahead, a pit glows like a burn barrel submerged in the ground to the lip. Bonter stops.

"Careful when we get to the pit," I say.

I exit the Saxon, hold Bonter's gun on Sheriff Brooks. His face is wide with fear and his eyes flicker between me, the darkness, and the orange glow. The woods smells of scorched leaves and dirt.

"Get out."

"You're crazy."

Bonter leaves the engine running and the headlamps soften the overall blackness around us.

I rap the pistol barrel to Brooks' head, then press the end to his ear. I cock the hammer.

"Don't do it, Jonah. Don't. We can come to a profitable agreement, you and me. Like before. We'll leave things just as they was."

I grab Brooks' neck, back another step, check the ground. My path clear, I lunge from the Saxon and Brooks drops to the ground.

"Bonter—get him to the pit. Give him food for thought."

"I got plenty to think about—like how I'm gonna see you swinging from a post— Don't do it. You—what's your name? Don't do it, son. I'm the sheriff. Use the brain God give you."

"Not a religious man, Sheriff."

I hold up my hand. "You've never been clever, Brooks, but you kept your nose buried in the right fella's ass, and you got along. Now you got a decision." I speak to Bonter. "Take him in your arms, like a bear hug."

Bonter steps behind Brooks and encloses him.

I chin toward the flickering orange pit.

"Don't!"

Brooks wriggles, heaves back. Bonter wrestles him to the edge.

••

"Who was it?" I say. "Spencer? Thurston? Who?"

"Nobody. Like I said."

"You want to burn from your feet up?" I stand across the other side of the pit and peer downward. "Look there, Brooks."

The walls fall straight like a well. Eight feet down the orange glow is like a furnace. A draft moves my pant legs.

"That's a mine down there, Brooks. You know how this goes. That coal seam's been cooking all this time, turning the dirt below our feet into cinders. Every hundred yards or so it burns up through the ground. I've been tracking this one three months. You look close down there, the flames are blue. Fucking blue, Brooks."

"You'll never get away with it."

"Will that console you when you're dead? Just tell me which one it was."

"This isn't going to happen like you think."

I step to the vehicle, withdraw a coil of rope and drop it at the foot of the pit.

"You going to hang a sheriff, McClellan? That it?" Brooks says.

I connect eyes with Bonter. Nod at the pit. "Drop him."

Bonter stares at me, then looks to the sky as if God almighty says otherwise, and back to me.

I nod again—the last second chance Bonter will ever get, and he knows it.

Brooks struggles. Bonter knees him, collapsing him. Bonter lifts, steps forward, arches backward with Brooks over the glowing hole, and releases. Brooks slides down his chest and screams. Inside the hole, Brooks braces against the walls.

He shrieks.

I shift to one knee, by the edge. The sheriff's head is four feet below. He leaps, claws at the singed dirt wall, curses.

Screams.

••

Yellow flame flares at the bottom of the pit and Brooks convulses. Thrashes.

I dangle the rope above Brooks' head.

"This is to drag your stupid ass out, once you tell me what I need to know."

"My legs!"

Indeed I smell burning flesh. "You don't have but a few seconds."

"Leicester! Oh God have mercy! It was Leicester!"

I hand the pistol to Hawkins Bonter. "Use it."

Bonter kneels, places the barrel below the lip of earth. He fires.

"It's a crucible," I say. "He'll be powder in an hour."

∗∗

# Chapter Fourteen

Grace studied baked clay streaked with ocher, dried puddles surrounded by torn earth and green wheat. The sun nudged above the horizon, beams bright and hard. Her shoulders ached from scrubbing the barn but her knees felt worse. She'd taken a mug of coffee from a recalcitrant Rose, breakfasted on a hardboiled egg and a slab of meat left over from the evening before, and hurried to the field before Hannah and Elizabeth arose.

She studied the depression Henry had left in the baked dirt and followed with her eyes the ridge formed by a fold in his shirt. He'd left such a tiny hollow, the vales where his legs had sunk. The crater where his elbow had indented the mud—she stood a few feet away and the entire impression was like a single letter on a piece of paper—an aborted word.

Henry. She remembered carrying him. Consoling him, and wiping clean his eyes after he fell in the oil slick.

A wave of sickness crested within her stomach. Tightness constricted her breast. According to Rose, Jonah McClellan claimed Henry's face had been shredded by the Hardgrave dog—though

Rose was certain it was a lie meant to lure Hal into an outburst that would get him killed and deliver Devil's Elbow to McClellan.

Grace had thought of the night Hal became Hoot. "Why does he want that land?"

"That tree's on it," Rose had said.

"The walnut?"

Rose nodded. "The Indian tree."

During Grace's youth it had been an oft-told story, usually at night by the fireplace, before bed. Whispered when wolves howled and wind whistled through boards, and the flames in the fireplace crackled and danced.

Of course Jonah McClellan wanted the tree.

If a Hardgrave had defended his land against a band of attacking Indians, swinging a six-foot sword and cleaving screaming aggressors in half—then she would have wanted that isthmus to be passed through her family line so that every son learned his namesake's valor.

Unfortunately for Jonah, the land had been traded years before, when the giant patriarch was a child, for enough grain to stake his father through a harsh season.

Jonah could have easily bought it back. Hal Hardgrave's fortunes had always deferred to the next season. There was no sense in baiting him into a death match over a quarter acre.

To Rose, Jonah shot the shepherd dog to bait Hal into a losing fight. But Grace studied the ground where the boy had lain while the sun rose and set three times and came to a different conclusion.

Years ago, when McClellan threw her to the ground and pressed a pocket knife to her throat, she'd learned firsthand the way he made deals. Jonah destroyed men as often as he struck business deals with them. McClellan had come for Hal not because he wanted a piece of land with a walnut tree, but because his boy was dead, he was ruthless, and believed Hal had killed his son.

••

Her son.

She'd barely known Henry. She'd fled to Jonah's Clarion cathouse and worked his books for months until she delivered, and then she left Henry with Jonah. She'd told Hal that she'd run off with a man from Brookville, but it hadn't worked out.

She'd given her son to Jonah. She was the cat that dropped a litter and left.

Grace stayed at the Hardgrave farm where she'd grown up three more years, but Jonah wasn't a man to be avoided, and finally she fled to New York.

After delivering Elizabeth and waking to the profound responsibilities of motherhood, she'd come home. She wanted to see Henry, and even if the ancient feud would never allow her to be his mother, even if she couldn't be near Jonah for fear of his knife at her neck, she would at least check on Henry's welfare.

After a long train ride to Reynoldsville, she'd sat in the Moore House while patrons described the storm she was entering, and she'd fled back to New York.

Paw prints peppered the dried mud with scores of claw holes; they mingled with boot tracks, obscuring any print the boy's killer might have left.

She was glad the dog was dead.

Grace walked with her head down, searching back and forth in an ever-expanding circle around Henry's impression. So many feet had trampled the baked mud and wheat that she felt foolish hoping to discover a clue Jonah or the sheriff hadn't.

She widened her circle to un-trampled wheat and looked between green shafts. Dew wetted her dress.

A silver glare the size of a fingernail caught her eye. It was the angle of the morning sun—she moved and the light vanished. Grace shifted to her knees. Leaned forward on her hands.

Her neck tingled.

∘∘

She picked up a pocket knife with a faint trace of rust forming at the edge of the metal-capped end. She turned it over in her hands, opened the blade.

The blade was ocher. Rust, or blood? And sooty as if used to cut charcoal.

She closed the knife and slipped it into her pocket, then sat in the wheat and wept.

*

Hoot Hardgrave rested in bed listening to kitchen sounds, smelling coffee, sizzling fat.

Worries rustled through his mind.

He inventoried his earthly possessions: he had his wife and sons, his sister and her girls—suddenly attached to him like toadstools on an oak—two horses in the barn, a dozen hogs running loose in the wood beyond the chicken coop, the chickens, the house and barn and land.

His dog and cattle were dead. His niece, who had sought his protection, had vanished. He could barely walk and hadn't the money to hire help. The coming fall's grain harvest, if sold at a fair price, supplemented by all the smoked beef they could eat, would ensure survival. But Jonah McClellan was more antagonizing than any winter storm.

Weather was indifferent. McClellan wanted him dead.

Sweat beaded at Hal's brow. If he could ease out of bed without jarring his back, and maybe follow along the wall for support, he might not lock up entirely. Might gin up the conviction to sit outside with a rifle and defend the hogs... for as surely as he knew

●●

the sun would rise and set, he knew Jonah McClellan would be good to his word. He'd kill everything Hal had, and then him.

His sons were responsible for all this. They were a curse.

He'd told them to leave Henry McClellan alone, had warned them their families didn't get along, never had and never would. But how does a man make his boys understand some men manufacture conflict to satisfy their lust for it?

Rose was right. It had always been about Devil's Elbow and that cursed walnut. He'd have gladly sold the land, but the tree had given him the appellation Hoot, and someday he'd have the wherewithal to cut it down, burn it, blast it, something.

But how do you tell Angus and Ian, don't play with Henry because his father is brute evil and he'll figure a way to lure us into trouble? Instead he'd said, "Avoid the McClellan boy. The farm hands. The men in the woods. Just stay clear of the whole clan, their land, don't even think of them."

But neither boy listened. They were unruly—nothing Hal could do about it.

Angus.

In his mind's eye, Hal saw his son with a finger crumpled inside his nose, a lock flaring from his hairline.

Angus—going after Jonah with a rifle.

Angus and Ian had befriended Henry. Jonah McClellan couldn't suspect the boys. They were only pups. But he blamed the Hardgrave house, and if it wasn't the boys, Jonah must have decided it was Hal.

He had to get out of bed. In a practiced move, Hal tightened his stomach. He tossed aside covers and rolled from the mattress. Nice and easy, in case Rose walked in. His feet hit the wood floor and he braced hands to knees, rocked forward and when he was standing, bent, walked his hands up the wall and straightened.

••

Hoot washed in the basin Rose had left filled with gray water, dressed and stepped sideways down the stairs. He crossed the fireplace, glanced at the Sharps carbine on the mantle. He'd left his .30-30 by the door—and it was gone.

Rose was around the corner in the kitchen; he could tell from the way she walked on her heels. The thud was the same as a cow that got loose once and wandered into the upper barn deck.

There was no other noise. The boys were doing chores. Not as many, without the cattle.

He entered the kitchen, sat at the head of the table.

Rose wiped her hands on her apron. "I just finished breakfast for everyone else and I got laundry to do."

"Didn't you cook any extra?"

"There's coffee, though your sister took enough."

"Where's she?"

"Off in the field where they found him."

Hoot braced against the table and rose to his feet. He carried a mug to the coffee percolator and emptied the last of it, waited for the grounds to drip to his cup.

"You want to put on some of that meat so I don't have to stand over it?"

"I suppose."

"You better do more than goddamn suppose. Had enough lip for the morning. So cook already."

She lifted a paring knife and pointed it at him. Her eyes were strong and if she ever got in her mind she was going to hurt him, she'd hurt him bad. But somewhere inside, Rose thought she was a frail woman.

She spun to the countertop and trimmed gristle from a cut of beef, slapped it to a pan. Broke eggs into another.

"Where's Grace's girls?" Hal said.

"You gonna keep track of them any better than Dot?"

\*\*

"Goddamn, woman."

"Not that you didn't keep your eyes on her."

"She run off. Probly found her way to Walnut last night. Hell, she saw what was going on here and didn't want no part. Surprised you ain't left too."

She stood at the stove with her back to him. She trembled at her shoulders.

Hoot took a dirty knife from the adjacent place setting and held it under the table.

Rose turned. Her eyes were puckered and her lower lip protruded and the whole of her shook. "Hoot, what'll become of us? We can't fight McClellan."

He looked at her, searching him for courage, and anger swelled.

"We ain't gonna fight McClellan. I'm going into the woods. I'm going to sit there day and night, and the first son of a bitch that comes after my hogs is going to die. That's what I'm going to do. Soon as I get some breakfast."

"We can't win," Rose said. "We can't win."

"I got to win!"

"Win? You can't walk. Can't farm. Can't cook a damn egg. Can't defend family or property or nothing, and we have to wait here for whatever fate Jonah McClellan decides because you can't stop him and you're too pigheaded to make a deal."

She slapped the rare slab of beef on a plate, tipped the other pan and the eggs slithered on top.

Hoot cut the meat. Chewed. "You tell Angus when you see him. Tell him I want him in the barn with a rifle, all day. And not that damned twenty-two rifle. 'Fore they come after the horses."

"You'll get us all killed."

"If we get killed it ain't me that done it."

"That's a comfort, Hal. You got to make a deal."

●●

*

I look down slope to the ancient walnut and see a dream vision of Dot, writhing beneath an invisible gang of long-dead Seneca. Her giggles break like water against rocks.

Those spooks devastated her.

I watch from a short distance, almost sensing whatever resides in the tree is not yet fully aware of me.

Whatever's in there, I'm stronger.

Every society must tend to its dead or face the havoc of wandering spirits. One of my still men, Buzzard, told once of a Caribbean tribe forced to bury a shaman in a basket of crabs to repay the spirit he'd failed to send off with adequate flourish. Truth is universal.

I knew from the first I heard my grandfather's story of the bludgeoning and hacking, each limb hung next another from a different carcass—that wasn't the way to send a spirit to the next world. A spirit insulted in such fashion would linger in the fabric between the wind and the leaves and the crevices of the bark; it would leach into the walnuts. A wounded spirit would be forever oriented toward revenge.

That's how I'd play it.

Look at the way them spooks went after Dot, like to destroy her. It'll be nothing to bring a supply of women—if the specters have something to give in return.

I step toward the tree, careful to not lose my footing on the damp leaf cover, and stop on the outskirt of the canopy as if passing underneath commits me to a deal without my obligations made clear.

I get a shiver and don't know if it's me or them.

••

I step forward.

At the tree I bring my hand to the bark. My fingertips tingle—but it's nothing. It's seventy-year-old nerves, hoping with the same ferocity as a ten-year-old boy to connect with a ghost. I let my hand glide across the rough bark and glance upward to the rich greens of the crown. Light sparkles through. Hard to imagine this being the place that turned Hal Hardgrave into Hoot, or Dot into a slavering whore.

I place my hand flat, and wait.

Laugh. Look to the lake and along a broad sweep. Old man talking to a tree.

"I know you're in there. I was there that night. I come here to say I want to dicker with you god cussed savages. If you're of the mind, I got a fair supply of women likes to fuck and I'll parade em through one at a time. I'll hitch em to this limb like a horse. But I need to know what you got in return. So you specters think on that. You spooks must have some advantage over the seen world. Some invisibility or clairvoyance. I'll stack the ground with women like a cord of logs—you got something I want."

I step back from the tree and brush bark dirt from my hand. Bring a girl here every night—that'd shut their mouths for a change.

The leaves are still. I look for a wavering bough or some movement in the ether—some shade or glimmer only I will recognize to indicate my words have been received.

I'm like any other man falls upon his knees and unburdens his soul to the sky, and afterward seeks acknowledgement in a cloud or queer pond ripple.

"I know you're in there," I say. "I know you hear me. I'll be back and we'll come to some damned terms."

*

Hal crutched to the woods and sat on a stump at the edge of a meadow where sunlight warmed his face. His view extended a hundred forested yards in any direction. Of the ten acres fenced for his hogs, his line of sight allowed him to defend the terrain where most now wandered. The other acres were higher on a slope wooded with maple—useless to a hog. A crick split the acres below, the soft vales populated with white and red oaks, walnuts, beech, hickory. Plenty of forage in the fall, with all them nuts falling. Plus a hog would eat roots and grass, carrion, deer shit.

Five sows, one boar, three gilts and two barrows. He hadn't decided which three to slaughter come November, and now with all his cattle gone and the extra space in the barn, and not needing pork except maybe for a change in flavor, maybe he'd keep them all and see how long it'd take to double the count.

Hadn't thought of that—but there was redemption right there. The animals would breed. He wouldn't have to manipulate anything. All he had to do was let them live. And raising hogs wasn't bad work. Hog shit, cow shit, not a hell of a lot of difference. It was chicken shit that made his guts roll.

And pork was good meat. Easy to smoke. The whole thing started to make sense. Hal picked crust from the edge of his nostril and his mind drifted. Ahead, in a ravine, the two barrows dug side by side for roots. Hal laid his rifle across his knees and leaned forward, stretching his back muscles and closing his eyes until the tightness eased and he could think straight.

Five sows and three gilts. That boar would see a lot of action. Hal smirked. At least someone would. Eight new pigs—and he wouldn't castrate one of em. He'd keep separate teams, and any subsequent males he'd turn into barrows, but not until the herd was

∗∗

growing strong. If he could keep meat on the table by hunting and putting Rose to work with a vegetable garden, he might pull the ends together for the two or three years it would take to bring a decent income from the hogs.

It would work.

Hal Hardgrave would be a hog man.

The barrows scampered away, almost playfully, and Hal nodded. Just getting away from that never-ending clucking—getting away from Rose had allowed him to conceive a solution. He didn't have to turn tail. Rose wanted a coward she'd have to look elsewhere. And he'd cut her loose, too. See if any man'd ever come sniffing around a woman couldn't hold her tongue. One lonely day she'd 'fess how wrong she'd been.

Twenty year ago that ass was something to behold. If it wasn't for that ass—wasn't that the damned awful truth?

Three sows and a gilt scampered between the trees—Hal leaned forward and to the right—maybe they'd cornered a rabbit. They disappeared behind a boulder.

A rifle blast shook the woods.

Hal ducked. Felt blood spike in his eyes and fingers. He peered for the sound's origin—but with only one shot...

From ahead, where the barrows had run, came the grunting peals of a wounded hog.

Hal whispered, "You son of a bitch!"

His heart trembled.

Hal pressed lower on the stump, leaned deeper into the tree at his back. He raised his rifle stock to his shoulder but left the barrel low.

Another shot—he'd been right. Dammit! He'd been looking right at the shooter, except for all the trees and the distance. A few hogs were on this side of an ancient rock—protected from the

\*\*

rifleman. But if Hal waited for the man to come find them, most of his animals would be dead.

Blood rushed hot to his cheeks.

Son of a bitch! The rifle fired again, followed by a quick screech that ended abruptly, as if the hog's life had emptied in a single spurt.

That was what? Three?

Hal cracked the .30-30's lever and observed brass in the chamber. He closed the breech, cocked the hammer, and lifted the rifle, pointing where the reports had arisen. He sighted over the barrel and studied the terrain for any indication of a man.

His adversary couldn't know he was there. Hal would get the drop... if he waited.

He closed his eyes and forced his breath out slow. His heart clomped so hard it ached and his mouth was gooey like he'd been chewing slippery elm bark. Hal looked aside, spat, and saw he'd mistaken altogether the other shooter's direction. There, two hundred yards off, a man scuttled between trees. He had to know his shots would bring Hal , and Angus and Ian sooner—since they could run.

The man walked stooped as if to lessen his profile, with his head angled for the longest view. A hunter who knew he was hunted.

Hal swung the rifle around and lined the front and rear sights, then followed the striding man. How much of a lead? He'd always done it by instinct, but this was different. A deer couldn't shoot back. He had to be right. Two hundred yards... A foot?

Damn! Up against a sapling. Hal raised the barrel around and brought it level, and the man had vanished.

Three shots in rapid succession: like a whip cracking, each report drawn out with a whoosh and crack and rolling thunder echo; each shot piled on the last and Hal counted six, that's six hogs he's killed.

..

I got to find him and put a bullet in his head before he does any more, I got to kill this man or I'm nothing at all; I got to kill him now…

\*

Eddie pulled the rifle stock from his shoulder. He'd been firing a thirty aught-six and each shot aggravated the ache where he'd been sliced by a .22 bullet.

He stretched out his arm and watched for another hog to present.

Wouldn't be long until that little shit firecracker Angus was along.

Six down, six to go.

He'd seen where Hoot had stationed himself below a tree, rifle across his knees. He'd noticed how, out in the open around other folk, he walked with his hand on his back, but in the solitude of the wood, stood upright.

Hoot Hardgrave wasn't exactly shrouded in mystery. He was a coward and a fool. In matching wits with Jonah McClellan he'd accepted a fight he had no business taking, and his fate would rightly rely on Jonah's mercy.

Eddie eased around a tree and saw Hoot had stepped out from his tree, and held his rifle like to jab a man with the barrel rather than shoot him with a bullet. Well, he'd better figure out which, because Jonah McClellan wasn't likely to stop until every Hardgrave on that sorry plot was dead and buried.

Shooting livestock was a pathetic exercise. Butchery. Eddie brought the rifle muzzle to his nose, breathed deep the acrid scent.

••

Shooting hogs wasn't as repugnant as slitting cow throats and feeling blood squirt on his forearm, but it was distasteful.

Before he'd started killing cattle the night before, Eddie had never been reluctant. He followed instructions. His employment required willingness to perform unsavory acts without second thought.

He knew the moment conscience crept in.

Bernadine.

The whole mess arose from Jonah McClellan's false accusations against Bernadine. That's the only way Stokes could have swayed her judgment and bedded her. Couched her. A hard pressed woman will go to the first place she can earn pay, so she went to New Money Stokes. Selling herself wasn't a strike against her loyalty. Jonah McClellan had forced her to make a hard decision. It wasn't fair to blame Bernadine.

A barrow wandered alone, two hundred yards off.

Eddie glanced back to Hoot. The whole exercise seemed designed by Jonah to rub Hoot's nose in his cowardice.

Eddie rested the aught-six barrel on a dead tree, lined the barrow in his sights, and slowly pulled the trigger. The rifle barked and the hog died. From Hoot's direction came an anguished curse.

Working for Jonah McClellan had given Eddie plenty of gray work. He'd been brought up to believe a man owed complete fealty to his master's operations. Self-worth was a reflection of how closely his actions anticipated his master's wishes.

The rub came when Jonah McClellan's wishes ran afoul Eddie's obvious self-interest. Eddie couldn't anticipate what would come next because for the first time in his years with Jonah, the man made no sense. He'd always been two shades shy of pure evil, but predictably so. Now, there was no rhyme or reason to it, except he wanted more of everything—even when more of one made less of the next inevitable.

••

More violence against the Hardgraves. Yes, and more cathouses. Stills. More men under his control. Women too. Seven foot two and he wanted eight. More and more. Money and power; anything and everything. Eddie remembered tracking down Jonah one day last week, finding him brooding over an oil slick in the woods on the other side of the wheat field where, eventually, he'd found Henry.

He remembered the look on Jonah's face, like a man waking on a prison cot the morning after incarceration.

Eddie edged around the tree. Hoot had disappeared.

Hair stood on the back of Eddie's neck. Had he just shifted into the line of another man's rifle? He glanced over the terrain, tiny dells and giant boulders. No Hoot. He looked for a break in the outline of shadows, a splash of red or green against the muted browns and blacks of the forest floor and tree trunks, a flicker of motion too big for a squirrel and too small for a bear.

Nothing.

Eddie eased back behind the tree, rolled, and peered around the other side. He spotted another hog, rooting in the dirt about fifty yards off, oblivious to the carnage.

Eddie stared at the hog.

But was he in Hoot's sights? It'd be idiocy to take the shot while in Hoot's plain view. It might give him the pluck to pull the trigger.

But why not? Hoot was a coward. Eddie had work to do.

Eddie shifted his rifle barrel over his body and swung it to the other side of the tree. He'd aim unsupported. He looked out the corner of his eye, almost feeling Hoot Hardgrave's sights on him. Perhaps it was judgment—but it felt like rifle sights. Eddie aimed. Wavered.

Eddie shifted his elbow and wriggled until he could draw a comfortable bead.

••

Sweat burned his eyes. He touched the trigger. Motion flickered to his side. He pulled the trigger and in the same motion as the rifle's recoil, rolled back behind the tree.

It was Hoot, across the way. He'd shifted to the other side of his tree and had drawn his rifle.

Protected by the beech, Eddie watched the hog flop and shriek. He'd jerked the rifle and the bullet had gone off mark.

"You son of a bitch!" The voice rolled between the trees, pushed a frantic tenor at the forward edge.

"Take your kids and wife, and go," Eddie said. "You're next."

Behind the cover of the giant beech, Eddie stood and pressed his back to the smooth bark. He scanned ahead for a route that would avoid Hoot's sights. If he walked forward with the beech blocking Hoot's line, Eddie would enter a dry stream bed, and then move laterally to the cover of a boulder that disappeared into a copse of brush and briars.

Eddie looked back to the left for any new hogs, then to the right.

It'd be a hell of a lot easier to put a bullet into Hoot Hardgrave and be done with it. That's where things were headed, anyway. The wife would bolt and Jonah would get what he wanted. Then Eddie could take a little time. Maybe find Bernadine and let her explain being ass-up on Stokes' sofa.

Eddie spat.

Now, Hoot's pretty sister... she'd be welcome to stick around.

Eddie adjusted his crotch. Rubbed. Recalled Bernadine's special way of pleasing him, a method she'd heard of long ago from a madam visiting from Morocco, she'd said.

Bernadine had never found a man special enough to please that way, except Eddie.

Losing her because of Jonah's wild accusations was a ball breaker, but it didn't increase his fear of Jonah. Eddie's fear was circumspect and rational.

••

While Jonah's business was stills and whorehouses, legitimate business killings were the best work Eddie could ever expect. That kind of slaying was honorable—or at least, understandable. No one would demand a businessman such as Jonah suffer unsavory or sneaky competition. But Jonah McClellan had lurched a new direction, an unthinkable and unpredictable direction, and Eddie would never have stopped to notice if not for the personal cost of losing Bernadine.

But hell. With a man like Jonah, you don't just quit. You want to live, you disappear. Or make your last kill count.

Eddie had worked for Jonah a long time. The whoring operation spanned six towns, and the stills supplied liquor to clients in five states. Jonah joked he was bigger than most big label distillers, and produced better quality and more quantity.

"Why don't you go legal, then?"

Jonah had studied him with a smirk.

Eddie had overseen both operations; he'd learned each trade from his master. He'd been comfortable doing the gray work behind the scene because Jonah's job required panache Eddie didn't possess. Highbrow talk with bankers and politicians. Eddie easily read the strategies behind the moves. He was Jonah's equal, there. But ascending to town aristocracy—Eddie couldn't conceive of how to swing it.

With Jonah ready to destroy the Hardgraves, a plan that relied on an act so wicked, no law enforcement, no matter how in the pocket, could overlook, Eddie's choices narrowed to finding a new name and set of circumstances, murdering Jonah, or killing livestock—and hoping Jonah had a plan bigger than the madness that seemed the only explanation for his recent actions.

For now Eddie would kill hogs.

◦◦

*

Hal exhaled. Again Eddie emerged. He was making quick work of the hogs—the few remaining had scattered and it would take time, on ten acres, to find them all.

Hal aligned the sights and led Eddie by a foot and a half. Hundred and fifty yards. Not an easy shot, without support.

He'd best wait until—

Eddie raised his rifle and snapped off another shot, and another. A hog squealed.

Hal would have to wait for a closer target or he'd have to shift sideways and brace the rifle against the sapling. That might give him away; he'd best not risk it.

His only advantage—with his back the way it was—was surprise. That advantage would disappear with the first shot.

Don't squander your advantage, Hoot. No, I only got one advantage and I'll wait. Damn skippy. But this bastard's going to die.

More shots. Eddie was closer now; Hal discerned the plaid pattern of his shirt, the sheen of his dark hair. Looked like he was carrying a Mauser.

Jonah McClellan didn't have the stones to come do the dirty work himself. Just like the rich, buy somebody to do the deed, then claim the spoils. Well I'll be damned if I'll sit and take it. Wait for the right moment. He's looking for hogs, not Hoots. Ha! Stay calm. There, like that.

Hal had the sight picture. Eddie was still, ear cocked.

Hal's front sight post came half way up Eddie's head. His nose seemed to rest on it. It was the same picture he'd used forever, all three posts level, the middle centered, and the target floating on

••

top. This son of a bitch was going to die. No room for accidents or errors.

Hal had the edge.

But what would Jonah McClellan do?

Or Sherriff Brooks?

Was Eddie shooting at you? Directly at you? If I say yes, Brooks says, well let's count how many shots he fired. Appears he dropped a hog with each shot. And I say I defended my property like the goddamn Constitution says I got the right—and Brooks comes back with sure you got the right. But I got the jail. I got you for murder, 'cause I take my money from the dead man's master...

There was no way to fight all of them.

Hal glanced away. If he fired, he might as well go put a bullet in Jonah too, or go to the Sheriff and give himself up for a hanging.

Unless it was self-defense, there was no way they'd let him live. He couldn't fight all of them. A prudent man would let the killers do what they would do, and when they moved along, look over what was left and find something to build again.

And the Bible said the meek would inherit.

As if hearing Hal's thoughts, Eddie snapped his rifle to his shoulder and dropped another hog. He stood, looked to Hal, dusted his        legs,        and        wandered        away.

••

# Chapter Fifteen

I drop a spade of dirt to Henry's coffin and wonder how it would sound inside, could the dead hear.

Pastor reaches for the shovel. His wrist has more hair than his head. I give him the handle.

The service was a few words. Most these folks didn't know Henry and only come because one way or another, I got their economics by the short hairs. I watch their faces as I pass, seek a pair of eyes to impress upon the grief in mine, the fury. But none will meet me.

Hawkins Bonter follows a step behind. At the Saxon he swoops ahead to open the door.

I climb inside. Bonter starts the engine.

"A minute," I say, watching men and women grouped at the grave. They wait for me to leave. A pair of men stands close and speaks with their backs to my car.

"You see them two?"

"By the rhododendron?" Bonter says.

"That's our pair, right there. Thurston Leicester and the man you promoted."

"What?"

"By murdering his boss. That's the next sheriff, Stokes. You see men talking up close like that, they're talking about you."

"You think they're here because they know something?"

"They know something. But they're here so it looks right when I'm gone."

Thurston Leicester places his hand on Stokes' back. Looks over his shoulder and points his grim face at the Saxon.

Bonter says. "You think they found the shot woman yet?"

"Thurston knew about Bonnie soon as she hit the floor. And Stokes knows he'll never find Brooks."

Bonter nods. "You know, last night I dreamed Brooks got out of that pit."

I snort.

"Honest. I had to kill him again."


I fill a flask with my best whiskey, aged in a burned oak barrel in my basement. I drink. It's afternoon. Eddie comes down the steps, rifle in hand.

"Hawkins said you was down here."

"Whiskey?"

"Nah. I'll be back in the sun in a minute."

I chin at the rifle.

"Hoot's hogs are dead."

"The horses." I enjoy a long sip. "The chickens next."

"I got other work too."

"But you like this work better. What? You aren't still grousing over Bernadine?"

Eddie opens his mouth and looks adrift. Closes it.

••

"Well, get back to your overseeing work."

Eddie backs away.

I sit next to the whiskey barrel. The air is dank and the stone foundation, built thick enough to support a barn, is damp.

Brooks reminds me: when a man pays for loyalty he only buys obedience, and that, for a time.

I sip.

Bonter's a good kid the way Eddie was a few years ago. They come in, glad for the break. They work hard to show it. One day their eyes are like metal with all their secret thoughts etched for the reading. They do the work; put their asses on the line but don't wind up wearing the suits and silver tipped boots. Short order, they know more than the man who built the empire.

I climb stairs, grab a rifle and go outside. Cross to the woods.

Specters—that's the kind of commerce no Eddie or Hawkins would ever conceive. A businessman sees the same world as anyone else but his eyes work different. He spots linkages. He sees what men want and contrives to supply that exact thing. Not just any man's wants. Any damn man wants all sorts of things, all of them outsized to his worth. The businessman looks for the man who has something of value, and then seeks to discover what he wants even more. That's the key to wealth:

Find the man whose wants make him mistake the value of his assets.

Of course, the easiest to identify are cooch and alcohol. But there are plenty more. Just happens the ones cater to vices pay better because no man introspects his vices. He writes them off as his creator's mistake—gladly—and if he wants to lead a life of virtue, seeks some other kind.

Take Thurston Leicester, a miserable banker. He works under the same principle, but corrupts it. He provides men credit on the principle they want money today more than they want money

∙∙

tomorrow. That's fine, as far as the principle goes. Take every penny a fool will part with. But where you get your money for the loan, Thurston, you goddamned thief... that's the corruption. You loan money that ain't yours, and cry for help when some old woman wants her deposit back. And walk up and down the street like a goddamn social benefactor.

That's what I should have told the shoeshine boy, Marshall.

I cross a small crick that leads to the corner of Devil's Elbow and stand at the walnut tree. The air is warm, even in the shade, and the still lake pretends the ghosts of screaming Indians don't skulk in the leaves and breeze. Nor the ghost of my granddad who put them there.

"C'mon down out there! We got to talk!"

I lean against the tree. Bark crumbles in my fingers. I prop the rifle against the trunk, fish my flask and drink a deeper pull than the last.

"I got something you want. I'm in the puss business."

I turn but no one is behind me. Seemed like Bonter followed me down.

"I got what you want, and you got something for me."

Nothing.

"C'mon, you fucking savages. Let's dicker."

I gander across the lake through air that feels thick. Lift my flask.

Something hard raps my head. I swat, spin. No one. A green walnut rolls and stops on a tuft of leaves. I look upward, then a full circle. I'm alone.

I pick up the walnut. "I come for a deal, you fucking spooks."

Rearing to hurl the walnut, my thumb mars the rind. I break it away with a fingernail. The scent is potent, antiseptic.

••

In the leaves there's dozens. Hundreds of the lime green pods. I examine the shell in my hand. Recall the specter's hand on my back.

Them fuckers are in the tree. One way or another they're in the tree.

I don't like whiskey so much, these days, as in my youth. During the war when I was sixteen I could drink myself blind and outshoot the sober boys. I came home after Gettysburg and family said on July second, they heard cannon and knew it was me, and I said I didn't shoot goddamn cannon. These walnuts... something not right about the whole thing. My head is cloudy as the air over the lake. Walnuts. Maybe I'll gather a mess and have a whore bake a pie. Leave it on the tree.

Or bring a gizzy from Walnut, leave her under the tree. Maybe...

I turn the walnut over in my hand, screw the cap on my flask. Too much whiskey for one day.

A rifle shot echoes.

The hillside follows the bowl of the lake and limits visibility. Twenty yards off, a crick arrives from a distant corner of McClellan land—back before my father sold Devil's Elbow for a few buckets of seed, you could draw a straight line out for a mile and everything on the right was Hardgrave and on the left was McClellan.

The rifle shot came from my land.

One of my stills.

I have many operations, the oldest in the wood below my house. As years passed competitors sought terms, sick of the fight, hoping to form a cartel under my leadership. I bought the bigger operations and hired their owners to operate them, and now control all the alcohol that gets made in Walnut County.

••

Four men produce whiskey in Jefferson and Clarion counties. When I fold them into my group, I'll set prices as far as Philadelphia.

I hear another rifle shot, and though I ordered Brooks to hit us hard, Brooks is dead.

This operation bears Thurston Leicester's fingerprints.

I slip into undergrowth where lake meets woods on the side hill leads to my house. Keep the rifle barrel pointed toward the still, a quarter mile away, and creep through a dale and loiter with my eyes level to the crest.

Stokes fires a rifle. Another man, by his suit and spectacles a traveling revenue agent, uses a shotgun. Together they ensure no square inch of metal survives without holes. Riggle—the newspaper man—has sent his photographer. Behind the shooters, the man works a camera box set atop a tripod. He'll record the men posing when the damage is complete.

The smell of fermented mash washes over me. I clench my rifle and fix my mind on the end, instead of the means.

\*

After the last rifle echo faded and McClellan's man Eddie strode off through the woods, Hal Hardgrave stood erect, studied the spaces between the trees as he turned a circle. Then he stumbled down a tiny depression and clawed up the other side, tiptoed across mossy stream rocks, and knelt at the first hog he found. He withdrew a knife from the sheath on his hip, found the hog's breastbone and sliced the corpse deep through its neck. Blood spilled in clumps. Hal grabbed the hog by its hind legs and reoriented its head to a downward angle on the slope.

••

He was almost too late.

Hoot glanced through the woods, placed his hand on his back and allowed his gaze to traipse over the terrain until it alighted on another hog.

He hurried over leaves like a native, the knife never returning to its sheath. He slit the throats of twelve hogs and positioned them to allow gravity to pull the blood.

These hogs needed to get to town.

Hoot looked to the sky, found the sun two-thirds across. Keep two hogs dripping in the barn and haul the rest.

Through the trees came a crashing of twigs and leaves. Hal lifted his rifle and drew a bead in the direction of the noise—and saw Angus followed by Ian.

"Here!" he called. Whistled. Placed his hand to his back.

Angus skidded to a stop and Ian ran over him.

"We heard the shooting!" Angus said. "But Ian wouldn't come." Angus looked to the dead sow at Hoot's feet, the blood on his boot. The gaping slit at the throat. He stared at that.

"Who's in the barn, standing watch on the horses?"

Ian punched Angus. "Told you!"

Angus hit him back.

"Nevermind. Go get Lucy. Fit her with the harness and bring a rope. We don't got all day."

The boys hurried away.

Hoot kicked the sow and a dead gasp escaped her mouth.


The boys returned leading Lucy, a twelve-hand mare. Angus held the traces and Ian walked a few steps ahead with a coiled rope over his shoulder. The horse splashed through the stream and Angus led a wide circle, halting with Lucy's hind five paces shy of the hog.

"Cinch a slip knot round her ankles," Hal said.

**⁂**

Ian worked the rope and finished, handed it to Angus. Angus secured the rope to the harness ring.

"Drag the hog to the barn and come back. Tell Rose to put on coffee, fill the dipping drum, and start the fire underneath it."

"You want I should get the scrapers?" Angus said.

Hoot nodded. "Tell Rose to get the scrapers and everything else."

The boys left and Hal moved to the next hog.

*

Angus led the horse and Ian walked with the hog to the barn, then stationed in shadows, worked at undoing the knot at its feet.

Angus said, "Tell Mam about the coffee."

"You tell her."

"I'll beat your ass," Angus said.

Ian met his eye a moment and slipped away to the house.

Angus knelt at the hog's head, pressed his finger to its eye until the orb popped sideways and his finger sank into the socket. He snorted and shifted his attention to the slit that ran from the hog's neck to breast, severing the great artery beneath and allowing the blood to drain. A clot was lodged at the bottom, partially obscured by flakes of dried leaves and black humus.

Angus removed his finger from the hog's eye and ran it along the length of the slit, registering the tough hide edges, the soft clotted hair, the clammy silken meat. He inhaled the scent of blood. Fell back on his haunches. Tasted his finger.

Ian approached.

Angus clambered to the hog's feet and untied the knot. He led Lucy out of the barn.

＊＊

"What's with Pap?" Ian said, waiting at the entrance. "You see the way he was standing? Like his back didn't hurt."

"It comes and goes; he said before. You heard him."

They led Lucy around the barn and at the woods, Ian unfixed the barbed wire and looped it back over the post after Angus and Lucy passed into the woods.

"You don't got to do that," Angus said. "They're all dead."

Lucy snorted as Angus led her along a path of pig blood.

"You see him anywhere?" Angus said.

Angus stopped and Ian stood beside him. They faced different swaths of forest. Angus shrugged.

Ian cocked his ear. "Listen."

Angus stepped onto a stump. "That's him." He pointed into a ravine. "Follow that hemlock to the trunk. See his feet? Knees?"

"What's that sound?"

"Bawling like Mam. Let's get these hogs to the barn. Pap won't be       no       help       anyway."

••

# Chapter Sixteen

Grace held her hand to her brow and looked east, then rotated toward the orchard. Hannah and Elizabeth were playing—hiding—somewhere.

Rose hadn't seen them.

Another rifle fired in the woods. Grace fought a constricting fear in her chest. She ran to the barn, listened, called. She ran to the orchard. Another rifle cracked. She ran to the lake and the rifle fired again and again.

She should have turned around five minutes after arriving—the minute she learned Jonah McClellan was making war. Should have gotten on the train and paid for tickets clear to the other side of the country. Henry was dead and there was nothing she could do about that. Dot had never returned and Hal was more worried about his hogs than finding her.

The only smart thing to do was leave, and see to it that Elizabeth and Hannah never met Jonah McClellan.

They wouldn't have gone to the woods... Please God they wouldn't have gone into the woods...

Grace hurried upslope to the house. Across the field on the McClellan side stood a form she recognized. Hawkins Bonter stared back at her, hands on his hips.

From behind the barn came a joyous peal, Hannah, as if oblivious to the catastrophes that had besieged the Hardgrave clan. Elizabeth chased and the two raced toward the chicken pen and disappeared behind.

Grace exhaled but the compression in her chest remained.

Turning again toward McClellan's, she touched her pocket and felt her pistol, and below it, the pocket knife. She saw Hawkins' face as it was last night, a faint, bemused grin.

What stories had he heard since arriving at Walnut? About Hal? Henry?

Her?

Bonter waved.

She raised her head high—she would acknowledge him but not return his enthusiasm.

He stepped sideways.

Grace mirrored him.

Bonter turned and walked.

She paced him, absently, and they drifted toward the bottom corner of the wheat field that a few days before was Henry's deathbed. Grace looked to the field's edge, the sunlight-limned crowns that descended to the lake.

Bonter walked as if he'd forgotten her. She pulled a shaft of wheat and dissected the grains, tossing each aside carelessly. The pistol in her dress pocket bumped against her leg with each step.

"I heard a story about a woman last night," Bonter said, still twenty yards distant. "Pulled a pistola on Jorg. I said, 'There's no woman that crazy' and Jorg said she was Hoot Hardgrave's little sis and I should go get an eyeful before she pulled the same stunt on someone with less humor."

••

"It didn't happen that way."

"No?"

"Where were you? Inside, watching?"

"I was driving Mister McClellan last night. A circuit I understand is the regular rounds."

"Checking on his whorehouses?"

"The rounds."

They were a few feet apart, circling like dogs of undecided friendship.

"Where were you a few minutes ago, with all that shooting going on in the woods?"

"Greasing bearings." He showed her a black streak on his sleeve.

"It wasn't gentlemanly, sneaking up on me in the barn."

"I'm a working man."

"It isn't polite, stalking me in the fields here."

"Stalking isn't the right word."

"Why?"

"You took this path so we'd meet where we stand, that's why."

She turned. He followed. They walked from the field into the thinly wooded crest above the walnut tree on Devil's Elbow. Downhill, the forest grew denser. Bonter tended that direction. Grace glanced back toward the Hardgrave house. Her pistol knocked her thigh.

Grace said, "I went to see your cohorts about a girl that disappeared last night. My niece, Dorothy. Left all her worldly things here."

"They said you asked."

"You see her?"

He looked through her. "I didn't see her. That all you want to talk about? Other women?"

"You seemed on edge getting off the train."

••

"I tried six ways to Sunday to get a hello or goodbye and you wouldn't pay me any mind. I thought I'd have to—"

Grace stopped. "You're spinning a web, Mister Bonter."

"It's the Lord's truth. Let's walk." He reached short of her hand.

She looked ahead to the lake and the few remaining trees between, casting short afternoon shadows. "Lets don't," she said. His face looked baby-skin smooth—save the scars—like he'd been bathed in milk as a child and never yet had need of dragging a razor over his neck. The corners of his eyes held mirth. "This the first you been in Walnut? Your first work for McClellan?"

He nodded.

"What have you heard about the boy they found right over there?"

"His name was Henry, and McClellan is certain your brother did it. Killed him, that is. And he's hell-bent on tearing his life apart one piece at a time."

"That's what's going on with the cattle? The hogs?"

Another nod. "Maybe this isn't a good place for you to stay?"

"It could be a good place."

Bonter sank his hands in his pockets. "I thought come Saturday you might want to find a dance or something in Reynoldsville."

"I don't think so." Grace backed from him. "But if you hear news of my niece, Dorothy, I want to know. Or if you hear anything about Henry. Will you find me?"

Bonter nodded, his eyes pointed at her, unflinching, incongruous with his shy hands and aw-shucks grin. He pulled a hand free and took hers.

A tingle chased up her arm and down her back.

Grace backed away and a dozen paces removed, whirled and hurried toward the Hardgrave house.

••

Grace looked out the top floor window at the end of the hallway. As a girl she'd stood here at night, watched the moon and imagined what her future would hold. Whether she'd find a man and bear him sons. If he would appreciate the way she cooked. If he'd pinch her while she worked, or till extra space in the garden so she could plant flowers.

A few years later she'd looked out this window and had seen the McClellan house illuminated through a narrow band of trees—and had been curious.

Later still, she stood at the window with her mind swirling, and wondered about the man who had claimed her body, harrowed her legs so they folded apart like clumps of black dirt, and planted seed deep within the split soil.

She'd gone to Jonah McClellan after five months to tell him she carried his baby. Eight years later the baby died halfway between them, in the field she crossed to tell.

•••

# Chapter Seventeen

Hal sat to a second morning of steak and eggs, coffee. Enough to make a man feel rich, if he didn't have a rifle at his temple, forcing him to slaughter his livelihood.

Yesterday after hauling the hogs from the woods, Hal and the boys scalded them one by one, then scraped their hides—an all-afternoon and evening chore. Hal watched the boys' hands go pale from holding the bell scrapers and then red from the boiling water. His boys talked like this was the way things were supposed to be, that a man would slaughter all his hogs at one time and not save any for breeding. They talked like regular boys, keen to split the pig bellies open and look for tapeworms, eager to cook and eat the hearts 'cause they taste even better than cow heart.

Finally, Hal had positioned the wagon in the upper barn bay. Eleven scraped carcasses hung from crossbeams. Getting each in the air had been a trick—a combination of the boys lifting the hog and Hal heaving a rope over the cross beam. He'd run out of rope and begun using chains, and one of the chains had broken, leaving a hog contorted on the floor with one leg broken under. Hal had left it there until he could swap it out with one of the others. The meat was probably full of blood.

After hanging the hogs, Hal had moved the wheelbarrow under two at the same time and split their bellies open. He'd misaligned the wheelbarrow and most of the first hog's entrails slithered to the floor. Standing in the guts of one, he hacked the breastbone of another with an axe. Blood came out in clumps that looked like organs.

Night had fallen by the time they dumped the last wheelbarrow of guts in the field. Hal had the boys splash a few buckets of water over the wheelbarrow, but had forgotten about the barn floor, where the spilled intestines had broken and half-digested roots, insects, and acorns had been drink for thirsty boards.

Now after a fitful night's rest, Hal stood on the planks with the morning sunshine falling at his feet. The horses were hitched to the wagon and Hal was ready to take the hogs to the butcher in Reynoldsville. Angus and Ian watched him, their big eyes absorbing everything he did.

They'd remember all of this. They'd reflect on it someday when they thought about the way their old man raised them.

A quick breeze lifted the sharp odor of stomped pig entrails. Hal's cheek twitched and his eyes rimmed with water.

"This ain't the recommended way of doing things, boys," Hal said. "Normally a man don't slaughter and treat all his hogs at the same time. Normally it's one at a time, or two or three, and a man'll have the goddamn dignity of deciding to do it himself, and he'll have made some fucking preparations so he don't have his whole herd hanging from the beams at the same cussed damn time."

Hal slapped the side of a three-hundred-pounder and it didn't move.

••

"Instead, we got to deal with a brute bastard thinks the whole county belongs to him. And thinks he can do as he pleases with another man's property."

Ian looked at Angus. Angus stared at their father through narrow eyes.

"Well, I'm fed up. I'm goddamn through with it."

"What you going to do?" Ian said.

Hal exhaled. "I won't stand for it."

Angus walked away.

"Where you going? We got work to do."

"You want the rifle?"

"Yeah. Get it and come back here. No. Get my Smith and Wesson instead. Tell Rose to pull it from the drawer. Belt and all. Goddamn sick of this."

"Yessir."

Hal untied the first hog's rope from the eight-by-eight pillar at the side of the bay, and lowered the hog into the wagon. He untied each, moving the trailer, lowering carcass after carcass onto the pile. With all but four on the wagon, Hal led the team outside.

Angus handed Hal a bundle of leather. Hal unrolled the belt, revealing a holster and pistol. "Ma says you'll get yourself killed."

"She's praying right now." Hal snapped open the revolver cylinder. "Angus, hear me good. Don't ever let a woman be the boss of you."

Hal strapped the belt around his hip and cinched the buckle slightly off center. He dropped his hand to the butt of the Smith & Wesson, snapped the pistol free and pointed stomach level. Shoveled it into the holster, lowered his hat brim, and drew the pistol again.

"That was real fast," Angus said.

"Well, I'm about fed up." Hal climbed to the wagon seat, sat erect looking into the distance. He brought his hand to his chin and

••

rubbed. His shoulders slumped. "While I'm gone, I want you and Ian to move those four hogs in the barn to the smoke house."

"There ain't room with all the beeves."

"Make room. Use the block and tackle like I showed you." Hal looked ahead, took reins in hand. Studied Angus a moment and exhaled long. "Tell Rose I'll be back when I'm damnwell back." He snapped the traces and the horses lowered their heads.

The sun had risen a half-hour before. Its rays fell warm on Hal's wrists and neck. His cheek. His gaze flitted over pale grain on the left, corn leaves tinging brown at the edges to his right. Dew had fallen so heavily overnight the dirt caked on his wheels like after a rain.

All this death in the basket of plenty. His difficulties arose uniformly from one man's needing to possess everything he saw, without regard for another man's rights.

Someone ought to cut down a man like that.

A man went as far off keel as Jonah McClellan, it became the duty of the nearest able citizen to handle the situation. If McClellan suborned the law and stomped another citizen, then that citizen became the law. There was no avoiding the logic. Hal had to be the law. He had rights by God, and responsibilities. Civilized society depended on it.


Hal followed a curve and came to a four-way intersection. He swung leftward and after a couple miles, crested a hill and looked upon Sandy Lick, and beyond, Reynoldsville. Hotels, mercantiles, churches. Houses. At the far corner was the butcher who'd gotten the better of their dealings the day before.

A pair of geezers sat on a bench outside the barber on the east side. One elbowed the other in the ribs. The other gaped.

Hal didn't have to look. The hogs were three-high in the middle.

••

That's right, you old coot. Hal Hardgrave killed his cattle and killed his hogs. Next is the wife and chickens. Go fuck a knothole.

Hal snapped the reins. The horses trudged on. At the end of Main he turned left and after another block came fresh upon the smell he'd been outrunning since the farm: dead animals, blood, offal. The sound of swarming black flies.

Hal clicked to the horses, applied the brake, and climbed down from the seat.

Butcher Frank came to the glass door, stood inside the shop looking out with his arms crossed. He wore an apron smeared in blood and a pipe stem peeked from his breast pocket. Hal waved. Frank flung open the door and approached with a slump to his shoulders and a sideways cant to his gait.

"They clean?"

"Bled, scraped, gutted."

Frank peered into the trailer. "No man shoots his animals like this. Here and there, chest, neck, head, ass."

"I didn't shoot 'em."

"Be better if you did. Word's out not to do business with Hoot Hardgrave."

"Figured as much. You got to move these hogs. It's the principle."

"Dollar each."

"I'll burn 'em on the road, first."

Frank turned. Waved his arm. "Do it down a-ways."

"You got to do better than a dollar."

"Yeah? I got fifteen beeves for crissakes. Town only eats so much. I don't have the salt or the barrels to pack eight hogs. Or the time. Got to sell it cheap to move it. Like to help but shit, you losing your ass can't mean me losing mine. A buck apiece."

"I got eight in here. Give me twenty."

"Ten."

∗∗

"Fifteen."

"Eleven."

"Twelve, you fucking thief."

"Twelve."

Hal sighed. "Done. That'll buy enough lead to kill every McClellan in six counties."

Frank shook his head. Almost frowned. "Bring them round back."

Hal led the team around the corner. He waited for Frank to come through the shop and move his truck, then pulled the wagon alongside the rear door.

Another man from inside joined them, a surly, Polish fellow built like a bull that walked on two legs. The Pole embraced the hog closest the edge, lifted, and danced it inside. Frank climbed into the bed. He slid the next hog to the lip and the Pole returned.

When the last was unloaded, Frank dropped twelve coins into Hal's hand.

"Don't come back with dead horses. I don't butch horses." Frank stepped close and lowered his head. "Some of McClellan's boys is in town. I was at Joe's and they was milling around. You think they knew you'd be here with your animals?"

"Joe's?"

"Uh-huh."

"Which fellas?"

"Don't know em by name. The foreman, Eddie, I suppose. Couple others—young fella I never seen."

Hal nodded. "Thanks, Frank. Thanks."

The packed dirt road in front of the butcher shop became brick a few yards before intersecting Main. Horse feet clomped and the empty wagon rattled. The sounds bounced from buildings and

••

Reynoldsville was suddenly an eerie place. Hal pulled his Smith & Wesson, checked the cylinder and replaced it in his holster. He planted his elbows on his knees. Twisted to each side, in turn, to loosen the stiffness in his lower back. Watched the empty sidewalks and upstairs windows.

He swallowed.

Hal stopped the team in front of Reynolds' Mercantile—run by old man Reynolds' son. About to step down, Hal glanced up the street, saw no one, and twisted for the view behind.

In his back he felt a twang like a snapped bowstring. He cast his hand to the wagon frame. The muscle froze him half-twisted around.

His back locked the same way every time. Within a half-hour the muscles would cinch up so tight he'd have to crawl to move and he'd be praying for someone to come along and mash a chisel through his temple.

Steady, he eased to the ground.

"Hoo-hoo-hooot!"

Three men emerged from an alley on the other side of the street. The one in front laughed.

They approached three-wide. Their hands hung limber like knife fighters ready to move. Hal braced against the wagon. Closer, they diverged.

Hoot gritted his teeth. The youngest-looking man angled for the back of the wagon. He must have been the one Frank didn't recognize. Looked like a half-breed. The man on the left, McClellan's foreman Eddie, cut in front of the horses. The other— the biggest of the three—was the man Grace pulled her pistol on. He looked ready to plow through the wagon to get at Hal.

Hoot reached for the seat, threw his leg to the step. A second string in his back twanged and an honest cramp settled above the

&ast;&ast;

crack of his ass. Sweet Jesus this ain't the time. Hal pulled his thigh and stood on the step, hoisted his leg to the wagon.

A hand seized his shoulder and toppled him.

Hoot landed on his hip, jarring his vertebrae and firing a bolt of fear through him. He caught the face of the man who'd dropped him—it was the new one.

"What's this? Possum?" Eddie said.

The new man snorted and drove his boot into Hal's side.

The big man stepped behind the others onto the mercantile deck. "Careful. He'll crawl under the wagon and shoot your feet."

Hoot sat, rolled to all fours and climbed to his knees. He grabbed the wagon and pulled through the weakness and met the foreman face to face. Hal stared into his eyes, then each of the others.

"I don't understand," Hal said. "I try and do right."

Each face returned his stare without adding anything.

"I'm prepared to do what I got to do," Hal said, and realized his elbow abutted the wagon and he'd have to shift sideways to grab his pistol.

Eddie's breath smelled sweet with syrup and sausage.

Eddie stared into his eyes, stepped into him and delivered a fist into his stomach. Hal crumpled. The big man stepped closer and drove Hal down with a fist to his shoulder. Hal looked at the youngest man's boots. The silver at the toes—the metal tooled in a leafy flourish—how did a farm hand have money for boots like that? Hal landed on his hands and knees and torture flamed through his bottom back.

"I told you yesterday." Eddie's voice was soft like fat summer rain. "See, Jonah said we got to keep killing 'til you leave."

Hoot rose to all fours. The back spasm swelled and Eddie's soft tone encouraged him to remain on the ground.

"Not much left, save the wife. The boys. That what you want?"

••

Hoot's Smith & Wesson waited on his hip, obedient, silent.

From the west a spring-loaded door thwacked closed. No passers by. No wagons or motorcars. Sweat rolled from Hal's forehead to his nose. The Smith & Wesson was loaded—six with one ready to fight. A quick draw and three squeezes would end a quarter of Hal's problems.

He'd practiced his draw. Everyone would know he'd been fair and just. No man should have to suffer a threat to his life, to his family, his livelihood. It was an outrage—by God. It couldn't stand.

But three shots from the ground? This little embarrassment was no reason to risk everything. Not with the advantage so clearly on the other side. Not in the open daylight on Main Street.

"You pack what you got," Eddie said. His voice was easy, an old friend giving advice. "Pack that wife and your sons. Take your sister, before she digs into trouble."

"She's a good girl," Hal said.

Eddie nodded. He touched Hal's shoulder. "You take everything you love and get out of Walnut, Hoot. Or things get godawful worse."

A splotch of rain hit Hal's back. He smelled tobacco.

Hoot twisted, looked up and saw the young half breed rearranging chaw from cheek to cheek.

Eddie shook his shoulder. "Today. Tonight. Or you lose everything."

Eddie walked away. The others followed across the brick street and returned to the alley that delivered them.

Tobacco spit wetted his skin through his shirt. Hal pressed his chin to his chest and closed his eyes. He clawed road bricks.

He grieved himself.

\*

••

The morning sun warms the fields. I sit on the porch and watch the road.

Ideas swarm like stinging insects. Times of tribulation are rife with opportunity. When prudent men hunker down, great men deploy assets.

Lines have been drawn almost without my involvement. The hullaballoo with Brooks raised to prominence a conspiracy I had sensed, but hadn't quite grasped in full.

I strike a match and hold the flame to my pipe bowl, breathe in the hot smoke. Rock to my feet.

Hawkins Bonter works in the barn. His boots protrude from under the Saxon.

"Something wrong?"

"Oil's the secret," Bonter says. "Change it all the time and she'll run forever. Give you more power, too."

"Uh huh. I need to instruct you."

"Be right with you. I'm turning a wrench."

I piss outside the barn and come back. Bonter is still under the Saxon. "I want you to find another vehicle. Something fast."

"That it, Mister McClellan? Something fast?"

"That's it."

"You know what kind you want? Or just something fast?"

"You'll need cargo space."

"This for business?"

I hesitate to speak to a man's boots. "Business."

"Then you want a Simplex. Sixty horse. Nothing faster."

"Will it haul?"

"Hell. It's long, wide and low. Slicker'n ham-grease dog shit."

"I want one."

"New York."

••

"That far?"

"Far as I know."

"How much?"

"Sheesh." Bonter rolls from under the Saxon. "At least twenty-five hundred."

I turn, take a step. "One other thing. When you're done here, find the walnut tree by the lake—down at the Elbow—and gather all the walnuts you can find. This year's, last, whatever. All of them. Don't peel them. I want the rind."

"No problem." Bonter slides under the Saxon.

"And we're going out tonight. Normal run."


The sun nears noon and humidity clings to the earth the way sweaty nightclothes stick to the nape. I fight the temptation to roll my sleeves; instead, I unbutton my cuffs and allow wind from the Saxon's open window to blow into my shirt.

Three days have passed since I saw Ursula. Other than driving by to make sure the house wasn't rousted the night Brooks and I had a run-in, I haven't thought of her. Ursula will make the brothel hers, and for now she is loyal enough to play it straight.

No Mame Gainer, but no Bernadine either.

Earlier, while Bonter worked under the Saxon, I reconnoitered the remains of my smashed still. Eddie had reported there was little to salvage from the mess; I sought to view the evidence again, without whiskey in my judgment. Eddie was right. Stokes' enthusiasm was manifest in every bullet hole and axe gash. The area stank of a thousand gallons of dumped mash.

It will be telling to compare the zeal Stokes deployed against Buzzard and the others' operations.

With all the strikes against me, however, I am satisfied. Henry is buried and Hoot Hardgrave will soon be dead or driven from his acres. The Hardgrave side of the lake is prime farmland, sixty tillable acres and most of it fallow several years. Those acres could produce corn and wheat, and many times I have stood at the walnut and envied Hardgrave's apple and pear orchard.

In a single run my operation could convert every piece of fruit from those trees into brandy—and temperance or not, women like brandy.

The end has never been in doubt. The walnut, the specters. Hoot's ass-wiggling sister add interest to the game—but the end will be the end.

Witchy omen, Grace showing up now... as if some instinct clued her to Henry's demise.

I'll have to arrange a meeting with Grace Hardgrave. Survey her thoughts. Won't do any good to run off Hoot only to have Grace squat on the plot.

Maybe run into her like I used to.

I close my eyes and see her bathing in the lake—can almost feel binoculars press the bridge of my nose.

"You want to turn left up there. Here!"

Bonter cuts the wheel.

"Sixth house. Right side. Swing by the shanty and park in back."

Outside this house resembles any other except at night when it has a red glow in the window above the door.

Stokes sits on chair located in the shade of the patio.

Bonter parks.

I swing open the door. "Stay here."

Bonter kills the engine and slides low into the seat. Puts his head back.

"Stay alert. Sit up."

I exit the vehicle with a mild chub from recollecting Grace in the lake, and enter the house through the rear entrance thinking to

••

grab a minute with a bent over woman. Ursula's in Bernadine's old room. Passing I see no light escapes the bottom of the door.

I continue down the hall and Ursula steps from the office door.

"Mister McClellan—"

Her eyes flash a warning. I stop. Glance to the foyer, as much as I can see of it, but nothing appears out of ordinary.

"Mister Leicester's waiting for you. He said he took a chance you'd stop by tonight. He's in the office."

"That right? Just took a chance?"

She nods, steps entirely out of the office and into the hall. "Been here an hour."

I relax my hand on the butt of my pistol and enter the office. Thurston sits at the edge of the desk, his silver-tipped walking stick across the desktop and aimed like a rifle at the entrance.

"Thurston. Get any puss? Or did you come for liquor?"

His face remains somber. He shifts sideways but offers no obeisance to the proprietor entering the office.

Fine. I wouldn't in his.

"I've received word from Mayor Spencer and Sheriff Stokes that, in light of growing public disaffection with alcohol and the baser necessities of life, they've embarked on a campaign to purge Walnut of businesses that cater to the seedy impulse."

"Shit. What do you charge for a sentence like that?"

"They're going to put your cathouses and stills out of operation."

"Sheriff Stokes? What happened to Brooks?"

Thurston smiles thinly and his brow crinkles. "It's a mystery. Nevertheless, the stars have aligned against you. My being here isn't altruistic."

"I'm sure you'll find any of my girls superior to the frump you've got at home."

Thurston shifts and I notice the sheen of sweat on his cheeks. He adjusts his jacket and, composure regained, meets my eyes.

"I'm here to coerce you, Jonah. I've got you by the balls and I intend to squeeze money out of them."

I pull my pistol and bring a slow aim at Thurston's head. "That's not where I keep money."

"Oh, I know you'll do it," Thurston says. "What with Brooks missing after he was charged to convey my message—I guess you murdered him without giving him a chance to speak. But if you have a mind for business—you do fancy yourself a businessman?— you might hold off and hear my terms."

"Talk."

"There are four whiskey operations in the nearby radius including Jefferson and Clearfield counties. Three outside your control."

"Fact."

"You are the largest producer, by far. You've bought most of your competitors, and for some reason, have tolerated the remaining three. Yesterday and today, the sheriff's office, assisted by an intrepid revenue agent, destroyed all known illegal distillation facilities in Walnut County. That same revenue agent is taking action tomorrow on the producers in Jefferson and Clearfield counties."

I motion with the pistol toward the door.

"If you rebuild, and we have not come to an agreement, you will find the local and state law are most persistent adversaries. They will destroy what you rebuild until they—we—grow weary of you."

I flick the pistol. "Outside."

"The upside is that this entire country is going to be dry. Lot of profit for a man with access to credit. And protection from the law."

I lower the pistol.

••

"That's right, McClellan. It's going to be you, or one of the three you haven't broken. One of you will choose a partner with a deep pockets and powerful friends. The others won't be as fortunate."

"I understand," I say. "You come into my establishment and sit your fat ass on my desk. Scratch the varnish with your silver stick. Threaten my business. And the gall of it—you can't rub two dimes together without taking them from someone else." I wave the Smith & Wesson. "Outside."

Thurston opens the door. Stokes steps forward with a hard glint in his expression, feeling his oats. "You might point that somewhere other than my face."

Thurston steps toward me. "I'll expect an answer tomorrow. If you're amenable to talking, we'll come to an understanding based on numbers. If not... I don't have to threaten you."

I lower the firearm and nod as if Thurston Leicester and I have arrived at a compromise. "Afternoon, Stokes. And congratulations on                             your                             promotion."

\*\*

# Chapter Eighteen

Grace scrubbed the barn wall. Cow blood had dried to the whitewashed stone and she wondered if she'd have more success cleaning with a chisel and hammer. Only a few stalls remained. The labor gave her time to think.

"Mommy?" Hannah arrived with a bucket of water. She carried it stooped, not quite strong enough to let it swing from her side, nor tall enough to dangle it between her legs. She splashed half of each bucket to her clothes bringing it from the well.

Angus and Ian had worked all morning hanging hogs in the smoke house, and Rose had permitted them to sneak off for a couple hours hunting rabbits—why, Grace couldn't fathom. More meat? Not that Hal would have stopped them. His back was flaring up again. After returning from town he retired to his room.

"Thank you, sweetie," Grace said. She dropped her brush and took the handle from Hannah, then held the lip to the wall and cascaded the water over the blocks. "That'll soften the blood."

"More water?"

Grace nodded. "Don't hurt yourself."

From outside, a rifle echoed. Grace paused. It arrived from nearby, but not so close as to cause alarm. There wasn't any livestock to worry about other than the chickens, and the shot originated in the woods between the barn and the road, not the chicken coop.

It was one of the boys hunting rabbit.

Elizabeth arrived with another bucket and Grace pointed. "Soak the wall there, like I did."

A large shadow fell across the barn's open gate. Rose appeared, frowning as if she'd taken great care constructing her countenance before turning the corner.

"Run along and get more water," Grace said.

Elizabeth and Hannah carried their empty buckets past Rose.

Outside there were two more rifle shots. The echoes rolled into a single fading sound.

Grace scrubbed the wall. "It'll take a while, but I believe I'll get all this blood up."

Rose clasped her hands at her belly. Sighed. "We ain't hardly talked since you arrived."

"Oh?"

"You come at a bad time."

"I know." Grace waved the brush, its bristles gleaming red. "I wanted to help a bit."

"You've helped. But these are hard times. You got to understand that."

"I understand. I was prepared to move on, the day I came. But being here has reminded me of some things."

Grace scrubbed the wall. Cow blood frothed pink under her bristles. Rose brought everything into focus. Grace had fled Walnut but now she was back, and she knew why she'd returned, and why she worked.

Her labor was claim-staking.

..

She worked here because she wanted to be here—because she had a longstanding right here. These acres were where her pristine childhood was defiled. Where Uncle Elmer and then Jonah McClellan subjected her to vulgar whims. She'd run away and almost been tricked into forsaking her birthright, but she'd turned a corner. She'd been at the absolute bottom of the heap, scrounging for survival, but God sent her a gift: outrage. She'd found the courage to face the root of her twisted life; she'd come home to wrestle her past and if the present jumped in against her, then she'd tear it asunder as well. In coming to Walnut, she'd come to take back the life that had been stolen from her when she was powerless.

She had come to confront Jonah McClellan.

Now Rose was telling her to move along.

"I don't know what Hoot's going to do," Rose said. "But it's going to be harder on him if he has to worry about you and feeding two more younguns."

"Seems to me he needs all the help he can get. The boys aren't big enough for most farm work, and Hal can't do it. And you keep plenty occupied with the house and kitchen."

Rose twitched below her left eye.

Grace said, "Maybe Hal hasn't said anything because he's glad for the help."

"Hoot's just a man. He's got no spine and that leaves me to say the difficult things."

"Why do you call him Hoot? You know that's disrespectful."

"That's your answer."

"How can a man have a spine with his woman constantly undermining him?"

"You'd better go. You're not welcome."

"Have either of you given any thought to Dorothy? Has Hal stopped at the sheriff's, or cabled family? She disappeared and it doesn't trouble anyone?"

••

"It troubles him." Rose turned away. "She's gone back to her family and I'm glad she had the sense to see the trouble she was causing. This house has plenty enough already."

"You don't think it peculiar she left all her things? She could just as easily be floating in the lake as wandered back to family."

"What would you have us do? What would you have Hoot do? We'd all appreciate if you'd finish up and gather—"

Rose halted.

From the woods opposite the pasture came a shout followed by the screech of tearing underbrush. Angus burst through, dropped to all fours and crawled below the barbed wire. He sprinted across the pasture. Inside the barn, he stood behind the wall at the gate and pointed his rifle back to the woods.

Rose lurched toward him. "Whatever—"

"They shot Ian!"

"What!"

"Ian. Right here!" Angus thumped his chest.

Rose's face drained.

Grace ran to him. She dropped to her knees and took his arms. "Where were you?"

"'Tween here and the road, watching grays." He shifted the rifle to indicate he'd been hunting. "Someone shot Ian."

"Where is he? Lord, no!" Rose screamed. "Where's Ian? This is Hoot's fault."

"Did you see who?"

"I shot back."

"I know. Did you see who shot Ian?"

Angus shook his head sideways. Rose grabbed Angus by the shoulders and plunged him against her belly. "You're safe? You're not shot, too? What have they done?"

"Take me there," Grace said.

••

"They're still there," Angus said. He pushed away from his mother. His eyes were big and aware. "But Ian's alive."

"They? How many?"

"Don't know. Maybe one."

"You can't go back there! Send Hoot. I'll send Hoot!"

"Take me there," Grace said. "Rose, go inside. Get Hal out of bed. I'll go for Ian."

"No! Wait for Hoot. Don't go, Angus! Grace can go!"

"Rose! Hurry!"

Grace grabbed Angus's hand. With the other he carried his rifle at the breech. Rose rushed behind, clasped Angus's shoulder but he tore away.

"Ian's out there dying!"

"Get my girls into the house, Rose. Go now! Get Hal—but get my girls into the house! Go!"

Angus raced into the pasture with Grace behind. They paused at the fence, beyond which stood a briar barrier that gradually faded into forest. Grace placed her finger to her lips. They waited with ears to the woods. Grace looked back; Rose shuffled toward the house with Hannah and Elizabeth corralled before her arms.

"Angus, how many men are there?"

"Just one, I think. I don't know."

"How many rifles did you hear?"

"One."

"Did you see the man who shot Ian?"

"No."

"See what color clothes he had on?"

"No."

"What did you shoot at?"

"The sound."

"Did Ian say anything?"

"His mouth was full of blood. He was coughing."

••

Grace knelt. "Hold the wire up so I can get underneath."

Angus lifted it with the barrel of his .22 rifle. "I rolled him on his side and come for you."

"Me?"

Angus held her eyes. Grace swallowed.

She crawled below the wire and when she stood, he led.

"This way," Angus said. "We don't have to go through briars." He stopped. "You think he's gone? The rifle man?"

"I don't care. We have to help Ian."

Angus led to a footpath that penetrated the dense thistles and blackberry briars that sprouted all along the edge of the forest. Under the canopy the shaded air was cool. The soft ground gave way to moist humus. Grace searched ahead but up close the leaves were broad and green and impenetrable; rare apertures to the forest ahead revealed only dark brown tree trunks and ancient moss-covered boulders. A man could hide behind any of them.

"How far?"

"Just ahead."

Angus crept swiftly, the rifle pointed ahead and his arms ready to fetch the sights to his eye. Grace stooped and lifted her dress from dragging in the leaves, but noise was unavoidable. "Whoever did it must be gone. Let's hurry, Angus."

Angus moved quickly but cautiously, and Grace wondered if she ought to keep her mouth shut and allow the nine-year-old to lead his brother's rescue.

What a man Angus Hardgrave promised to become.

They came upon Ian. Grace stopped ten feet away. Angus stood beside his brother and stared into the woods with his rifle ready. Blood splotched dry leaves. Ian's face was white—all his color had spilled out his chest. His eyes were still. A black fly crawled at his lower eyelid. Ian's rifle lay inches from his fingers.

"Jesus," Grace said. "Oh Lord, Jesus. Embrace this poor child."

..

She stepped to him and kneeled, placed her fingers to his neck. Grace looked at Angus, nodded ahead, toward the road. "Is that where the shot came from?"

"Uh-huh."

"How many times did you shoot back?"

"Four."

"See anything out there now?"

"No."

Grace snaked her arms below Ian and lifted him. Her hand slipped through blood on his back, and his shirt soaked through her sleeve. The wound went all the way through. He'd been shot with a deer rifle.

She carried Ian. Angus followed like a soldier guarding a retreat.


Grace climbed the steps with Ian in her arms. Rose opened the door.

"Put him on the table so I can work on him," Rose said. Her face glistened.

"He's... he's past that."

"On the table!"

Rose cleared a lantern and pepper grinder. Grace rested Ian on the tabletop as if he was asleep and she didn't want to rouse him. Rose shouldered her aside.

Hal had come down from upstairs. His face was blushed and swollen about the eyes. He wore overalls and an undershirt, but no shoes, and leaned against the wall while keeping one hand on his back. His toes were crinkled.

"Angus?"

The boy looked at him.

"You get off any shooting?"

⁑

"Four." Angus stepped into the kitchen. "Don't think I hit nothing."

Grace noticed Rose's hands were on the table beside Ian.

Hal came around the table corner. He shared a long look with Rose and finally turned away.

Hannah and Elizabeth hesitated at the kitchen entrance.

"Girls—stay in the other room," Grace gestured away from what should have been a burst of Hardgrave grief.

"It's all but done, now," Hal said. "All but over. I thought we'd have more than a few hours but that's all we get."

"What?" Grace said.

"I'm broke." Hal reached to a chair at Ian's feet and rested his weight upon it. He sat, slumped with elbows on knees, head hanging like a weight from his neck. He spoke to his chest.

"I'm done with it. There's no fighting a man that'll do this. Not when he's got the law stuffed down his pocket." Hal's voice firmed. "We're going tonight. Angus and I'll dig a grave by the lake and you women can gather what you need to take. We'll find land west somewhere. I don't know. We can't stay here."

"Have you lost your mind?" Grace said.

Hal looked up. "That's all I got! I'm broke. I'm beat. I got enough money to leave and if I don't go now, I'll lose that. He'll kill every miserable one of us."

"You got to talk to Jonah," Rose said. "He wants the land. The Elbow. You give him the Devil's Elbow and everything's better."

"No," Grace said. "If you make a deal because he makes you miserable, he'll give you more misery and make another deal tomorrow."

Angus stood at the foot of the table beside his dead brother. He looked from Ian's head to Hal. "Kill him."

"Kill who?" Rose said.

"McClellan."

••

"Agghhh." Hal waved his arm. "Go 'long. Get the shovels from the barn."

"You want me to kill him?"

"I want you to do as you're goddamn told!"

Angus stepped backward, watched his father with each step. He looked at Grace, turned and left the house.

Grace studied Hal and Rose and Ian all together. The dead boy shared features of both parents; he had Rose's oval face and her broad, tall brow. Ian had Hal's wide nose, proudly passed down through generations of Hardgraves. Growing up, Grace had teased Hal that picking his nose had shaped his nostrils that way... Ian had the same wide nose, not like Angus, whose beak was narrow and sharp—peculiar on a boy.

"God," Grace said. She cleared her throat.

They looked at her.

"God have mercy on this boy. And all of us. Hal, you have to fight. You have to defend your family. I swear right now, in the presence of this dead angel Ian and God above, that if you run away I'm going to stay here." Grace looked Rose in the eye. "I was born in this house and it's as much mine as yours—I'll stay here and I'll deal with Jonah McClellan myself."

Hal slammed his fist to the table. Opened his mouth but kept the words inside. He rose, slapped a hand to his back and hobbled to the front door. "I'm going to bury Ian. When I come back I want to see women doing what they were told by the god-cursed man of the house."

Hal slammed the door but it hit his heel and bounced open.

Grace circled the table and peered out the window. Angus entered the barn, probably to find shovels. Hal sat on the front porch steps.

Grace turned. Rose had been watching her.

"Ian has your face," Grace said. "Oval, and a rounded nose."

\*\*

Rose nodded. Her eyes brimmed and glistened.

"Angus doesn't."

Rose's jaw opened.

"If you're on Hal's side, make it plain."

\*

I sit on a stump with a Mauser across my knees. Hand on the barrel north of the breech. It was warm until a moment ago.

Angus. What a hellion. The way he moved, returned fire. Almost made me shoot him.

Wasn't surprised to see him lead Grace to the body. I watched her skinny frame, her quick motion. I can see her now.

Makes the scrotum roll.

She hasn't changed at all, maybe a little thicker in the good places. And now she's come back to Walnut four days after Henry departed.

I look over my shoulder. I'm near the road, hid by a tangle of rhododendron, grape vine, and briars.

Hasn't always been this way. I stomped here in my youth, when the road cut through forest and only moss grew in the shade. I hunted squirrel here. There was a population of black squirrel until I took a liking to their pelts. 1858 or thereabouts. I asked my father what made the squirrels black while others were gray and the small ones red. I asked if it was the tar coming up through the soil on the piece behind the Hardgrave barn. Nah, it wasn't that, my father said. That black stuff just makes a mess of your boots.

After the war, after wives and children and labor—came the Standard Oil and Rockefeller. I worked different businesses. I

••

labored at the farm and did mill work. Eventually I happened on selling whiskey and women.

Through the newspapers everyone knows Rockefeller. Everyone knows of the black gold. Derricks have gone up and wells gone down all through Titusville and Oil City, Franklin. No one thought a mess of that black gold might be in the ground so far to the west, in Walnut. Not my father, dead before Rockefeller consolidated all the producers into Standard. Not the Hardgraves, lazy bastards that never walk their own land, never get their boots stuck in it.

Beside my foot is a teaberry plant. I pull two leaves and chew them.

That oil isn't twenty yards away—and in all this time, there still isn't a Hardgrave with the foggiest notion.

But Grace is one to watch. She ran off when Henry was a toddler but she must have hid on a mountain of mettle and soaked up half of it. Just when I have Hoot Hardgrave about broke, Grace shows up with enough spine for both of them.

If Mame Gainer doesn't pan out, maybe Grace? Some women, you grab an arm and drag her. Others, you root around in her head and find what to break.

She turned her back on Henry but I bet she's soft on those other two.

The girls.

I look out across the trees.

My eyes move to the crowns; I follow a beech from almond-shaped leaves to elephant-skin bark. My heart's burned for decades. Burns like after a good woman. That little shit, Angus... if I could drop him on my lap and whisper knowledge in his ear, I'd say, you cherish the way your first woman smells. You nibble on her ear, and you never forget the way she trills. Remember the taste of salt on her neck. Think of it first thing in the morning and last thing at night—soak her up like you're mad for her, even if she's a tramp and you don't care. Refresh the memory every day because one day you'll be old. Your bones will squeak like mice, and most mornings you'll lay in bed wishing someone would come along and end you, and the only thing that'll get you up will be the idea of grabbing something that isn't yours. You'll lay there with your eyes closed, mind wandering in a half-dream. You'll try to remember your first girl. Whether her kiss was sticky-scared or wet like a handful of brook water. You'll think of her thighs. The smell of her underarms. Snatch. You'll wish you'd memorized every freckle so you don't have to get out of bed.

Son, if I could tell you everything...

I run my tongue across my teeth. Chicken gristle—small, from the knob of a leg bone—wedged between incisor and cuspid. I reach into my pocket for my knife.

*

Angus arrived at the porch steps carrying two spades. He stopped, studied the worn leather at the toe of Hal's boots and his torn, faded pants. The frayed sleeves of his shirt, and the red spider webs across the whites of his eyes.

"Down by the lake, I think," Hal said. "Ian liked the lake."

"Is that the way we're supposed to do it?"

"What?"

"Up and bury him? Not an hour past?"

"What else we gonna do? Pay someone else?"

"How do you know he ain't coming back?"

"He ain't."

"You don't know that."

**

"Come here." Hal stretched his hand.

Angus watched.

"Come here. Listen to me." Hal took Angus by the hand and pulled him in a one-armed embrace.

Angus smelled his father, an acrid scent.

"You got to listen." Hal sniffled, wiped his nose on his sleeve. "They done pure evil to him. Pure evil. Ian only got one chance. It's gone and he'll never have another. It's evil, and you got to get your mind around it, and put it behind you."

Angus wrestled away. He stared at the lake.

Hoot sniffed.

"Take the shovels. We'll pick a spot by the walnut down there."

Angus flashed a look.

"Well, I know I don't like it down there, but Ian never minded. He always liked it."

"You said there was ghosts."

"Well, what the hell do I know? Ian was fond of the tree, and he had a pugnacious spirit. If there's ghosts, he'll lick 'em."

Angus was still.

"Go along. Take them shovels and pick a good spot. I'll be down."

Angus carried the shovels along the trail from the porch. He stood at water's edge.

Killing Jonah McClellan would solve the family's problems, but it wouldn't make his father whole. The Hardgrave situation was precarious and desperate, but there was another solution. Jonah had killed Angus's dog, but Hal, in failing his family, had killed Angus's brother. Maybe the best answer was to let Jonah McClellan kill Hal.

Or hurry things along and do it for him.

Hoot arrived at the lake with Ian in his arms, swaddled in a white bed sheet with a red blossom. Hal's face was drawn as if he

••

battled physical pain. He leaned way back and dragged his feet. His eyes wandered. His face was blank.

Hoot passed Angus, turned at the lake and followed the path to Devil's Elbow. He paused at the edge of the ancient walnut's shadow, tilted his head toward the tree's crown, and stepped into the gloom.

Angus absorbed every detail.

Hoot knelt at the walnut trunk and rested Ian on the ground.

"I was your age once. I thought everything was pretty. We had the farm, and we eat ham all winter long, and in the summers it was corn straight from the field, and fish from the lake, and butter from the churn. I was just like you. My pap was simple, like me. He did what he could, and passed all this on. And if things was different, I'd pass it to you."

Angus spiked the shovel into the dirt and balanced his weight on the back of the blade. He wiggled the point deeper.

"But the world ain't as simple as a man, his land, his work, the harvest of his labor. Not a damn bit. You'll see. I wish I could keep it for you. I wish I could make this farm the only place you'd ever need to see, and family, trustworthy folk, the only you'd ever have to deal with. You're my—I put stock in you just like Ian. Just as much, exactly. But I can't do what no man's done before. Someday you'll see the world for the giant leach field it is. I see you looking like I'm a fool, and I know you think it's as simple as putting a bullet in Jonah McClellan."

Angus pitched aside a spade of dirt.

"I seen the way you look sometimes, like you got a coward for an old man. But I ain't a coward. I see a train coming like to bust me into tomato soup and I step off the tracks. That's all. You're different'n me, though. You got a wild streak."

Angus drove the shovel into the dirt.

＊＊

"But what I was saying is this: the world's full of men who'd rather steal the cherry of your labor than do the labor themselves. The way they see it, life's about seeing how many men they can get under their boots. And they got rules in place. You wonder why I don't put a bullet in McClellan's head? Well, no matter what evil he done—Ian here, the livestock—I'd be hanging from a tree in a day and it'd be the law that done it. They'd say I was wrong, and since the whole fucking cabal works together, you and your mother, and Aunt Grace and her girls—you'd all be left in the cold to starve without a man to see after you. They'd probly say that whoremaster's son Mitch, wherever the fuck he's hiding, deserves all this land instead of you. That's how they'd do it."

Angus stuck the shovel, clung to the handle and leaned.

"Angus, you ever see a group of men, and they got money, and they're in town, putting on airs—be prepared. They'll do any kind of evil they want. You'll never be safe. It's a shame that's all I've accumulated in my sorry goddamned life to pass on to you, but it's the truth. You tell that crowd to go to hell, and you keep away from 'em."

"What if I don't?"

"If you got no better sense, you do what you got to. But someone will come along cut you down."

Angus jumped on the back of the shovel blade. Through the corner of his eye he saw Ian's swaddled feet. His eyes grew wet and his brother's form grew blurred.

Hoot said there was nothing an honest man could do.

He didn't explain what honesty had to do with anything.

••

# Chapter Nineteen

It is morning. I cross the fresh grave with wonder. Buried their boy at the walnut?

Some kind of message?

I kick the mound of dirt, stamp my boot in the middle, and continue to the trunk of the walnut. Hand pressed to the bark, leaning, I feel a connection like Ursula dragging a feather across my balls. Except I see.

They are five, Seneca with skin like stream-bed clay, decked in a feathers and wampum at their chests. Bows at their backs and eyes set in cold faces. They stare at me through a hundred years.

I know these men. They bled the dirt black under the walnut, dripping from legs and arms; chunks of men made into meat and left to rot in the wind. My soul surges at the thought a single man butchered them, and that man's blood courses through my veins.

They know me.

The image fades and I press harder to the bark. Lift my other hand and push into the tree as if topple it.

"You got something for me? Damn you."

An image sprouts from the fog in the back of my mind, not a picture so much as an awareness. I can't see, but I know. I close my eyes and the thought resolves into visible form. The tingle, the electric, is unmistakable; the source is not in doubt. The specters have sent me an image of a woman.

Mame Gainer.

She stands with me at this very tree; she sweeps her skirt at the knee and kneels to a blanket spread at the trunk. Beside her a wine neck protrudes from a basket. She smiles like a new wife. She wears a ring and in a dream-way I understand the specters are telling me Mame Gainer will be my wife, and I will bed her here.

"Tell me about the oil!"

The image vanishes.

My mind is hollow and I can't fill it. I steady myself. Think of who I am and where I am and it comes to me that I've opened a doorway to someplace uncanny.

"Oil," I say, and step toward the wooded slope to my house. "Gainer?"


I find Eddie at the still, bossing Jerome, the underling with women problems. I study the bullet-riddled boiler, copper pipes blasted into chunks that look like squirrel guts strung across the ground. Jerome gathers sections of coiled tubing in one arm and drags another section away from the site into the woods.

"Where's he going?" I say.

"Dumping out there a ways."

"You there!" I call. Swing my arm. "Take that up to the barn."

Jerome looks at Eddie.

Eddie nods.

Jerome reverses himself, labors uphill, the shortest distance to the barn.

••

"He worth a shit?"

"Dense like ironwood, but once an idea takes form it'll hold."

I watch Jerome, aware that Eddie's eyes search my face.

"Yesterday..." Eddie says.

I clear my throat. Spit.

"I—uh. I couldn't take orders like that. I killed the cows and hogs and all—"

I wave my hand. "It's done."

"You got to know it was—I just—it was a boy." Eddie leans against a cherry tree and looks at the ground. "How long I been working for you, Jonah?"

I shrug.

"All that time I never said I couldn't do what you said. And some of those things was nasty. Bad nasty."

"Where you going, Eddie?"

"You run off Bernadine, start in on Hardgrave. I don't know what you're up to. This don't look like business. Since Henry... Things were good, making whiskey and selling puss. That's honorable, decent work. But killing a boy—that's a damn sight different."

"Best to let things like these settle. What I'm building will make whiskey and puss look like selling flowers at a funeral parlor. You'll see."

"Hawkins said something about Oil City."

I clamp my teeth. Exhale. "I'm going there tomorrow. See about another cathouse. Meantime I want you to see our new Sheriff—Stokes."

Mirth flickers across Eddie's lips.

"I want you to find out if I can buy him. Put aside your little man-hurts and lay it to him straight. I'll cut him in, but Thurston's out."

Eddie watches me. "What if he wants numbers?"

••

"Find out what his number is. If Thurston's throwing him nickels, I'll throw him dimes. Use those words with him. You find out if it's money driving him, or what. See to it tonight. He'll be at Fifth Avenue. Always is."

"I will. And Jonah—Mister McClellan—I'm loyal. I couldn't—"

"You'll soon see how I value your loyalty."


Late afternoon I arrive in the barn and find Hawkins Bonter sitting cross-legged and slumped forward. Brim over his eyes. I rouse him with a boot to his knee.

"Going to town."

Bonter jolts erect. "Where to?" He swings his arms like his shoulder is stiff. "You want to see them other stillers?"

"Buzzard?" I say. "Other stillers?"

"I see what that banker's up to. I figured you'd outflank him."

The man is acting queer. "Out flank, huh?"

"That's right."

Bonter beams. Rubs his knee.

I climb into the Saxon. "Why in hell would I resurrect my competition?"

Bonter starts the Saxon. Before the road he says, "Where to, Boss?"

"Walnut."

I withdraw my pipe and pack it with leaf.

After a man's first kill he grows fond of the man that walked him across the line. His speech assumes an affinity. There's a nod, a too-long glance that says we're brothers, you and I. And soon his eyes get dreamy and say, I'm a killer—and ought to be respected as such.

If he survives, he'll learn there's no kinship born in murder.

••

Bonter steers and I drift in thought. I stand at the cusp of meaningful achievement. I've spent my life, my strength. I've sacrificed.

"Stop in front of the barber."

We arrive in town and Marshall Brady, the boy I lectured in economics, sits in front of the window below the striped cylinder, his shoe shine box between his feet. Marshall stands when the Saxon stops.

"Stay here, engine running. Glass up."

I remove a five dollar paper note from my wallet and fold it lengthwise. Marshall Brady watches the greenback. I close the Saxon door.

Marshall gestures for me to sit. He snaps his rag. "I'll make your boots shine like snot on a glass doorknob."

I grab his shoulder and squeeze until I have the boy's full attention. "You got the line down. How's it working?" I release him and he edges away.

"Well, I still get every man that needs a shine. But it's funner than my old line."

"Just rolls off the tongue." I sit. "Hold up. Don't need a shine. Want something else."

"Yes sir?"

"Come here." I lean. The boy steps closer but his stare is beyond me. Quick to fear. I like him more. "I got this fiver here—I need a job done and it has to be done right."

"What kind of job?"

"I need you to get a message to Deputy Stokes. You know who he is?"

"'Course."

··

At the cathouse, I have Bonter let me out in front before he circles behind to park. I enter through the front door. The office is empty; I poke around the papers on the desk.

Ursula appears in the doorway.

"Rutting mood?"

I reach to her elbow and pull. She comes against me plump and warm and the air that arrives with her smells of perfumed powder. The scent strikes like an arrow. Her breath is peppermint from hard candy. She places her lips to mine and presses the sugar rock into my mouth. I growl and push her from the office, pull her down the hallway toward Bernadine's old room.

Spit candy to the floor.

I got naked Grace Hardgrave bouncing the corners of my head. I want to take her by the hair.

We stop at the door.

Ursula is silent.

I study her eyes. Listen.

"Who's inside?"

"No one."

I gesture. She opens the door and I peer around the corner. The room is dark, save the bolt of light from the door. Ursula moves to dresser, strikes a match and holds it to a lamp.

The room is empty, bare except the bed and dresser, which sits unadorned by photos or accoutrements, like a plain woman made all the more forgettable by her lack of paint or jewelry.

"You entertain Thurston last night?"

"I don't entertain anymore."

"Who did he see, last night?"

"No one. He waited for you in the office. I threw him out and Stokes was on the step, said every one of us'd spend the night in jail if I didn't play nice."

"Why didn't you say that last night?"

..

"When did I have a chance to say anything at all, last night?"

I sit on the bed and Ursula stands before me, her hands behind her back. I watch them in the mirror, navigating knots and countless textile obstacles before finally she stands before me in a corset, and it falls to the floor.

I glance at it. "I like that corset."

She kneels on her clothes.

I close my eyes.

Grace.

∗∗

# Chapter Twenty

Marshall Brady raced into the alley between the bank and the adjacent clothier. Alone, he skipped to a stop, threw his hand into his pocket, withdrew the bill and snapped it taut. He examined the front and back.

Jonah McClellan was Walnut's own Vanderbilt.

As swiftly as he retrieved the bill he stuffed it in his pocket. Though his years had been short he'd seen every kind of thievery. No one could be trusted—even gentlemen carried pistols.

Marshall sprinted and emerged at the back of the bank. He turned left on a backstreet that eventually crossed Fifth Avenue.

He slipped inside the Tavern through a rear entrance, ducked between men stumbling to the pisser. The noise was formidable as a block wall—men shouting, catcalls, women braying—Marshall made himself invisible against the bricks and studied the barstools, the booths, the men on foot who rested on neither. He emerged at Deputy Stokes' booth.

Stokes was a Teddy Roosevelt barrel of a man with cropped hair and a bristling mustache. Pugnacity glistened on his skin like sweat. He sat alone.

Marshall touched his arm.

Stokes turned. His face was bland, pale. His eyes seemed to do a great amount of seeing.

"I got a message for you."

"From who?"

Marshall winced. Mistake. "From me."

Stokes drank water. "Beat it."

"There's a man coming for you."

Stokes clicked his fingernails on the table. Looked at the door.

Marshall slipped into the opposite seat, climbed up on his knees and leaned across the table. The polished silver of Stokes' badge caught his eye and he hesitated.

"I heard men," he said, "I shoeshine at the barbershop—"

"What? Get down from the table!" Stokes' face splotched red. He looked across the bar and then at Marshall.

Marshall swung off the seat and around by Stokes. He placed his cupped hand to Stokes' ear. "I heard men at the barbershop. There's a fella coming for you named Eddie. He's mad about some hoor, and he's coming to kill you."

Stokes pulled away, looked in Marshall's eyes. Put his ear back to Marshall's cupped hand.

"That's not all. He said he'd pretend to talk business first, so's to get the drop."

Stokes nodded and Marshall backed away. Stokes held Marshall's stare for a moment, then flipped him a coin. "You keep an ear out, son."

Marshall back-stepped toward the rear entrance, sat still and small. Stokes drank from his glass of water but otherwise remained motionless. Patrons roared and sang and passed Stokes' booth, and

••

Marshall noticed that men sobered long enough to give a nod and receive one in turn.

Marshall watched men's boots, women's polished shoes and lacy black leggings. The men outnumbered the women by a wide margin but the noise was mostly clucking and whinnying. Some of the men paid the women no mind, but only stared into their brews looking like they needed sleep. Marshall grew fixated on a fine, laced boot—he saw the sculpted curve of her ankle, the flare at the genesis of her calf—all accented by her merry voice—she was beautiful as he imagined maybe his mother was beautiful—and then her voice trailed into silence and Marshall realized that while he'd been watching her feet, the shuffle around her had stilled, and the sounds had died, and two men now stood facing each other.

Stokes and Eddie Bonter.

Marshall saw Eddie look downward and followed his eyes to Stokes' right hand, which held a revolver level at hip level.

Bar patrons backed away and Stokes stepped into the cleared space.

"Outside, Eddie."

"You got this wrong," Eddie said. "I come to talk."

"Then talk outside."

Eddie lifted his hands and backed away.

Marshall ducked out the rear of the building, circled the Tavern and crouched behind a giant oak in view of the sidewalk.

The Tavern's front door busted open. Eddie stumbled out as if shoved. He backpedaled across wood planks and landed with his back on dirt only ten feet from Marshall.

"You son of a bitch; I speak for McClellan."

Stokes emerged on the wooden landing, pistol still belly-high. Marshall shrunk behind the tree and watched with one eye.

Stokes said, "I know what you come for."

"McClellan wants to talk."

●●

"You're sore over Bernadine."

"Bastard. Where is she? Where'd she go?"

"Right. You come here to talk for McClellan."

"You gaming me?" On his back, Eddie sat up on his elbows.

Stokes stepped closer but still blocked the door. Patrons stood behind him but Marshall couldn't see a face.

Stokes glanced along the road, both ways. "Don't pull it, Eddie!"

He jerked and a flash of orange spat from his gun and the boom knocked pain straight through Marshall's ears.

"He went for it!" Stokes said, "Son of a bitch pulled on me from the ground."

Stokes emerged and men fanned behind him on the porch. The bewilderment on their faces became curiosity. Marshall looked at Eddie. He'd fallen flat with his elbows still partly tucked, and his right hand rested near the butt of his holstered pistol. His head rolled sideways and his eyes pointed at Marshall. His leg jerked once and then folded outward. Blood trickled from his mouth and he was still.

A voice said, "Everyone knew he was soft on that whore."

"Hey boy, you seen what happened?"

Marshall looked. It was a lanky and whiskered man from the bar. He wore a railroad cap and stood on the porch next to Stokes. "You seen it, boy?"

Marshall stood and stepped from behind the tree. A smile paused at the corners of Stokes' lips.

"It's like the sheriff put it," Marshall said. "Eddie here went for his gun. No way could he've got the drop, but he surely went for it."

*

••

Grace stood at the porch edge. On the horizon a cloud-halo circled the evening moon. The lake reflected its rippled parody. A gust fluttered through leaves and as abruptly as the wind came, it vanished, leaving only crickets to serenade the fireflies. The house was silent.

Hoot had proclaimed everything lost. They'd leave in the morning. Then he'd gone to bed. Rose had lingered a short while with Grace, and had entreated her to take up the cause of Hal seeking terms with Jonah McClellan.

When she was a girl and had just birthed a son she ran away from her problems and consoled herself that fleeing meant survival. A child fathered by a devil had no just claim on her future. But after years of scraping by she learned flight only postponed the ultimatum. She would either remain meek, or hew to a code that demanded sacrifice and risked death, but promised honor. No question was more fundamental, because no evasion would permanently forestall the consequences of a predatory world. She fled Uncle Elmer and Jonah and replaced him with another beast, and another.

Now she watched Hal suffer at the end of the trail of meekness. God in his mercy gave her a lifetime of opportunities to learn.

"McClellan's gathering walnuts on Devil's Elbow."

Grace started. It was Angus. "I didn't hear you creep up on me."

"He sent his new man down there to gather them, but he's there most every day, at the tree."

"Shhh. Everyone's asleep upstairs." She thought a moment. "Why at the tree?"

"He talks to it."

"He talks to it?"

"He mumbles and closes his eyes. Feels it."

"Why are you telling me this?"

••

"No reason." Angus sat on the porch edge. His legs dangled. "But he's down there alone, most every day."

"Are you thinking of something?"

"I could pop off the back of his head nice an' easy."

"Don't say such a thing."

"No one else will."

"Your father—"

"Phhh."

Angus's eyes had an intelligent hardness, as if he understood the way the world worked. He was what they called an old soul. There was no glitter in his eye, like he had some dime-novel, Billy the Kid concept of killing a man. Angus was steady and strong-willed and seemed to instinctively understand the same lesson Grace had spent almost thirty years learning.

She extended her arm and brought Angus close. "There would be consequences to shooting Jonah."

"We got to—"

"Let me finish, Angus. If you shot him, things would get worse. No one would believe it was you, and they'd come take away your father so they could hang him from a tree."

Angus shrugged. "I don't know. But he's down there every day, alone."

Grace woke with anxiety in her chest. Hal had said they'd leave this morning.

Though he was her brother and she dutifully honored him, and schemed to destroy their mutual nemesis... and though Jonah McClellan was a monster, a slave master, a thief...

Jonah believed Hal had killed her son, Henry. He believed it strongly enough to bring utter destruction on their household.

Had Hal killed him?

••

Had Angus or Ian, or all three?

If they were responsible for Henry's death, shouldn't she rightfully align with Jonah against her brother?

Grace gathered her clothes and donned them while Hal, downstairs, shouted at Rose. Grace heard fractured sentences. She tried to un-garble the syllables and parse them, only to miss what words came after. She eased down the steps, avoiding the creaky middle and tiptoed out of the house unseen.

Angus squatted at Ian's grave.

Her legs grew wet with dew from the grassy slope. Grace stood beside Angus. He stared at the dirt mound, his face canted low and his cheeks streaked with tears.

She touched his shoulder.

Angus shrank from her. Grace rested her hand on his back.

"What are your thoughts?" she said.

He shook his head sideways.

The ground before them was loose clay, some still holding the curved plane of a shovel. In the center was a giant footprint. Her mouth fell open. She closed it.

Angus held a clump of dirt in his fingers and crumbled it.

"Why did this happen?" Grace said.

"It was Jonah."

"But why?"

Angus was silent.

She rubbed a small circle with her thumb on Angus's neck. A mosquito flrrred next to her ear but she ignored it.

"Angus?"

"We didn't do nothing."

"I found your knife."

He pulled away. "What knife?"

"Your pocket knife."

"Lemme see."

∗∗

She pulled her hand from her pocket and opened it.

"That ain't mine. I got mine."

"Let me see."

Angus extracted a knife from his pants. He unfolded it and held it beside the other.

"You didn't have two?"

"Who has two knives?"

"Did Ian lose his?"

"It was in his pocket when... he went in there."

Grace shifted to her knees beside Angus. She grasped his shoulders, turned him, and lifted his chin. She studied his puffy eyes. "Tell me the truth, or let God strike us both down right now."

"With God or without. That ain't my knife. Nor Ian's." Angus pulled away. He stepped to the walnut trunk. "This is what you should see."

Grace stood. Angus swung his hands to the corrugated bark. He took a hold and in a moment balanced above the crotch with one foot on each rim. "You see down here?"

Grace took the same path as Angus and climbed. A foot higher and she could see into the tree center. Angus sat on the opposite rim, split his legs against the inner walls, and back and forth worked inside the rotted hollow. He vanished inside the tree. Grace climbed higher. She looked down and only his head showed. There was room for several boys amid the shadows.

"How do you know that isn't full of snakes and spiders?"

"There's tons of spiders in here," Angus said. "Fuckers bite."

"Angus!"

"They do."

"Come out."

"This is where he comes," Angus said. "He stands beside the tree and speaks his mind like the tree is going to talk back at him."

••

Grace climbed down. Angus knew more than he was saying. He dangled information in front of her, playing her, and she could do nothing but play along.

"You've heard Jonah speak his mind?"

Angus threw his arms out, pulled and scraped until he sat on the lip. He tousled his hair. Smacked his arm. "He's here most days, sometimes right off in the morning. He's been here this morning."

"Angus... where are you when Jonah unburdens his mind?"

"Down there."

"Oh dear." Grace looked to the lake. "What's he said? Secrets?"

"He got his troubles." Angus leaped from the tree and rolled on the ground. He brushed his pants with his palms. Smacked his leg. "Fucker."

"Angus! Your mouth... What has Jonah said about Henry?"

"He don't talk about Henry much. But he's said enough."

"Did you know Henry?"

"'Course."

"Tell me about him."

"Dumber'n a bushel of air is what Jonah says."

"Angus."

"What?"

"He's passed on," Grace said. "Show respect."

"Everyone's dead lately. No one wants to do anything about it." Angus crossed his arms.

"Tell me about Henry. Who killed him?"

Angus shrugged. He looked away. "Could've been any of them. Maybe that man that was out waving a stick around, in the woods."

"What man?"

"A few days before Henry went missing. Me and Ian saw a man in the wood by the road waving a stick around in front of him, shaking all the time. He kept looking back over McClellan's place, and eventually that's where he went."

••

"Divining water?"

"Is that what you call it?"

"There's plenty of water right here." She looked at the lake.

Angus stepped away. He nodded at the walnut. "He's so tall I could crouch in the bottom and still take off his head. He leans in with his eyes closed." Angus held her gaze for a second. "That's what I'd do."

He walked the path to the house.

Grace watched his back and rolled the pocket knife in her hand. He was being coy.

She studied the knife. The handle was ocher, stained with blood. She probed the blade spine with her fingernail Opened it. The blade was caked—was that Henry's hair? She touched the steel with her fingernail, as if to rub away the blood, and stopped.

Without the blood, there was no way to say the knife had anything to do with the crime. But it could be deer blood, as easily as Henry's. Hal came to mind—and his argument. Would the law care about evidence?

Grace froze.

A windborne scream arrived from the house. Elizabeth? Hannah?

Running uphill she slipped on grass and caught herself with her palms. The cries were high and piercing. Joyous? Frightened? Grace's heart thudded.

She crested the hill and spotted Hawkins Bonter at the edge of the yard.

With Hannah.

He held her wrists and swung her in wide circles. Her hair flew; her dress flapped. Her peals suggested horror but her face said glee. Grace watched Bonter's face with each turn. He beamed. Elizabeth stood a dozen feet away, leaning forward as if eager for her turn.

Grace hurried closer.

••

Rose opened the front door and crossed to the edge of the porch. She peered around the side of the house.

Grace took a deep breath and placed her hand over her heart as if to calm it. "Put her down! What are you doing?"

Bonter slowed. He lifted his arms and when he stopped spinning, Hannah was vertical. He lowered her, and then with an explosive move, tossed her into the air. She shrieked with merriment and he caught her, then vertigo took him. They collapsed together into the grass. He fell back, grinning.

"I'll thank you to leave my daughter alone."

"I came to see you, not the sweetheart."

"Well, you see me. What do you want?"

"Let's walk..."

Grace snorted. "Come here, Hannah." She led Hannah a dozen steps from Bonter. She knelt with her back to him. "Are you okay?"

Hannah nodded. Her face was flushed. Her eyes seemed to spin in their sockets.

"Did he do anything to you? Hannah, look at me... Did he... did he touch you?"

Hannah shook her head.

"Go inside." Grace spun. She strode toward Bonter with her hands on her hips. She met his eyes and marched past him. "All right, Mister Bonter. Let's walk."

Bonter jumped to her side. "I thought you and I got on real nice the other day."

She stopped and faced him. "You stay away from my girls. What kind a man does that? Come unbidden and twirl a girl in the air. What kind a man?"

"I come to say hello—"

"You've said your hello."

"Well—actually, I haven't."

"Then say it!"

••

"Hello. I'm taking the train to New York."

"Have a nice trip."

"I'm going to buy a new motorcar for Mister McClellan."

"I'm sure you'll enjoy that."

"Isn't that where you came from? Wasn't you on the train the whole way?"

Grace brushed a lock of hair from her face. "I—It's none of your concern where I came from."

"I wanted to mention I was going back on a quick haul—there and back in two days. Thought you was from New York, and I'd tell you now... In case maybe you forgot anything and wanted to pick it up. Or have me pick it up for you. See what I was thinking?"

"Are you—" she stopped. Shook her head and blinked—squeezed her eyes closed to focus her thoughts. She needed a moment with her mind and turned around and walked toward the house. She heard his pants and boots as he hurried behind.

Hawkins Bonter might have learned something about Henry. He might know who shot Ian. He'd been plain about his interest in her, and if a man's lust made him disloyal to his employer, was it the woman's fault? Was there a reason she shouldn't encourage him?

She'd robbed a man in plain daylight and here she was having trouble with the ethics of flirting?

"Grace, hold on!" Bonter ran beside her then stood in her way. "What the hell's got your back up?"

"You come here, twirl my daughter in the air. Proposition me? Are you daft?"

Grace resumed toward the house. She'd seen his eyes... she hadn't gone too far. He placed his hand on her shoulder, light.

She twisted. "Take your hand—"

He'd already removed it. "That's not what I meant. I was being polite. But you got some bug up your ass like every time I say hello

••

I'm here to do you harm. That ain't the case—but it won't ever matter with you. So have a good day."

"Wait!"

"What?"

"I—need to think."

"Think all you want." He strode toward the McClellan farm.

"Stop!"

Bonter halted.

"Your boss is trying to kill my family. And there's history—"

"What? Your history?"

"Me, Hal, Jonah. This isn't the beginning. It isn't realistic to think you can swing my daughter by the arms and all of a sudden your boss hasn't put my family in crisis. Ian's buried right over that hill! Just last night! You don't have a right to expect a particular demeanor from me. Who the hell are you, anyway?"

She steeled her thoughts. Hawkins Bonter was a man, special in no regard. He'd earned Jonah's trust, if he was being sent to New York City with enough money to purchase a new motorcar. Was Bonter clever enough to hope Grace might purchase his secrets with the only commodity she had?

She couldn't possibly go.

She couldn't take the girls; nor could she leave them with Rose and Hal. She'd return to find the farm deserted. The girls gone. The barn burned to the ground.

"I'd like to go with you to New York—"

"Come by in two hours—" he nodded and the wrinkles above his brow vanished. "—we'll saddle up and my brother'll take the horses back from the train depot—maybe, I guess. If I find him. We'll get it done either way."

"No, Hawkins. I'd like to go but I can't. I have the girls... But when you bring back that car from New York, come find me. Maybe we'll drive someplace."

••

Grace stood at the doorway. Rose wrapped a plate in newspaper. A wooden crate sat on the floor partly under the table. Rose moved as if numb from the cold reality of her actions. She placed the plate into the box and grabbed another from the dishes and pans stacked on the planks above.

"You're going to give up your home?"

Rose stooped to the box. "Or wait to get killed. Some choice."

"You believe that?"

"There's nothing else to believe!" Rose lurched, stood inches from Grace. "Ian's dead. Livestock's dead. Tomorrow, tonight, maybe in five minutes I'll be dead or you'll be dead."

Grace wiped Rose's spittle from her cheek.

"You're better off. You don't have a man. When you got one there's nothing to do but wait on him and if you spend forever waiting, that's all your life amounts to. You're nothing but your man, and mine's broke. Someone murders everything you love and the coward you're hitched to hides in the corner, you got to hide there with him."

"That's not what I meant."

"Somehow I'm sure you'll tell me exactly what you meant. But the only way this family gets saved is when it leaves this farm to Jonah McClellan."

Grace retreated a step. She dragged her sleeve across her face, again. "Angus has the gumption to handle Jonah. Why don't you?"

"Angus?" Rose leaned into the table. The legs barked sideways. "A boy? What are you saying?"

"That boy has more courage than—"

"The rest of us? Of course he does. He's got a mean streak a mile wide. You want to take on Jonah, you go right ahead. There's rifles in the cabinet, and Hoot said you was a tomboy knowed how

••

CLAYTON LINDEMUTH | 235

to use them. I'll wait here 'til I hear the shot, and then start unpacking. Why I'll—"

"You'll be a hundred miles from here and still pretending your fight's with me. All because you lack the courage to see the truth."

"Truth?"

"You can't outrun evil. That's it. Fight it. Kill it. Or die from it. You can't outrun it."


Grace stood at the edge of the porch looking over the lake. Her clothes stuck to her arms and back.

People like Rose—

She should have said you either kill evil or every inch you give, it becomes you. You wake up and stand for nothing. You can't barter with it. And Rose would have answered there's the gun cabinet, High and Mighty. You take the biggest gun your skinny ass can carry, and go say hello to Jonah. Then tell me what I ought to do with evil. That's what Rose would have said.

A plate shattered.

Grace jumped, turned about and a moment later kneeled beside Rose. She picked shards of porcelain from the floor with trembling hands. Grace touched Rose's shoulder. She leaned until their foreheads met.

"Rose. We're almost sisters. We'll get through this. Let's be strong."

Rose wept.

"I'll do what has to be done," Grace said.

Rose shuddered, exhaled until she couldn't have any air left in her.

"You have to give me a couple of days. There's a man working for McClellan... he fancies me and maybe it'll loosen his tongue."

••

Rose snorted and plopped on her behind. "Here two days and spreading your legs."

Grace stood. "It starts with Henry. I want two days. Everyone stays in the house. You keep an eye on my girls. In the house. And you stay in the house. I'll be at the bottom of this in two days."

••

# Chapter Twenty-One

Before leaving for New York, Bonter reported the Hardgraves were packing boxes.

I lean close to the driver wheel and slow the Saxon, study the trees ahead, ancient rocks, the thickets—all of it cover for a stilling operation. Soon I arrive at the remnants of Gunnar Buzzard's business. I park, shake the vibration out my wrists, and step from the Saxon.

Beside me stands once-rival Gunnar Buzzard, master stiller, wild man, rumored to have created a still out of a clay pot and tropical leaves while shipwrecked off some isle during his days in the merchant marine. Buzzard settled to Pennsylvania and perfected what people say is his invention—maple rum, distilled every spring at the thaw. Other men collect sap and cook it down to syrup. Spread it on flapjacks. Buzzard adds yeast and a secret he won't reveal, and cooks maple sap into a smoky miracle.

Ten years ago, I sent Eddie to Gunnar Buzzard with a message. Sell your operation or face the wrath of Jonah McClellan. Gunnar said he'd ponder it and deliver his reply in person. That night, I woke with a machete blade pressed to my neck.

At my bedside, Gunnar Buzzard said, "No."

I said, "That's agreeable," and Buzzard withdrew the blade.

Any other man, I'd have ripped him limb from limb. But Buzzard alone knew the recipe. I said, "You'd be dead if not for maple rum. You ought to make more."

"Only so much sap."

"I'll give you the goddamn sap."

The bargain was struck. Every spring thaw, my men tap each maple on twenty acres and deliver the sap to Gunnar Buzzard. He stills maple rum and we split the product. Our relationship is careful. Gunnar's happy to live on his own terms and knows I could have destroyed him. He produces corn whiskey, but only for a pair of local shot houses. And I remember the feel of cold steel at my throat, and appreciate the profitable balance that stays it.

I take in Buzzard's site. "Rebuilding?"

"So they can bust it again?" Gunnar sits on a stump, whiskey jug propped between his feet. He's three sheets. He packs tobacco into a corncob bowl.

I step to a boiler, a copper kettle with a clampdown lid and a sink fixture brazed to the top. They axed the sides, and I count three peppered shotgun holes. The greenish copper pipes are chopped into two-foot sections, and the doubler appears to have been placed on top of a log and hacked in half.

"Thurston call on you? Brooks?"

"Stokes."

I consider that. "Said they'd set you up again?"

Gunner lights his pipe, tosses the flaming sprig back to the fire. "They want to bend a man over a loan."

I find Buzzard's eyes above his pipe bowl. "I figured they'd already cut a deal with you."

••

"I suspect they's places south of here more friendly. Maybe I'll find one." Gunnar drinks from his jug and offers it to me. I decline.

Gunnar says, "You and me's been at each other's throats how many year? Always thought if I got snookered, it'd be you. Now these boys come in from the side—"

"Without lifting a finger—that's what grabs me by the balls."

"Without lifting a goddamn finger!" Gunnar drinks again. "One's got the money and the other's got the law, and neither one makes a fucking thing but trouble. Well, that's what you and me understand. We ain't city, so we're alone. But if a man don't own his labor, then fuck it, he don't own nothing." Gunnar lifts his jug, props his feet on a log, and leans against a tree. "May as well find a gun or take a long ass walk. Fuck 'em."

"That's one approach."

"It's do as they say, and be a slave, or try to hide an operation they already found."

"There's the other thing."

"What's that?"

"You still have that blade you put to my neck?"

Gunnar grins. "I could find it easier than the sober to swing it."

"They have money and the law, but only two people. Thurston and Stokes, it looks like."

"What you have in mind?"

"Maybe nothing. Next time they come see you, play it soft, like you're ready to think on it. Send me word."

# Chapter Twenty-Two

My teeth ache. I bite them listening to a wildcatter named Sprague.
I drove to Oil City feeling the gears of my plan were beginning to
mesh. But this oilman throws sand.

Sprague wears denim and a white shirt; a tie and a mustache, all
lopsided.

"You don't know if that seepage is a splash or a spring. And you
won't, without we drop a hole." Sprague smirks. "Might be muddy
water."

"It's oil, you cussed—"

"We drop a hole, that's your expense. You say there's oil and
that's fine." Sprague shrugs. "If it was here, I'd look and buy the
land. But you from Walnut? There's no oil in Walnut."

"And after I pay for a derrick?"

"I take fifty percent, or I buy the land if you want to cash out.
That's very smart; less risk for you. But there's no oil in Walnut."

"What's a hundred-acre farm worth? Presuming it's sitting on
more oil'n you ever saw in your life?"

"Fifteen hundred."

"And, in your best estimation, what is the cost of standing a derrick on my land?"

"Ten thousand."

"Robbery."

The oilman lifts a ragged cigar stub to his mouth. "Nah. If there was oil we'd make the deal sweet. But there ain't, and you ought to save your money."

"I hear Oil City's run dry. Nothing in Franklin, Titus, all dry."

"You heard a lie, what you heard."

"You know—"

The man tilts his head.

I close my mouth, measure the pugnacious oilman. I remember a derrick I spotted on the drive to Oil City. "Never mind. There's no oil in Walnut."

My route home will take me through Clarion and I intend to visit my new goldbox, Dorothy. There's a gusher in Clarion.

But first I slow as I approach the field I remembered while talking with the wildcatter. The derrick is situated in the middle of a wheat field, recessed from the road a quarter mile. It is a cable tool rig, an eighty-foot derrick designed to slowly pound a pointed metal bit into the ground. I swerve into a mud entryway, drive half way to the rig, and park.

Even from this distance the derrick engine sounds strained. I exit the Saxon.

The flywheel spins, the walking beam rises and falls like a drunk giant's shoulders. Men move like ants, each knowing the motions of the rest. One stands apart—any observer would assess him the man upon whose shoulders the entire operation rests.

I approach.

••

The foreman barks. His voice carries over the racket of the engine, the pounding drill, the friction between men, steel and mud.

I have found instruction on the function of each element of an oil derrick. I watch the sand line down from the top of the derrick. The walking beam rises and falls, the band wheel spins, pulleys and cables and belts, sweating men. Cursing men. They are oil, wheels and belts of the machine and the whole thing is magnificent. Each man performs his function with myopic perfection; his lot is to toil, to make his back and legs into steel and fire.

I'll supply the vision.

A Model T passes and parks closer to the rig, near several other vehicles. A man jumps out and advances without a backward glance.

"Hey!"

The man spins. His brow is arched. He looks at his pocket watch then to the man on the deck. I stand beside him. "Who is that man?"

"The driller?"

I nod. "That's right."

"Whelpley."

I pass the man a double eagle, twenty-dollar gold coin. "Give him that and tell him I'll have a word."

The man stares at the specie then hurries to the derrick.

Whelpley's shouts penetrate the noise but come through garbled. My messenger must have been tardy; he weathers a barrage of curses before leaning to Whelpley. He passes the gold coin and points.

I dip my head. "Put it in your pocket."

Whelpley holds the coin sideways to the sun.

"Put it in your pocket."

••

The tardy man posts at the bull wheel. Another man disappears into the structure of the derrick and emerges a moment later climbing a ladder within. Whelpley waves me to the rig.

I watch the goings on and walk easily.

Whelpley resumes his labor, equally willing to hurl a command or his body to get a task done. He assists hoisting and threading a pipe to the drill, in the time I walk thirty feet.

I join him on a wooden pedestal. He plugs his right ear and leans.

"I want you to build one of these for me."

"One of these? For who?"

"Me."

"What company?"

"Me."

The man steps back.

"What'll it cost to have you right one of these on my land?"

Whelpley shakes his head. "Sprague handles all that." He tosses the coin to me.

"Sprague didn't want to talk, so I'm bringing the proposition to you." I take his hand and slap my coin in it.

"You ain't serious."

"I am."

"Then you ain't hooked up right. And this ain't the thing to talk about, here."

"Where can I find you?"

Whelpley peers into the distance. The derrick clangs. Metal bangs. He slips the gold coin in his pocket. "You know Franklin?"

I nod.

"Well Digger Saloon. Seven."

I step from the platform and Whelpley barks commands. From twenty feet away I stand on packed dirt and watch the men operate.

••

The rig is an old design that drills by repeatedly dropping a pointed bit into the ground. The derrick, the wheels, belts and walking arm, contribute to the singular function of shoving the earth aside, crushing rock. Human willpower batters terra into submission. I can't discern the weight of the bit, but some scale at more than a ton. Given a far enough drop, they deliver a fifteen-ton blow to a space the size of a hog teat.

Most wildcatters man their rigs around the clock and average thirty feet per day. Their native limitations force them to sell their only asset, their labor, at prices that enslave them for sustenance. I was once a man of brawn, and but for my superior wiles, still would be. Some of these men have nothing else, and are the exact sort I want working for me.

I'll buy every one.

I drive to Clarion. My mind swirls, intoxicated with focus. I see smiles, hear challenges, voice rebuttals. I see everything the way I want, and the images flash to the sound of a steam engine and leather belts flapping on derrick pulleys. Spinning wheels like spinning schemes. The money. My ambition. I'll reckon with Mame Gainer and she'll oversee the whorehouses. Hawkins Bonter will take his brother's place. I'll devote my newly freed attention and cash flow to pulling the oil from the earth.

I'll meet with Thurston Leicester. The banker has one more play.

It'll be a thrill to take a man with an ego the size of a ship's prow, bend it around backward, and shove it up his ass. I'll do that before visiting Mame.

I arrive in Clarion committed. I'll hire Sprague's man Whelpley and show those wildcatters something about the oil business in Walnut.

It is dusk, too early for a brothel to bustle. The girls ought to be readying for work. Alberta sits inside the office, feet propped, her legs a dazzling varicose array under gray fuzz. A cigarette dangles from her lip.

"She run off."

"Who?"

"Dot."

"How you let her run off?"

"Let her? I can't keep watch all day and night. She run off."

I smack her feet from the table. She looks up.

"I told you—"

"Well, you did! And that don't change nothing!" She flattens her dress.

"Where is she?"

"Hell if I know."

"When?"

"Yesterday. She took to the life all right. Enthusiastic. Just when I trusted her, she was gone."

"With a man?"

"No reason to think so."

"Other'n her being a fresh whore. You're going to find that girl."

"How?"

"You'll think of something." I fish my pipe and tobacco.

Alberta pulls a fold of paper money from her brassiere and passes it. I remove the outside bill and return it to her. I tuck the wad into my billfold.

When she has put away her money, I strike her. She looks up from the floor and I leave her there.


Men knock elbows at the bar, but the tables are open. I sit. A skin-and-bones blonde pauses beside me long enough to nod. I catalogue odors, dirty men, oily men. Sweat and crude and dirt. The light is

••

low and the men are dim, save rare patches of teeth behind awkward black grins. The lamps flicker.

Thurston Leicester is a new breed of nemesis; he buys power with other people's deposits. Men crave credit and Thurston is in the business of balancing risks. He borrows from regular folks in the form of deposits, then lends to others and charges interest, and leverages the whole cockamamie scheme with the mayor and new sheriff.

Power created from a vacuum.

The mayor will be the darling of the temperance movement while being part owner of the very stills that supply the liquor he helps make illegal.

The starchy new sheriff will take protection money from the chosen stillers.

Thurston will offer loans, except the new enterprise will be a cartel, aligned in purpose to the temperance movement to make product scarce and buyers desperate.

Craftier than my plan—Thurston's adding a company store as the controlling arm. Must have a lot of faith in Stokes. Without protection, a cartel becomes an ash heap of debt.

When I started stilling, I eliminated the closest competition. Some folded their operations into mine. Others disappeared. When it was down to four of us in three counties, peace set in. Relationships with local buyers became sacrosanct. Each operator is free to expand in different counties, but upsetting the local balance will result in bloodshed. I accepted the arrangement knowing I was the only producer who had integrated my businesses; in time my efficiency would win out and the growth rate wouldn't distract from my other business arrangements.

But oilmen are an established lot of players. Bigger, millions of dollars at stake. I'm the swinging dick in Walnut, but Rockefeller's got the cock of a whale.

••

Whelpley will be an asset. Eyes cold as shale. He's a lynchpin, and moving him will move his crew.

The blonde emerges from behind the bar. She stops at a table, brushes her lips against the cheek of a bedraggled drinker, and drifts to me. She braces against my shoulder and leans; skinny tits hang under a thin top like bait worms come unhooked.

I say, "Proprietor here?"

"Back room. Ted. He'll be along later."

"Tell Ted that Jonah McClellan wants to see him."

"Uh-huh. You thirsty?"

"Whiskey. Two."

She disappears. I remove my pocket watch.

Whelpley stands at the doorway scanning faces. I nod. Whelpley ignores me while getting the lay. Finally he sits.

Whelpley places the twenty dollar gold piece on the table. "I ought to buy."

"Got two coming already." I say. "Keep that."

"What's this you're building a rig?"

"I'm not. You are."

Whelpley leans away. He lights a cigar. "Your gold piece buys twenty dollars of truth, so here goes. You don't want to dance with these boys. I don't care who you are, you don't got the guns."

The blonde wench returns with a tray. She places two glasses on the table and eases behind me. I turn but she shifts. Hair stands on my neck. I twist the other way and she dances aside, then presses against my back. Lips at my ear she says, "I seen you looking."

"Get off me!" I thrust backward. Her feet shuffle. I crane sideways to watch. She slinks away.

"Easy." Whelpley smiles, but his eyes are more plainspoken. "She's a favorite."

"She best keep them tits off my back."

••

"Hell. She probably knows who you are. Maybe looking for a new occupation."

Whelpley knows my business—in one afternoon. He's interested enough to investigate, but is it his interest, or his master's?

Whelpley gulps his drink. "I gave you my advice." He pushes back.

"Sit a minute. I want to understand something."

Whelpley studies me.

"I got a patch of oil on my land. Seeps out of the ground on its own."

"You willing to spend fifteen thousand to find out how much is under it? And then have another operator smash your rig, or steal your land right there legal in the courthouse, or just dispense with the trouble and pay you a nickel a barrel? Leave you bankrupt or dead?"

"I'll worry about that."

"Ahh. You've had a wildcatter poke around."

I sip whiskey.

"Did he use a doodlebug? Bunch of voo-doo horseshit. Dips a stick in oil and tells it to find its kin. He'll shake like he got religion, and you'll pony every penny and by and by when your money's gone you'll see the divining rod don't spot oil, it spots fools with cash."

"But you know how to find it."

Whelpley is silent.

"Well, I got oil on my land and know exactly where it is."

"Odds are against. But even if an experienced crew cuts a hole, you're as liable to come up with water as oil. And all the while you got the big boys in Oil City, who answer to even bigger Rockefeller boys in Cincinnati, playing all sorts of tricks on you."

"That's why I want you and your crew."

••

"No way possible. And if Sprague hears about you poaching his men, he'll come for you."

I tip my glass. "Have another."

"I'm through."

"I want you to look at the land before you say that. I'll come for you next week. You take this while you think on it." I slide a fold of bills across the table.

Whelpley looks at the far wall.

"Cover that money with your hand. See how it feels to have a year's wages all at once. Go ahead." I press his hand to the money, mine on top. "See? Now. As long as my hand is on yours, you know that's my money, and you're the same man as walked in here. A worker with no claim. But when I lift my hand, you're a man with a stake in business. A man with means, and a future."

We lock eyes. His fingers shift under mine, but hold steady.

I lift my hand.

"Look around this room. Cash like that puts you in a different class of men. Now I need a man knows what the hell he's doing. I need a man ready to step up and forward. I need a man who can build one rig, and then another, and then a field, and oversee them all. Then help me find more land and more oil. I need a man wants a stake in the whole goddamn thing. So you spend a few days thinking about being the cock and balls of a new company. That's what I'm talking about. The cock and goddamn balls. You think on that a few days, and I'll come find you."

I stand. Nod at the blonde. "Come here."

The whiskey wench stands beside me.

"I want to see Ted."

••

# Chapter Twenty-Three

The two days Grace asked for had passed. She helped Rose clean dishes after supper. Hannah and Elizabeth had been upstairs virtually the whole time.

Hal had sat in a chair next to the bedroom window, rifle within reach against the wall, surveying McClellan fields and trees for activity. Because he'd complained about his back, she'd brought him food and drink when he asked.

"You out looking for answers on Henry's death and it don't matter who done him. Could a been the hand of God Almighty and Jonah'd still be after us. You down there, talking lies to my wife, turn her against me..."

Grace had left the room.

Earlier she'd revisited the mud where McClellan had found Henry. She'd hesitated, feeling she ought to remove her shoes, or somehow recognize her son had died because she was one of those animals unsuited for motherhood. She'd told herself she was a sensational fool, but bitterness constricted her chest until she had to force deep breaths into her unwilling lungs. The accusing voice would not stop. She was the trollop who had conceived Henry, the frightened mother who had abandoned him, and now, the scarred woman who must confront her failings.

Grace had circled the impression left in the dirt by Henry's frail body and wiped tears from her eyes. Already, bent grass was righting, and the next rain would remove any reminder her son had died there. Her shoulders folded inward and she felt herself about to collapse in grief—but it was a luxury.

There would be more killing before those who remained were clean.

She'd collected herself and stared through the thin line of trees at field's edge, overlooking the lake, and imagined she was a girl. Almost exactly twenty years ago she was blameless. Almost. The sky was the same, but bluer, the clouds purer. The green scents gayer.

The pungency of the present overwhelmed her memories. Had she ever been clean? She'd looked to McClellan's white house glimmering through the trees. While she had been away, she had loved her son. Or longed to love her son. What was the difference?

Rose placed a stack of plates to the left of the sink and lingered beside Grace. "You want to dry them?" Rose said. "I can get these scrubbed ten times faster."

"I'm thinking." Grace placed an iron skillet on the drying rack. "Any more iron?"

"No."

Grace sprinkled detergent into the water.

Rose plunged her hands into the sink and beat the detergent frothy.

"You've had two days," Rose said. "I got our belongings separated and packed so's everything important is in those boxes."

••

She lowered her voice. Hal was on the porch, rifle in hand, and the window was open. "And the boxes are small enough Hoot don't have to carry them."

Rose's voice carried a new lilt. A melody Grace knew rote. Rose was ready to run.

"Sounds as if you're set." Grace said. "Got somewhere picked out?"

"Nowhere in particular. Of course we got family scattered through Iowa. But I don't know the first thing about Iowa. Always heard it was flat, but the people ain't highfalutin, like in the city."

"Not like those city people."

"We're going to Iowa, and pray God we find peace there. All our mistakes done and gone with."

"Mistakes?"

"We'll leave all this death behind." Rose held Grace's eyes for a moment. "You don't have anything to say?"

"What do you mean?"

"You've had your two days."

"I've spoken with a couple of people. One of Jonah's farmhands I saw rinsing socks in the lake, the other night. I even spoke with Angus. You'd be surprised how little things don't mean anything to one person, but a bunch of little things start to make a picture."

"What little things?"

"Well, did you know your dog knew about Henry long before anyone else did?"

"Could've been any dog left dog prints. It could have been one of the dogs that hang around McClellan's."

"But it wasn't. Jonah followed those prints from Henry's body to your doorstep."

"All I know is he shot that dog and swore he'd kill us all." Rose splashed water from the sink.

••

"Did you ever go out and look at where they found Henry's body?"

"Why would I do that?"

"I did. Nothing struck me right off. But the ground was indented and the grass was broken, and it left a clear mark of his position."

"So?"

"He was on his back."

Rose passed another plate. Grace took it, and began drying.

"Not just that, but the ground was wet. Muddy. His arms were at his sides, and his legs straight, and together."

"I don't see."

"Did you know Henry?"

"He played with Angus and Ian."

"Was he a normal boy?"

"Normal, I guess."

"You ever see a normal boy lay like that? Straight legs and arms at his side, on his back? Why, every boy or man I've ever seen wants to throw his legs and arms all over the place. He's got one leg cast way out, an arm way over here, and elbow propped over this way and his hand on his crotch, and one boot up and the other down. A man has to control his space, and he does it by spreading body parts all through it. It isn't natural that Henry was on his back with his arms and legs straight. You have to figure he tried to do something, no matter who was attacking him. He wouldn't just stretch out like he knew he'd be put in a coffin, so he'd be thoughtful toward the undertaker."

"I suppose not."

"Well, then somebody moved him."

"Moved him?"

..

CLAYTON LINDEMUTH | 255

"And if he was moved one inch, why not a hundred yards? Why put him right there in the middle of the field? And why reposition him to make him look peaceful."

"I suppose guilt is a natural enough feeling."

"Really? I don't think so—not for just any old killer. Imagine some man came wandering through from some city. Would he feel guilt and position him nice and restful?"

Rose scrubbed.

"So when I see all these things, I wonder. If Henry wasn't killed by someone wandering through—then it must have been someone over here or someone over there. And not just anyone—but someone who knew Henry, and felt guilt."

"One of Jonah's farm hands, maybe?"

"Can't say. Anybody. But I've only seen two people acting strange since it happened."

"Who?"

"And I can only think of two people who might want to leave a dead boy between Hardgrave and McClellan land."

"Grace, who?"

Grace nodded to the open window, where Hal sat on the porch with a rifle. She spoke quietly. "Jonah thinks Hal did it. He's got it all added up, and he's been acting on his evidence for a week now, killing everything and person he can, step by step."

Rose leaned closer. Hushed. "You're his sister! How can you say that? And Hal ain't man enough! Won't raise a hand to protect his family from pure evil? And you think he went out and murdered a boy?"

"I believe any man, even a coward, who suffered injustice like Hal, he'd reach a point where he'd die to stop it. A just man, an innocent man, even a coward, would risk lives to protect them from unjust suffering. And my brother hasn't reached that point—that's

••

not how an innocent man would act. Not even an innocent coward."

Rose's nostrils widened. Her hands were submerged and Grace half-expected them to erupt from the suds clutching a knife.

"All that's speculation. Foolishness." Rose's hands worked under the water and in a moment she raised a dish. "We'll be leaving tomorrow."

"It might be speculation. But I've got proof."

Rose halted. "What?"

"I have the knife that killed Henry."

Rose's head twisted. Her eyes went wide.

Grace said, "We'll know the truth soon enough. If you think Hal didn't do it, you may as well stay. I'll have my answer."

From the kitchen window drifted the sound of an engine, tires on rocks. The bleat of a motorcar horn. Grace looked up and saw headlamps sparkle, a fiery starburst sheen at the front fender.

Hawkins Bonter.

Grace turned toward the sound of shuffling feet. Hal stood at the jamb, arm braced, tired. His brow hung like a wet rope across his eyes, and his shoulders sagged as if from a supernatural burden.

He'd heard everything.

Grace tossed her hand towel aside and at the door, fleetingly met her brother's eye. She ducked under his arm and hurried toward the car. It would be a relief to get away.

She had planned to stay until the ghosts that haunted her were vanquished. She'd confront Jonah McClellan and by her wits and tenacity subdue him. Fate would inform her actions. Afterward, she would be free. The pain that addled her decision making throughout her adult life would be gone and she would forge a new, clean future as a new, cleansed woman. She would leave Walnut forever. That had been the plan.

••

But she could also stay. If Hal abandoned the farm, who could contest her birthright? She could spend the money on livestock and bullets.

Bonter parked midway between house and barn. Billowing dust rolled over the car and then Grace. White wall tires. Fenders and pipes and chrome and spokes. The vehicle gleamed even under a coat of dust. She squinted and in a moment Hawkins stood with his elbow on the roof, his face uncharacteristically downcast.

"You said you'd take a ride," Bonter said.

Grace studied him. The familiar breeze from the lake reasserted over the car's dust and the humidity was cool on her skin.

"It's getting late," she said, "so not very far."

"Grab a sweater. I did maintenance all afternoon, after riding back from the city, and I got to take it for a spin and make sure everything took."

"You don't sound like yourself."

"Little bit of news. That's all. Bad news." He forced a grin to his lips, but not his eyes. "Let's take a ride and see where we end up."

"It looks very comfortable."

"Like you're floating on air. Even on these roads. You get her on the bricks and she sings. Go on, grab a sweater. We'll have a bully time."

She studied him and he seemed more convinced than a moment ago. Grace turned to the house. Hal remained in the doorway, with Rose now standing behind, blocking the way.

Grace trotted the steps to the house. She stopped before Hal and said, "This man's brother has been working for Jonah forever. I'll know everything he does."

"Thought your mind was made up," Hal said. "Thought you'd figured me out." He raised his arm.

Grace passed beneath.

∗∗

# Chapter Twenty-Four

Grace watched Hawkins from the corner of her eye. The car was fast—a thousand times faster than traveling by horse, but with the same unlimited view. It was like rushing headlong into fate, and she could raise her arms for protection but the road, the fields on the right, the trees on the left, kept racing at her. She squirmed into the seat, scrunched low for a moment, and decided the excitement was too much, she was going to enjoy it. She poked her head out of the side window and squinted into the evening wind.

"You'll get a mouthful of bugs," Bonter said.

His voice carried the mournful note she'd first heard when he arrived. Grace pulled back inside the car.

"You're troubled."

"You know Eddie?"

"Your brother. The man who met you at the station."

"That's right." Bonter cleared his throat. "They shot him. New sheriff. Stokes shot him the other night. Called him out of the bar and did it just like that. Eddie was there to dicker on Jonah's behalf."

"That's horrible." Grace said. "Did Eddie shoot Stokes?"

"He didn't shoot at all."

Bonter sat with one elbow out the window and one hand on the wheel, at ease. The engine hummed and the tires crackled on rocks. They entered a copse, turned left, and emerged in another world of cool air below a heavy tree canopy.

They emerged from the neck of forest and the air was again warm. Fields at both sides of the road.

"Walnut?" she said.

"I want to show you something. A little farther out."

"Where?"

"Closer to Reynoldsville."

"It's getting late..."

"You'll forget all about how late it is when you see it. Or feel it, maybe, is a better way to say it."

"I've got the girls back at the house, and with everything that's gone on..."

He clamped his jaw. She closed her mouth and thought of the knife in her pocket. But her fear was irrational. Bonter was anguished. It was an innocent drive. She wanted information and he wanted consolation. His brother had been killed.

Her son had been killed.

"Well, let's get there quickly."

"Just this side of Reynoldsville. You won't ever forget it."

Grace swallowed. "You spoke to witnesses about your brother?"

Bonter was silent a long while. He exhaled. "Eddie found Stokes at the bar on Fifth. Jonah told him to set up a meeting. There's things going on—Jonah's affairs, and I ain't at liberty. But Eddie was there on official business, and all of a sudden, word is Stokes has his gun pulled and Eddie has his hands up, backing away, 'cause Stokes got the drop. No one's faster than Eddie, and if Stokes got his gun out first, he was the only one thinking about shooting."

••

Bonter was silent. They came to a crossroad and he slowed, then swung left. "Eddie stepped all the way outside, hands in the air, and when Stokes was blocking the door, he put a hole in Eddie."

"Stokes blocked the door?"

"No one could see past, and Stokes says Eddie drew on him."

"Outside? So Eddie would have been shooting into the tavern?"

Shadows cloaked the forest. The headlamps became suddenly relevant—or maybe she had just noticed them. Grace gripped the door handle.

Bonter glanced to her hand.

Bonter said, "That's right. Stokes says Eddie went for his gun— even after Stokes had the drop."

"And no one but Stokes saw it." Grace lowered her hand from the door. She breathed slowly. She'd keep her wits. He sounded focused and withdrawn—in a man, the peat of violence.

She touched the pocket knife with her index finger.

Bonter shook his head. "It won't stand."

"Where are we going, Bonter? I have to admit I'm not keen on being in the middle of nowhere..."

"Just a little ways farther."

The road ascended a gentle hill, crested and began a long descent to Reynoldsville. Though she couldn't see through the darkness, she knew to the left, across a few hundred forested yards, lay the railroad track that had borne her to the Sandy Lick train depot. Adjacent was the stream with the same name. Thick vegetation obscured her line of sight and gloom was oppressive. Grace fought the urge to throw open the door and bolt into the undergrowth.

Bonter slowed as they approached a narrow lane. He swerved. "I'm going to kill that son of a bitch," he said.

"What?"

**

The trees swallowed them. Grace turned to Bonter and he was a black silhouette against the dusky grayness of the trees. Bonter sniffed. "Just what I said."

"You've killed men before?"

"Being right helps."

The headlights cut a swath into the woods. Briars leaned onto the trail Bonter followed, a pair of tire tracks through pale yellow grass. Thorns screeched as they passed.

"So much for the shiny paint."

"Jonah didn't want this car to look good. He wanted it to go fast. He told me to make it less of an eye-catcher."

"What's Jonah need another car for?"

"Deliveries."

"Delivering what?"

Bonter paused. "Liquor. That's about where we're going right now."

"A still? What on earth made you think I'd want to see a still?"

"Hush." He smiled. "It ain't the still. We don't want to go back that far. We're just about there."

Grace peered into the forest, glowing yellow in the headlights. Dark tree trunks, thickets, some silver, some browns and rushing blackness.

Bonter pulled off the trail beside a smooth-barked, lightning-blasted beech. He turned off the engine. Every sound was amplified, the rustle of his pants as he shifted in his seat, his sleeve against his vest.

"Why stop here?" A ravine off to the right emitted a faint orange glow. "That's strange."

"You've been away quite a while? I mean, you were brought up on the farm, but left a while ago?"

"That's right."

••

"Then you've never seen one of these. I never did. You won't believe it. C'mon."

A moment ago she'd looked to flee into the woods, but now she craved the safety of the car. "It's dark. What could I possibly want to see in the dark?"

Bonter exited and the door slammed. As he passed in front of the headlights, she noticed fresh nicks on his neck—he'd shaved before coming to get her. His stride was quick and his form... bold. Was it some kind of dance?

After so many years of accepting men's advances based on the economics of food or protection, or the temporary cessation of abuse, Hawkins Bonter presented a test. It didn't take being alone at night in an orange-glowing forest to admit he was attractive. He'd been handsome on the train, and after surprising her in the barn, and now, all but tantalizing in the headlights with a smooth face, billowy sleeves and pomaded hair.

Just how much did she believe in her right to control her destiny? Did that extend to every area of her being, even to taking satisfaction from a man for no other reason than that she wanted it?

Grace squirmed into the seat.

Bonter turned the corner and shadows crossed his face.

The window was down. Bonter placed his elbows on the door and rested his chin on his crossed arms. "That driver's side door—the hinge is awful slick. I greased it because it was noisy and I knew Jonah would gripe at the first opportunity. I didn't mean to make such a ruckus."

"It's okay."

"I wanted to show you a sink hole. There's a coal mine on fire underneath us, right now. If you get out and put your hand on the ground, it'll feel warm. That's why all the grass is yellow. And over there the ground plum give out, and there's a hole to the fire."

••

"Underneath us? Are we going to fall in?"

"Nah, not here. They say the mine's been burning for eight years or so. It's likely out, or moved farther up the shaft. It ain't as bright as a few days ago."

Grace relaxed. He'd greased the car door. He'd brought her to see a natural wonder. He was trying to impress her. "You want to show it to me?"

He opened the door.

"I'd have worn slacks if I knew you were taking me on a wilderness expedition."

He placed his hand on her knee and lifted her dress a half-inch, slowly. "This is fine." He took her hand and after helping her outside, wriggled across the seat to the back. He reemerged with a folded blanket under his arm, and a small basket.

"Oh," she said.

He took her hand and guided her through the ravine to the source of the orange radiance. The closer they approached, the warmer her feet felt, though it could have been her fancy.

The pit glowed like it held a sunken bonfire, projecting light into the canopy and softly around them.

"Don't stand too close," he said, and nodded toward a patch of ground that resembled the collapsed tunnel of a giant gopher.

"This is such an amazing phenomenon."

"There's stuff like this all over. Natural stuff. There's a hill near Pittsburgh, I swear, you park at the bottom and gravity will pull your car up the hill. I swear it's true."

"Well, this is a lot easier to understand. Just coal burning underground."

Hawkins spread the blanket and placed the basket in the center. "Better than taking you to a county fair. Don't you think?"

Grace stood at the edge of the blanket and went to her knees, sat sideways.

..

"They say the snow won't stick above these mines, and if they keep burning, in a hundred years they're going to be all over, and half the state'll be on fire, underground. Won't that be something?"

"Your job for Jonah McClellan is to deliver his whiskey to different places?"

"That's right."

"Have you done it yet? I mean, you just got the car."

"He's got operations all over three states. Four. I don't know. I haven't made a run for him yet." Bonter looked into the trees.

"You've done this work before? Other places?" She kicked out her legs and sat with her hands behind, bracing. Ground heat spread through her.

"Sure. Florida to Chicago, New York, all over."

"Florida—tell me about Florida."

"It's always warm, even in the winter, you just put on a sweater and you're fine. Strangest thing. And the woods are wet and green. You'd never spread a blanket. Hell, a crocodile'd get you."

"You've seen crocodile?"

"Seen? Hell. Shot, skinned, cooked, and ate em. I only wish I'd have made some boots."

He sat at the blanket's edge, then sprawled back. Their shoulders were closer than their feet; the basket a barrier between them.

"You miss the south?"

"Nah. Different people is all. Not better. This Jonah McClellan—I don't got to tell you, but ain't he something? I mean, six foot seventeen, and got his thumb on every critter with a heartbeat in six counties."

"You like working for him?"

"I'll learn what I can." Bonter looked at the fire pit. "I got my own ambitions."

Bonter reached for the bottle in the basket, and glasses clanked.

••

"That's wine?"

"Uh-huh. Eye-talian. From New York."

"You know your boss killed my nephew. And my brother's livestock—and is promising to kill every one of us. You know that, right?"

"That's why I wanted you to go to New York with me. Talk some sense into you."

"What on earth-—"

"Get you away from your brother."

"Why?"

"He's a killer. Now Jonah, way I see it, is doing what any man with gumption would. Justice."

Bonter poured wine into a glass, stopping half way. He passed it to her.

Grace said, "On what evidence?"

"Evidence? Hell, your brother and his boys killed Jonah's son."

"Were there witnesses?" She sipped from the glass. Grimaced.

"I dunno. Wasn't my place to ask. Man like Jonah don't brook fools."

"Did Eddie—" She stopped. "Did he tell you anything?"

"He did. Mortician did, too. I had to handle a couple things for Jonah. He didn't have the stomach to be around his dead boy. You sure you want to know? His being a child and all?"

She nodded. Bonter's face was Halloween-colored shadows.

"The boy's throat was cut..."

Grace fought the urge to touch the knife in her pocket.

"...and there was a dog that chewed on him. You sure you want to know all this?"

"Go on."

"There was bruises on him. Arms and legs, and probably his head, but the mortician couldn't see that too well. So your brother and his boys beat on him before they cut him."

••

"You keep saying that, but you haven't made the connection to Hal."

"Well, I don't expect that boy to matter to you. You didn't know him. I didn't know him either. But there's no other way it could've been. There's history between your families, what I gather. And your brother, let's just say he ain't much in the huevos department. Uh, that's Florida-speak for gumption."

"It ought to take more evidence than that to destroy a man."

"You know what? It don't matter if I'm wrong. Jonah McClellan thinks Hoot killed his son—and that means the same thing for you whether he did or didn't. Henry was Jonah's youngest boy, and the only one with any promise, as the story goes. He'll see to it that everything Hoot loves is dead. He's going to take his property and burn it. Salt the fields. There's no end to Jonah's anger—he's cold and when I'm driving I look over and I see him dreaming of making things right, and that's why I wanted to talk some sense into you. Let's say you're right. Maybe a bunch of gypsies came through and killed Henry. It don't matter. You got to go away 'til Jonah runs out of revenge."

Grace stared into the thin orange glow. She sipped from the wine.

"You don't like wine too much," he said.

"I guess not."

"I got it because I didn't think you'd drink hooch." Bonter chuckled. "Jonah's got some new recipe. Mixes walnut oil, and a bit of stain from last years' rinds. Looks like you're drinking tar, but it damn sight gives you a jolt. You want a sip of what I got in the car?"

"I don't think so."

Hawkins drank an amazing gulp from his glass. He lowered it and his face was taut with a frown. He swallowed. "Excuse me."

••

He rolled away, dumped his wine to the dirt, and when he came back he was much, much closer.

He wore cologne. She shifted back.

A part of her craved a man's caress, abandonment in a tangle of arms and legs. Warmth and the smell of oil, sweat, and clove shaving soap. She'd pressed those desires deep within, hoping to smother them, because physicality with a man had always been transactional. Even before her single act of whoredom, bedding a man was about securing protection or favor.

Now, two daughters depended on her. Her son demanded justice.

But her girls were this moment secreted and safe, and the boy was already with his maker.

Hawkins Bonter wanted to take her on this blanket, and she wanted taken. He'd have her if she allowed.

And maybe if she didn't.

Bonter kissed her. His mouth pushed hard. His hand pressed her back, crushed her against him. She wriggled but his mouth was warm, and the wine—the shave soap, the candle orange glow—she parted her lips. The ground was hot below her hands and behind, and she wanted to recline and feel its heat up her back and on the sides of her thighs. She held him and he was a thin hard reed with dark habits and mysterious history, and that made his hardness better. He kissed her as if completing his kiss perfectly was more important than anything else he would ever attempt, as if it consumed his entire focus, and he was as helpless against his desire as she against hers.

Forest air chilled her bared flesh. A breeze washed over her, around her, through her, in her hair and every square inch. She lay naked compressed between volcanic earth and a ravishing heat above. His mouth moved with angry passion. She gnashed back. He thrust and she absorbed the worst of his bawdy wrath, and gave

••

it right back. Sweat dripped from his neck. The forest air chilled. She clawed and he arched. Bonter weighed against her hips and battered a place inside that sent a paroxysm up her spine, down her legs. His shoulders caved and he tucked his head to her arm.

He was a mere animal; the ground scorched and his body burned but between she was detached and chilly as the forest wind—and aware, ready to venture out stronger when her tarry concluded. She curled and quivered. She gasped and clutched his back. It was grand for a moment and the moment was gone. Her son was dead. Her daughters waited. Her purpose could no longer be delayed.

Hawkins Bonter shook. He shifted from her and rested on his side. Sweat lay on her skin and a mosquito hovered next to her ear.

"Whoooeee," he said.

"Whoey," said she.

# Chapter Twenty-Five

I sit across from Thurston Leicester in a hardwood chair designed for slight men. The cross supports are close to the floor, as if Thurston had the legs sawn short. I cross my leg, place hat on knee. My hips press against the sides.

Thurston sits behind a dark cherry desk wide enough to host the battle of Gettysburg. The banker smokes a cigar and silver clouds roll across the table like smoke from Rebel canon. They heard Gettysburg canon in Reynoldsville—a hundred fifty miles—my father said. When I left I was sixteen but stood six foot six and my height made them mistake me for a man. But they were not mistaken. And this tycoon of usury sits across the smoky field, pompous and gorged on fatty steaks and potatoes and gravy, sits in an elevated chair—

Fuck this piss ant.

"You're a day late," Thurston says. "I struck a deal with another. You're out."

I look through a side window. "Who?"

"Buzzard."

"Buzzard works for me, and if what you say is true, he'll be dead by noon and we'll have this conversation at one." I lock eyes with Thurston. "No, this is what's going to happen. I'm bringing you in as equity."

"I detest equity."

"You put up equity to rebuild my operation and the others I'm taking over—six thousand."

"Six thousand!"

"That's your part. Should have thought of that before you had those stills smashed to hell."

"I own Stokes. The money is in my vault. If you want to do business in this town after Prohibition passes, you'll do as I say."

"No loans. No papers. No rents for you, based on wheedling other peoples' dollars into loans. You're equity. And the deal's sealed with a handshake, and a bullet if things go wrong."

Thurston looks over his spectacles. Behind his eyes, the schemer turns, mills, crafts new pieces into the old puzzle. He's thinking I'm the same pawn regardless, calling it loan or equity means nothing when one holds the power and the other is the chump.

I agree with him.

"I suppose you understand the bullets can fly either direction?" Thurston says.

"There's always that."

"Equity." Thurston opens his right top desk drawer. His hand emerges with a flask and two glasses. He pours into each. Slides one across the desk.

I lean, note a scar in the wood; grab the glass. I sniff. "Buzzard's maple rum."

Thurston nods. "Aged." He holds his glass in salute.

I sip.

"I'll make a deposit into your account, and you and I will conduct business as gentlemen."

**

"I don't have an account. I'll take specie—none of these paper notes."

"Our paper is backed by the new Federal Reserve. It isn't bank paper."

"It burns, it ain't money. Six thousand in specie, and we're in business." I finish my snifter and land it on the table.

"That will require a few moments."

"I'll wait."


"McClellan? McClellan!"

I halt on the sidewalk, four steps from the Saxon. Hair stands on the back of my neck. I didn't survey the sidewalk before stepping on it. Careless, with a bag of specie no less. I switch the money bag to my left hand and get my right to my hip before I turn.

"Mister Jonah McClellan? Sir?"

The man rushes toward me. He wears a black vest and a white shirt—the Western Union man. "Just got this now and thought I saw you on the street." His outstretched arm bears a note. He gives it to me, tips his hat and retreats.

I hold the note, glance a full circle, and read the type.


I stumble downhill with arm upraised to fend off unseen branches in the dusk. Clutch a maple, drop hands to knees and breathe, collect my awareness. Square myself. Resume, telegram in hand.

The walnut canopy is a perimeter, a Rubicon, and crossing means acknowledging to the specters I recognize their power, and want it—yet I have no guess what terms to expect. A half century of business has taught me never to rush into a contract. Bringing the paper to the tree is a consummation. A deal. What terms will

••

they demand? I've no muscle to tip the deal my way. I'm blind, and though I control the world theirs intersects at the walnut, I can't fathom how deep is theirs, beyond, and under it.

Yet, to see a vision and know the outcome in advance... Where to drill? Who to drill? To pierce the unknowns with certainty—the business applications boggle.

I step to the tree and press the Western Union telegram between my palm and the corrugated bark.

"She changed her mind! You fucking spooks knew!" Sweat stands cold at my brow. My knees tremble. "Gainer says she wants to get hitched."

No image arrives. I hold the telegram, brush away crumbled bark, angle it for best light. "Reconsidered. If offer stands, please return or send word for me to come."

I fold the note and tuck it into my pocket. Again I press the tree. "You hear that? You knew she'd do that. You knew, and we got to strike a deal. I want to know about the oil. I want to know where to drill, and how much we'll pull. You got to tell me everything. What do you want for information like that? What's it worth, in puss?"

I strike the tree with my palm. Wait. Calm my thoughts.

"You specters seem to parley when you want. That's fair. You want to control the business talks—only natural." I breathe more slowly. "Go ahead, you queer fucking spooks. Think on it. But I don't have all night."

The specters bide their time.

As should I.

"Listen, you goddamn savages. When I leave, I'm going to fetch an axe, a team of horses, kerosene and matches. And when I come back, I'm—"

Electric shoots through my hand. Bears an image. I close my eyes. The vision resumes where the first, days ago, ended... Mame

••

Gainer folds her knees on a blanket spread below the walnut. She invites me to her. Pictures flash through my thoughts, splashes of animal love that conclude with Mame Gainer writhing as if enjoying the sex of a half-dozen, while none are visible.

That's the trade.

"I'll bring her here. Let me see the oil."

A sound issues from inside the tree. A scraping. A hush.

The image vanishes and it's just me and a walnut tree by a lake. An old man unsure. Tree bark.

"The oil, you fucks!"

\*

Hawkins Bonter scratched his groin. Nerves, or last night's quif carried disease. He pressed against the stone foundation and concentrated on slowing his respiration. Above his head, a window opened to a room spilling forth with gaiety and smoke.

He remembered his employment discussion with Jonah McClellan. All that talk about running liquor out of Florida—the high-speed chases, the gunplay, making enemies of powerful men—all of it wordplay to strike a better employment deal.

If I'm willing to do it, what's it matter if I've done it before?

Until Jonah told him to drop Sheriff Brooks into the fire pit, Bonter had tended bar and soaked up stories. His resume: he'd bounced a couple of top-hat drunks.

Now he rode the cusp of a storm—but that's how fortunes were made.

From inside the house issued laughter, snifters clanking. Leaning back, Bonter observed cigar smoke floating at the ceiling.

&&

276 | SOMETIMES BONE

"They'll be inside making jokes about you," Jonah had said. "They think they own men like you. They don't like the way you smell."

Bonter slipped along the wall to the slope-doored basement entrance. He eased the wood bar sideways. Inside it was black. He had plenty of time. He'd allow his eyes a half-hour to adjust, and hazard a flame only if he still couldn't see.

Bonter felt his way down the steps and sat on the cement. Before closing the door above him, he pulled a .38 revolver from the holster on his hip, and checked the cylinder. Satisfied, he closed the door and settled into total darkness.

"Kill him," Jonah had said.

"I thought maybe the order would be for Stokes, first, on account of what he did to Eddie."

"That'll come—but not until I've exhausted his usefulness. That business with Eddie... you keep that ready."

Bonter rubbed his crotch. It could have been one of the whores, on second thought.

A scuffle broke on the rafters above—sliding chairs, stomping feet, an uproar of general hilarity.

"Enjoy it," Bonter said.

The boys at the lodge said Jonah McClellan was a bootstraps man whose list of exploits dated to the Civil War. The stories had Jonah shooting twenty-three rebels with twenty-three head-shots. He picked off artillerymen by anticipating when they'd duck and weave through their cannon firing sequence, timing his shots to their brief appearance at a known point in the order. Each shot at several hundred yards distance.

A man like that knew how to plan, and grasp opportunity while other men waited.

McClellan had entered the liquor business because it didn't make sense to sell corn on the cheap when converting it to whiskey quadrupled the price. And turning corn into liquid made it taste

••

better. He multiplied his earnings and then multiplied them again serving a corollary vice, man's universal desire for women of easy obtainability. And now, in his waning years, Jonah was set to do it again. Bonter was no fool. He added the trips to Oil City and Franklin and snippets of conversations. The farm hands whispered about the oil slick on Hardgrave's land.

McClellan needed a sidekick.

Earning that trust meant taking orders without equivocation, even at great personal risk.

Upstairs, Thurston Leicester whooped it up with hoity-toity blue noses.

Pure darkness filled Bonter's eyes. It seemed a half-hour had passed. A window at the top row of the stone foundation emitted a pale gray gloom that diffused into shadows. He'd have to crawl on the floor to find his way around. He would wait until the party abated.

Be damn nice to roll a cigarette.

An hour had surely passed. The upstairs noise had tapered but the front door had not yet opened and closed. Leicester's guests remained.

His buttocks cold as the cement upon which he sat, Bonter rocked forward onto his hands and knees. The pocked cement was gritty under his hands. Tiny rocks cut his knees. He'd have to remember to brush the dirt from his pants, lest someone know he'd been crawling around a basement floor.

Bonter cocked his head. Footsteps gritted above. The door latch clicked.

He had to urinate. If it got much worse he'd do it where he stood.

••

Voices and laughter erupted with a wistful winding-down timbre, a vanishing lilt. The party was ending. Bonter inhaled, held his breath, released. Moments. The door closed and the house was silent. The lock clicked. Bonter tracked a single pair of footsteps crossing above.

Jonah had warned there'd be a woman to deal with, as well.

Bonter waited, and heard a second set of feet.

He'd heard stories, tending bar. A rough man with a bare face would ask for spiced rum. He'd stare into his drink before consuming it, and Bonter would wonder what stories the man held, what hurts, what sacrifices he'd made that left his face flat and brooding. He'd fill the glass higher for a man such as this, and linger at his end of the bar when a slow moment presented.

What line of work?

The stories ended the same—a drunk man unconvinced of his exploits, taking a moment's retreat before returning square shouldered to a difficult world.

A man who wanted to get ahead had better make his choice early, and not wait until the advantage lay with another.

Bonter extracted his .38 pistol. He'd checked the load, but wanted to do so again. He dug a match from his pocket, felt the cement floor for dryness, and struck the match.

Silver gleamed—chest high—Stokes's badge?

Bonter moved by instinct. Sideways. His bladder broke. He swung his pistol-arm and pointed.

It was a lantern on a shelf.

Warmth spilled down his leg. He realized he was still urinating and cut off the flow. The wet heat spread through his crotch and down his left leg.

It burned.

••

Bonter snorted, perplexed at his stupidity. He'd almost had a gunfight with a glass globe and he'd pissed himself like a five-year-old seeing a ghost.

Easy—take things slow. Pay attention.

The match burned his fingers. He dropped it and crushed the blue flame with his sole.

He'd checked the revolver's load before setting out and again when he'd arrived at Thurston Leicester's house. He'd force himself to trust it hadn't unloaded itself.

The best of the storytellers in the bar made it sound like you walked into a room, said something memorable and pulled the trigger. They never mentioned being so afraid of a lamp they pissed themselves. The heat spread farther down his leg and the acid scorched his groin. It was his cross to bear. He'd wear these pants until Thurston Leicester was dead, and his woman, and Bonter would steal another set of pants for the ride home—but no way in hell would he confess to Jonah the act was accomplished in piss-soaked britches.

Hawkins Bonter holstered his pistol and crept forward. He probed darkness with upraised arms. Dragged his feet close to the cement to find the stairway. The grit was so loud he feared Thurston would hear it.

His right foot thudded on the stairwell. He lifted his left and probed the appropriate height. Finding the first step he shifted to the side where the boards were better supported against the wall. He dragged his hand along the stone blocks and one by one ascended the staircase.

Would Thurston see his pee-spot?

Bonter twisted the knob. After the basement's near-total darkness, the dim pantry was like a lighted room. He would have to pass through it to reach the foot of the staircase that led to the top floor. Bonter studied the layout looking for anything that might clatter or trip him. The path was clear. Glasses and bottles arrayed on a table; Bonter minded his elbows. He placed each foot with a rolling motion, prepared to abort at the first creak.

He should wait until he heard a man's snores. With all the alcohol that had flowed, it would be minutes. He would wait another half hour, now that he could see his whereabouts. He'd find a chair and sit, and wait.

Bonter stopped at the table and eased his hand toward a bottle standing taller than the rest, taking care unless his eyes played tricks. He grasped the bottle and from its weight decided the partiers had barely tapped it. He removed the cap. Tending bar he'd poured many a snifter of cognac, but had never drunk more than a hidden snurkle for the stolen pleasure.

Bonter carried the bottle to the sitting room.

A fading orange glow wavered in the fireplace. Upstairs, where Thurston bedded, was silent. Bonter crept to a plush chair and upon drawing his firearm and holding it at his lap, settled into the cushion. He studied his surroundings. Shifted to alleviate the burn of the urine at his crotch and down his left leg, to no avail.

Tobacco smoke might settle his nerves—and the air was already thick with it. Another ember would risk little. Likely, Leicester already slept upstairs.

Bonter extracted a cigarette he'd rolled beforehand and struck a match to his boot. He drew in the tobacco's richness. Euphoria washed through him. His fate waited upstairs. He would prove to Jonah that Hawkins Bonter was worthy of tasks that demand high rewards. He'd come a long way since traveling north seeking his destiny. It was time. Bonter drank from the cognac and replaced the cigarette at his lips. He left the bottle on the floor and carefully, slowly, walked to the stairs.

He heard his footfalls. If by chance either of his adversaries were awake, his boots would announce him.

••

Bonter leaned to the wall, removed one boot then the other, placing each to the side.

He thought. Unbuckled his gun belt and pulled off his trousers. Then his under shorts. He balled both and padded to the fireplace. Placed the cloth bundle against orange embers, and waited until the flare subsided and the garments were ash.

Naked at the waist, Bonter stepped to the next floor. At the top he waited but no noise disclosed the banker's sleep chamber. A single window at the far end of the hall allowed outside light to enter. Bonter discerned in the shadows four doors, two on each side. It struck him that a banker would be tardy to rise in the morning and would prefer the west side; Bonter crept to the first door on the left and without stepping before it, leaned with his ear close to the jamb.

He heard bedsprings—but from farther down the hallway.

Bonter inhaled cigarette smoke and exhaled through his nose. He pulled back the revolver's hammer. The click resonated. He dropped his smoke and let the cherry glow on the wood floor. Looking down he noted something strange.

He was hard. He thumped his manhood and the sting returned him to the moment.

Bonter walked on the sides of feet, rolling steps, balanced.

The floor creaked. He stopped.

A snore rumbled from the room to the right—the east. The banker was an early riser. Bonter crossed the hall, then shifted past the door. He reached back, thinking that if his quarry shot from inside, he would shoot through the door, not to the side.

Bonter exhaled. Grabbed his mess with his free hand and fought the temptation to handle his business now, first, before the killing. The hardness was unlike any arousal he'd experienced. Painful. Urgent—an ache that made him slightly sick in his stomach.

＊＊

Bonter wrapped his fingers around the door handle and twisted. The mechanism clicked.

He clenched his jaw until his teeth felt about to shatter. Who locks a fucking bedroom door?

A paranoid man who expects a threat to emerge from darkness...

On the other side of the wooden door lay a man. He might be asleep, or he might feign sleep and have a gun cocked and pointed.

Bonter stepped into the center of the hall. He turned toward the door and smashed his bare heel through. The door crashed inward.

He rushed though, gun arm high. He saw a moonlit bed. A chair with a jacket over the back—or was it Thurston, already risen to meet him? A shriek—the woman sat bolt upright in bed and Leicester was beside her. He wore a white nightgown.

Bonter pointed his pistol. His other hand found his tool and his mind swirled, wove thoughts of murder with the itch of venereal disease, the burn of piss on his balls and thighs, the purple pressure making him crave the thump of the head—

Leicester screamed a jumble of syllables like Sheriff Brooks when his feet and legs burned.

"Jonah says 'thanks for the specie.'"

Bonter fired three times, each flash illuminated Thurston jumping and thrashing, the last, with a red bloom on his chest. Bonter swung his arm to the woman and fired twice.

He waited with gun at his side. The room was silent save gurgling death sounds. His ears rang. At the window he looked. The night was still.

Beside the woman he placed her wilted hand to his manhood and rubbed until the desire released and all the muscles of his frame convulsed and he gasped for air.

Bonter leaned against the wall by the window until his heart no longer raced, then stepped to the bureau and yanked open the bottom drawer, then the second lowest.

••

Then the next. Leicester didn't wear normal underwear, but some silky frilly garments. Bonter grabbed a handful of the shimmery cloth, found an opening and stepped into it. He checked the top of the bureau for Leicester's billfold. He found a watch but the fold was nowhere.

Neighbors would soon arrive... but he'd murdered a banker and there should be cash handy. And he needed trousers. Bonter remembered the jacket hanging on the chair back. He fished each pocket and the second yielded leather. Bonter slipped the fold into his shirt pocket then stepped into Leicester's baggy pants, held them at his waist with his free hand.

Bonter retraced his route. Through the hall, down the steps, he rambled as fast as darkness would permit. In the great room he paused, cinched pants in place with his gun belt, slipped on his boots, grabbed the cognac, then crossed the pantry and hurried into the pitchy basement.

The new sheriff lived only a dozen doors away, and the sound of gunplay in the night would travel. But Hawkins Bonter would be gone before the first man cursed—if any man would curse the death of a banker.

This would make one hell of a story, Bonter considered. Walk in, say something clever, pull the trigger.

Nothing else to tell.

# Twenty-Six

I sit on the porch viewing the sun break over eastward trees. I'd have left for Pittsburgh last night after Hawkins Bonter returned, except I meet Whelpley this morning.

I pull my watch, check the hour, and replace it in my vest pocket. The wood chair is one I took from the dining room, and has a stiff straight back. I gulp steaming coffee, then press the hot mug against my shoulder.

Eddie Bonter had gotten thoughtful in his responses, since Henry died. Begun asking questions and offering opinions and that's always the end.

I've groomed no replacement—though Hawkins Bonter angles. But Hawkins can't see past his desires. These last weeks have been about unraveling my interests, not consolidating. Soon Mame Gainer will have autonomy over my cathouses. She will be my wife and property, of course, but primarily my foreman. And I will work with Buzzard, eventually—maybe—placing Hawkins Bonter in Buzzard's service as a shipment driver. If he pans out.

And Todd Whelpley will oversee my drilling venture. I'll complete those details in short order, soon as Whelpley sees the oil seep on Hoot Hardgrave's front acre.

I've built the biggest empire I could, and in time, maybe, will hand it over to my grandson.

Angus.

But before that, one more person exists, who needn't. Then the path is clear. A shame. I always liked her tits.

A rooster trail of dust billows a quarter mile away. I lean forward, eager.

\*

Birds had begun to sing. Down the hallway, Hal, or Rose, snored.

Grace held a pistol in her left hand and a rifle from the downstairs cabinet in the other. She'd checked the weapons to ensure each had a bullet in the firing chamber. Both were cocked. She left the rifle leaning against the wall outside Hal's door.

His snores continued inside.

Grace closed her eyes and thought of the last time she'd seen Henry, playing outside as she snuck down the road at twilight.

About to open the door, she paused. Surprise was better. She raised her booted foot and rammed her heel against the door next to the knob. The door burst open. She entered with gun raised.

Rose screamed, "Jonah!"

Hoot jumped from bed and stood halfway to his rifle leaning at the window, his stance wide and balanced.

"Your back not troubling you this morning?" Grace said.

"You lost your mind?"

"Get back in bed and keep your hands above the covers."

••

Rose drew the covers about her neck, her forearms exposed but her face hidden.

"Well I never expected he'd send you," Hal said. "He sent his man Eddie for the rest of it, but I thought he'd finish things himself."

"You've got to account for Henry."

"That boy?" Hal's face wrinkled. "What's that boy to you, more than your own—" His eyes widened. "You left. You was gone when he was born, run off with that feller..."

"Henry was my son."

"And you think I killed him."

"I know you did. Now get back into the bed and keep your hands above the covers." She motioned with the pistol, but Hal stood unflinching. "Move!"

Henry was dead and it was her fault. She'd left him because she loved her reckless future better than she'd loved him. And he was dead because of it. "Move!"

Hoot sat on the side of the bed.

Rose whimpered and it sounded like grotesque laughter, the whole insane ploy was crumbling at her feet. She had to have known all along.

Hal placed his hands on his knees, but remained sitting at the edge of the bed. His frown disclosed his complete understanding of his predicament.

"I just want to know why you killed him," Grace said.

Hal shook his head.

"Don't pretend any more. Don't act like it'll all go away if your back hurts, and you're too big a coward to defend yourself or your family. Say it! You wanted to destroy the man who's been your better your entire life, always extending his reach. And Rose? Was it Jonah you bedded or was it Mitch? Yeah, Hal, bow your head.

You knew he fucked her. Too bad you didn't figure he did me too, or maybe you'd have—"

"Enough!" Hal stood. "Do what you came to do, but when did you ever see me kill anybody or anything? When you ever see me lift a hand against anybody? I sat here and took it and took it and took it 'cause the minute I lashed out, I knew he'd ruin us, and you call me a coward. I been called that my whole life and it ain't goddamn true. Shoot your own flesh and blood and I won't flinch 'cause I don't care. I've had as much as I can stand. But I didn't fight back 'cause it would have made things worse, not because I didn't have the guts."

Grace pointed the pistol at Hal's chest.

"I didn't kill your boy, Grace. You did, when you left him with a cussed animal."

"You murdered him." Grace withdrew the knife from her pocket. Pitched it to Hal and he caught it with one hand. "That's Henry's blood," Grace said.

"May be. But this ain't my knife. Looks more like Ian's, than mine."

"Why'd you put Henry's body between your house and Jonah's?"

"Ask him that."

"Why'd you straighten out his arms and legs, like he was all peaceful, being dead?"

"Talk to Jonah."

"How'd you think no one would add it all up, how you've been raising a McClellan boy under your roof, and watching Jonah grow more and more successful, and you have to sleep next to a woman who every night wandered in her mind over to his place? I know what it's like to have something eat at you, all the time, never letting up! I know it Hal, and that's how I know you killed Henry."

••

"You don't hear a single thing you say. I'm out of fight. And patience."

He tossed the knife to the bed. Staring, Grace lifted it.

Hal raised his hands. Stood, and faced the wall. "Do it."

Rose said, "Grace? Don't, Grace."

Grace backed away. "You fucking coward."

In the hall she ran.

\*

"Have a slug of this." I extend a green-hued jug to Todd Whelpley. Black liquid sloshes inside.

"Nah, it doesn't do any good to see it in jug. I have to get a look where it seeps out of the ground."

"It's whiskey. Drink it. Consider it a gift."

Whelpley withdraws the cork with his teeth and sniffs. "Smells like pure unmitigated evil."

"Wait 'til you taste it."

Whelpley brings the jug to his lips and tips it back. His Adam's apple bobs. He coughs.

"That's a special mix," I say. "Secret ingredient is walnut oil, and enough stain from old rinds to make it black."

"Whiskey that looks like oil. You got the bug, McClellan."

"I got the oil, too."

Whelpley rests the jug on the porch. "Show me."

I flag Hawkins Bonter, working in a section of barn illuminated by the morning sun. I wave him forward. "Bring the car!"

Walking with Whelpley toward the barn, I turn and find him kneeling in driveway dirt, rubbing powder between his fingers.

"How far off is this seep of yours?"

●●

"Three hundred yards, maybe."

"I'd just as soon walk and get the lay. This oil seep," Whelpley says. "Thick like tar?"

"That's right."

He stands in the middle of the drive and rotates slowly. His eyes dwell on the far-off hills and near depressions, as if noting each geographic feature. He studies the forest behind the house. "That a lake, beyond those trees?"

"That's right."

"And you're on a dome here."

"I suppose. That good?"

Bonter emerges from the barn in the Saxon and stops beside us. The engine idles. Bonter reaches to the passenger side and releases the latch from inside.

"We're walking," I say.

Bonter turns off the engine and steps out of the vehicle.

"All right," Whelpley says. "Let's see."

"We won't be needing the car, Hawkins. Take it back to the barn and get ready for tonight's drive."

I lead Whelpley down the driveway and at the road turn right. The oil seepage is a hundred yards beyond the terminus of the field separating McClellan from Hardgrave land, where I found Henry. The oil is hidden in the forest between Hardgrave's barn and the road.

We walk. The Hardgrave place seems deserted, as if ridding Hoot of his animals and one of his sons has salted the fields. The farm is bare and stark.

Whelpley stops to glance different directions without rhyme or reason. He frowns, thoughtful. "That one of your men?"

I shield my eyes with my hand.

"Top window. Looks to have a rifle in his hand."

••

"Just the neighbor, time being. I'm buying this place out from under him."

In minutes we reach the mud lanes leading back to the Hardgrave farm, and immediately beyond, the forest.

"I take it the seep is off the road a bit?"

I nod.

"I'll want to study the woods."

I withdraw tobacco and pipe and fill the bowl. The trees are beech and oak, primarily, with silver-barked maple spread throughout. Whelpley studies several, stopping to dig with his fingers between the giant trunk folds, sniffing the dirt and spit-polishing small rocks he unearths. His frown grows soberer, his brow more thoughtful, and I read him as a man beginning to realize his bluff is called. He will have to decide whether to plunge into a new enterprise with me, or return to being a small cog in a giant machine.

At a rock seam Whelpley stands with one arm raised as if to prevent me from telling him what he will recognize on his own.

"We are here," I say.

But Whelpley has already homed to the seep. He moves in giant strides and upon reaching it, kneels, pushes aside leaves with his hands. The oil darkens a stretch of soil and rock so a ten-square-foot area is spongy with it.

"Hell," Whelpley says, "this is something. This is tremendous." He places a careful foot on the black soggy soil and sinks inches. "What you got here is maybe a dozen crevices, all saturated and seeping out." He tilts his head, looks down. "There's a whole network and they span maybe fifty or a five hundred and fifty yards, down to the oil."

Whelpley turns back to the rock seam he studied a few moments ago. "That rock seam'll tell me where to drill. It's the one thing that'll tell me."

＊＊

I follow his gaze. Hardgrave's barn is visible through the trees.

Whelpley grins. "You may not have to worry about that man with the rifle. If I'm right."

"What do you mean?"

Whelpley jumps back to solid ground. He wipes the sides of his boots against leaves. Closes his eyes for a moment and opening them says, "You ever notice any gas coming up through the ground?"

"Just the bubbles in the crick."

"That's exactly what I mean. Where's the crick?"

"Below my house, empties in the lake."

"Any on this side?"

"Not for another half-mile."

"Removed from the dome of this hill?"

"Right."

"Show me your crick."


Whelpley descends the slope toward the crick. He stops at every rock formation, every seam, and spends as much time turning slow philosophical circles as walking forward. When he does move, he lurches, only to stop as if possessed by some new insight. His behavior drives me mad with anticipation.

What did he mean about not bothering with Hardgrave in the window, and why search here when the oil is over there? I've been over every square inch of this slope, there are no seeps here. The oil is on Hardgrave land. That's been the whole goddamn problem to start with.

My pipe is burned out. I suck and the cherry is dead. I pat my pockets, remember my new knife at the jeweler for engraving, and break a sprig of birch to scrape the bowl.

••

Barely visible, Whelpley steps from a black shale outcrop and kneels at the crick. He stands where as a boy I watched bubbles percolate out of the streambed like bubbles at the bottom of a water pan, about to boil.

I light my pipe. "Come on, dammit." I pull my pocket watch from my vest. The ride to Pittsburgh will be long and the almanac calls for rain. "That's air coming out the ground, not oil."

Tobacco smoke eases my ire and I walk back to the barn. Inside Hawkins Bonter is bent over the engine of my new vehicle.

"Problem already?"

"Engine burns oil, but it didn't when I drove it back from New York. I'll need to break it down."

"What makes an engine burn oil?"

"Uh—oil. It mixes in the firing chamber. Just a leak, is all. Probly a piston ring. I'll handle it."

"Have the Saxon ready to go to Pittsburgh in one hour. Less is better. We might stay overnight but I'm doubtful."

"The car's ready now."

Bonter looks away, nods toward the open barn door, and the house beyond.

Todd Whelpley strides toward us.

"Looks like he found what he was looking."

"Why don't you get the bag I left at the door? We might leave sooner than later."

Bonter glances at Whelpley and back to me. He wipes his hands on a rag. Leans against the fender. "You got a minute, before he gets over here? I want to mention something, might bear on how you handle your business."

I study Bonter, the slope of his shoulders, the antagonizing looseness to his bearing that suggests he considers himself initiated.

●●

I turn toward Whelpley, extend my arm and lead him away from the straight-line path Bonter will take to the house. Whelpley angles to meet me, more gangling with each stride.

Bonter calls, "Maybe we'll have the chance to talk about a couple things on the drive."

I nod at Whelpley.

"We'll sink a hole right over there, best spot." Whelpley points toward the road, and the cornfield on the other side. "You got your capital where you can get your hands on it? I'll need to build a crew 'fore I build a derrick, and it'll take eight thousand just to get everything I need in one spot. Right over there. So pull your money out the bank and we'll come up with terms. Put it on paper if you want—Sprague knew my word was good but I suppose you're not Sprague. Whichever way don't matter; neither men nor material move on a promissory note—not when you're bucking Rockefeller's crew. I'll have to scarf equipment all over the state, and it'll take money in my hand to do it."

"Two things, Whelpley. It wasn't a week back you said I was a fool. Now you want to build my drill."

"I see a man every week in town, convinced he's about to get rich. But you was right; you got the bug and the oil. That's what you need."

"What about Sprague and his men destroying me?"

"That hasn't changed. They get wind—and you can't buy what you need for a derrick without them getting wind—they're liable to make a bid on your land. You don't sell, they'll try and stop your suppliers from selling you bits and belts. You beat them there, they might sabotage the derrick, or get the railroads to rob you, or if you're thinking pipeline, they'll buy all the land between you and Oil City, where you'd most likely send it. Make no mistake, these men are in the money business, not the friend business."

"Uh-huh. Well my friends are equally few."

••

"So what else? You said two things?"

"You said you'd put a derrick across the road, but the oil's over there." I nod toward Hardgrave's woods.

"No," Whelpley pointed to his feet. "You're standing on it. This whole dome's got oil under it, and the surest hole is right down the middle. Seepage shows up here and there in rock fissures, and that's where a body'd expect. From the slopes I'd say we put a well right where we stand, we hit gas. We go across the road a hundred yards and we'd likely hit oil. You won't know 'til you drill, but you damn sure won't do better halfway down the slope."

"The seepage is over there," I say. Turning, I see Hawkins Bonter close enough to hear what I hear.

"Yeah," Whelpley said. "You said that."

"What about—what about mineral rights?" My mind races. My stomach rolls. "What about pulling his oil from a derrick over here?"

"The oil's under your feet. Here, there. The other side of the road, or that farmhouse with the rifleman. Drilling's about the law of capture. Don't matter where it's under ground—the man who pulls it out owns it."

"You mean we can drill across the road as easy as down at the seep?"

"Easier. And more likely to hit oil."

I think of Henry's frightened eyes—

"Anywhere?" I say.

"I'll have equipment showing up in two weeks, you give me the cash to make it happen."

I shake my head but the ghost of Henry won't leave it.


The afternoon sun makes travel a speedy interlude, a few hours of needed repose from business. I ride in silence.

••

My thoughts drift. Whelpley said to drill on my land. On the dome. I feel now as I did when Whelpley uttered the words—numbness replete. I see Henry, feel my son under my fingertips, the softness of his wrists and arms, his shoulder dislocating like a roasted turkey leg. Henry's eyes—inflamed—yet trusting. Only when his body sagged did his gaze harden. Day after day I said. "We must find Henry," and Eddie looked at my hands until I inspected them for blood. The dog that stripped Henry's face—I couldn't have predicted the luck of it—

"Wanted to mention something, see if you was amenable," Hawkins Bonter says.

"I am not."

"Uh, it's about Leicester."

I shift in my seat, turn partly sideways. "Speed up. I don't want to be driving all goddamn day."

Bonter accelerates. He pulls a billfold from his pocket and passes it to me. "That's Leicester's."

"If I recall, I told you not to rob him, and leave no trace except holes in his chest."

"There's no problem; I can make that fold disappear. I just wanted to show it to you."

I am silent.

"You don't want to know why? I got to thinking, a man does the bidding of another, working in a field, labor, turning wrenches, that's a damnsight different than shooting people. That's a liability, and no matter the reward, a big ass liability."

I straighten in my seat and stare ahead, still seeing Henry, still thinking about the oil derrick. I always saw it on Hardgrave land. For years I saw it on Hardgrave land.

"I see what you're doing, Mister McClellan, and it's tycoon genius. You're going to be bigger than Rockefeller and Carnegie and a battalion of those gilded sons a bitches. You got the nerve.

••

Now, when I break all the rules of God and man, I need to know I'm your ace, that you'll never hang me out. That's why I went the extra mile."

I press my fist to my temple. "Is this about Eddie? Is that it?"

Bonter places the billfold between his knees. One hand on the wheel, with the other he opens the billfold and withdraws a folded paper. "This is about your new man, Whelpley."

Bonter hands the paper to me.

I inspect the handwritten document, which appears to be the text of a telegram Leicester was preparing, perhaps for an attendant to deliver to the Western Union man.

Six thousand in JM's possession. Anxious for its return.

Or had already sent.

"What I heard of it, Whelpley sounded damn eager to start buying equipment."

"Doesn't say 'Whelpley'. Doesn't say anybody."

"Well, all I know is somebody was in cahoots, and it don't make sense Leicester'd send a telegram to Stokes, two hundred feet away."

••

# Chapter Twenty-Seven

Rainwater has dribbled from the corruptly sealed passenger window the last two hours. An hour from home we drove into storm, and the afternoon has been gloomy, since. I shift closer to Bonter, who now considers me in his debt, and will expect repayment if only in loyalty.

The easiest man to swindle is the one who swindles himself. I have pondered Whelpley's character and enthusiasm. Grappled with how he—whom I located randomly—and Leicester might have been connected.

If Leicester's note was an unsent telegram, it was not to Whelpley. Regardless, I saw the oil—thought about it for years, and when the mechanism for securing title became apparent, I was intrepid. The foundation is laid.

I study the back seat. Water from the window, failing to soak my arm, spatters to the seat.

"I'll ride in the back with Mame Gainer on our return. See about drying that rain, and do something about the window."

Bonter nods. He keeps his gaze on the road. Normally compelled to drive with arrogant speed, he now appears overwhelmed with caution.

"You'll be making a right turn. Slow—here."

Bonter swerves.

"You can't see it from here, but down by that rail yard, a house'll have a line of men out front."

"A line of men in the afternoon, in a squall?"

"That's why I'm stealing the madam."

On the right, the rail yard is a center of bustle, scattered hoboes, the shock of steel on steel and sometimes bone. Hawkins Bonter slows and even through rain sizzling on glass and roof, the clash of coupling railcars and the shouts of yard bulls reaches us.

Men of the railway brotherhood stand dripping outside Mame Gainer's brothel.

"Drive on by, and stop under that red maple."

Bonter turns into the space.

"What's with the dick slapping his baton in his hand?"

"He knows this vehicle. I set him straight last time. Don't go anywhere. Get that seat dry and fix the window."

I gather my collar about my neck and exit. Heat spreads from the base of my spine up my back and through my limbs. I am here to take home a woman.

The copper approaches, still thumping his palm with his club. He stops at ten paces.

I stride past. Climb the steps in two bounds and rap the door.

It opens. I recognize the woman in the aperture—she brought coffee.

"I'm Jonah McClellan." I step into the gap.

The woman blocks my path. "Mame will see you shortly. She is not yet available." She lifts a mug and saucer from a table beside

••

the door and offers it. "Mame thought you would be happier in the comfort of your vehicle than inside. Here. Please."

I focus on the sounds around me, the pressure in my head. The sense that all eyes see my embarrassment. I take the mug, glimpse beyond the woman for Mame. The woman presses door to post and I block it with my foot. "Coffee for my driver?"

The woman glances toward the side office, backs an inch, then faces me. "Please, sir, if it isn't an inconvenience—will you wait on the porch?"

"Never mind." I pass the mug and saucer back to her, about-face, and return to the Saxon.

I wait a moment at the car door while rain trickles over the glass, then turn and step to the dick.

I offer my hand with a single eagle coin between my fingers. "You and I got off to a rough start and I won't fault you." He takes the gold piece. I place my arm behind as if to shepherd him, and turn him, thusly blocking our conversation from the men in line. "Tell me. A man in your post is privy to rumor. What have you heard about a change in management at this establishment?"

He looks up at my face, drags fingernails across chin stubble and glances back toward the house. "I know the owner and the first I heard of change is you."

"That's fine."

I return to the Saxon and climb inside. There are no rumors about, and to prevent them, Mame keeps me waiting. An acceptable caution—and by the time the dick has worried the men in line, Mame will be itinerant.

Those specters are amazing, though. To have seen it, a week in advance... I'll honor my side of the bargain and take Mame to the tree—though I would prefer to take another. Doubtful the spooks would know. Or care. And if by some error I held Mame in reserve,

**

to provide only if they demand, what's the harm? I need her in shape to run my houses.

"She not in?" Bonter says.

"Not yet."

"Look at that." Bonter points to the back of the house, where a young boy escapes the yard between broken boards in a white fence. "What do you suppose got him flapping elbows? Stole his first brassiere?"

I think of the industriousness of boys of low circumstances.

"That boy's a courier."

I glance backward. Bonter has wiped down the seat but new rain spatters even as we sit motionless.

Bonter sits with a rag on his lap. "I'll have to jam this in after you close the door. It don't mate flush."

"Do it now, and we'll enter from the other side."

Bonter smiles flat. Exits into rain.

I'll take Gainer back to Walnut tonight, and retire for the evening.

Tell the tree I'll bring a girl tomorrow.

Beholden to a tree.

I'll send Hawkins to fetch Whelpley, not saying a word of the intercepted note from Thurston. We'll meet and if I leave feeling all is well, maybe I won't take Mame to the specters at all. Maybe I'll burn that damn tree and be done with it.

"Look," Bonter says. "A gentleman not waiting in line."

A man walks alongside the men on the sidewalk. He wears a top hat and a black overcoat that flaps, exposing black pants and black shoes. His beard is white.

The same boy as before crawls through the fence hole, making his return.

I ponder the trap being set within.

••

Did the specters show me images they were certain I'd misapprehend? Or have they been fair, and this series of events bears an honest explanation?

The man in black is helped inside.

I wipe my palms on my pants. The hair on the back of my neck begins to rise. I think of how events have unfolded, the surprise telegram from Mame; Thurston Leicester's too-easy agreement and coughing up the specie. Whelpley's sudden desire to braze his fate to the oil seep on Hardgrave's front wood. Surprises all, and without them I would not be here this moment, sitting in hot anticipation.

While a trap is set.

It smacks of Bonnie and Brooks, though planned by a far more devious mind. A woman's mind.

I look rearward through the small window, study trees distorted by bulbs of water on glass into the elbows and knees of hiding men. I view the men in line, and think I spot a club or a rifle barrel.

"In a minute I'll be summoned," I say. Sweat bulbs at my brow. "I want you prepared. Keep an eye behind you, and keep the window down so you can hear."

The front door opens. The coffee woman waves. I study the shadows behind her in each curtained window. I wait until the tightness in the back of my neck relaxes, and then exit the Saxon.

I tramp through sodden grass to the stone walk. Unseen behind walls and windows waits Mame Gainer. After rejecting me she was overwhelmed by her better judgment. That must be the story. The rest of this apparent setup is the manifestation of nerves. A smoke will serve as tonic.

Standing on the porch I open my coat and extract pipe and tobacco. The coffee girl in the open door aperture studies me. She shivers, wearing naught but a sheer gown and slippers. I pack my bowl and hunch from the breeze to light it. She steps aside and

••

extends her arm. I look inside. The office door is open but the angle prevents view of its occupants.

"Mame is waiting," the girl says.

"As was I."

I enter, look right to an empty parlor and down the hall, then up the staircase. The foyer is empty of men and women. A whorehouse without sound...

"In the office." The woman glides opposite the entrance and again gestures me forward.

I peer inside.

Mame Gainer stands from an oaken desk chair. Her gown—she is stunning. Cleavage like a basket of grapefruit, hips like the girders of an iron bridge—

The man in black shuffles his feet.

I lurch rightward, away. Mame steps between us and extends both arms. Her face glows with warmth and her charms gleam up at me, and that damned confoundedness strikes me again, like sniffing some aphrodisiac flower or gulping a slug of moonshine. But the man in black—

I take Mame's hand. Master my thoughts.

"Jonah," Mame says.

"Mame."

"Never mind the judge," Mame says. "I hope I didn't trouble you, but appearances and proprieties, I'm sure you understand."

I nod; clear my throat. "Nice day to wait outside."

"We've only a few things to address. Your offer was so intriguing I couldn't put it away but it demanded I reconsider. You said I should control your houses and stand to inherit?"

I look at the judge. I understand.

"That was and still is the offer. I presume Judge... Judge?"

"Judge Whitmore Jackson," Mame says.

The judge nods slightly.

••

"Yes, I presume Judge Jackson has documents that will make it official?"

"And upon receiving your signature he is prepared to marry us."

I feel my chest swell, my mind. "Married in a cathouse." I say. Her smile, her eyes... Mame is intoxicating. "The documents?"

"The documents—" Judge Jackson swings his arm to the desktop. Beside him are two stacks of paper, each arranged in triplicate.

Mame leads by my hand. Humidity adds an animal pungency to the room's sweetness. How the judge maintains composure is beyond me. I stoop to the documents.

"You'll need to sign here," Mame says. "And the judge will witness it here."

I glance over the words, then as composure settles through me, read them again, and after the first sentence can't remember its beginning. Grapefruits. Girders. I lift the document and step back from the desk. Mame's hand falls away from my arm and I hold the document under the gray window light. "Stuffy in here," I say. I read the document the way a starving man ingests meat, and am satisfied with the documents' forthrightness. The papers leave Mame Gainer exclusive owner of the properties—each listed by address—and any business enterprises that may be located thereupon.

I sign the document.

"All three," the judge says.

I sign each and my son Murray is out. I'll have some shenanigans in store to bring in young Angus anyway. And I am an oilman now. I will leave the hens to the house.

The next stack is a marriage document, a summary making it legal, admitting forthwith and forever asunder and whatnot, and I affix my signature thrice.

"Is there a ceremony?" I say.

"If you want one. Otherwise, you may kiss your bride."

"Mame? You need any special words?"

"Just what's on those papers. Come here, darling."

I step to her summons. She embraces me and tosses back her head and I oblige with a kiss. I close my eyes and see the girl Dorothy under the tree, a quivering pool of ransacked flesh, and her face becomes Mame Gainer's—and I am jealous and mad.

But I want what that tree can tell me.

I'll honor my word to the specters; I'll take her to the tree. But not the first night. And not if I can substitute another. In any event, not until I get new papers signed in Walnut, bringing Angus into the line.

**❊❊**

# Chapter Twenty-Eight

Elizabeth and Hannah chased fireflies in the orchard, on the side hill visible from where Grace stood lake edge, at the inlet corner of the isthmus of Devil's Elbow.

Sharp autumn grass pricked Grace's bare feet. The sun floated above the horizon, sinking. Already the trees cast bold shadows across the water. Behind her, hidden in the up-sloping forest, Jonah McClellan had located a still. Between her position and the Hardgrave home was the rot-hollowed walnut tree, and all around her was stillness. Bass jumped at insects and occasional birds called to one another in their secret code. The water was flat and soon the sun would disappear.

She placed a rifle on the bank, pointed toward the wooded slope that led, two hundred yards removed, to Jonah McClellan's house.

Grace lifted her dress over her head, removed camisole and knickers. She picked up a rag from the ground, unfolded a bar of soap, and stepped into the chilly water. Mud oozed at her toes, but the shock began to make her feel clean.

She'd come to Walnut to face her past and re-create herself. To change her core so she would make better decisions for her girls and herself. On arrival, she realized part of demonstrating the values she chose relied on claiming something real: property, farm, livestock. A home—a place where morals are upheld, where rules associate with physical space, so when people drove by, they would say, "those are good people." Or, "those people are bad." The home tethers behavior to location, and if it is upright, being there is a comfort.

And if it is wicked, it spoils all who remain under its influence.

The Hardgrave homestead, from her earliest memory, was a place of warmth and safety. But with Uncle Elmer it became the dark, and with Jonah McClellan, something altogether worse: a prison.

Now Hal, Rose and Angus clanged toward Iowa in a wagon full of dishes.

The farm was hers to claim.

She looked to the side hill by the water, a hundred yards distant, where Hannah and Elizabeth chased lightning bugs under apple and pear trees loaded with ripening fruit. This would be a home for them, like it was for her, before Uncle Elmer.

Hal had left a rifle—stationed now at lake edge—and all the provisions Rose couldn't fit onto their wagon. He'd left almost everything he owned, and to Grace it seemed Hal was abandoning his life of cowardice to find his courage somewhere else. She wondered how that worked, how Hal would find his courage where he'd never been to lose it.

The water rippled at her knees and goose pimples rose on her legs and arms.

Grace balled the cloth rag in one hand, clasped soap in the other, and dove into the lake. In a moment the water seemed warmer. Electric.

••

As a child she swam naked in this water and emerged to find Jonah McClellan watching her. Through her dawning nubile awareness she understood he was transfixed by her, as he towered greedily among the trees beyond the walnut.

Her first thought was fear—but Jonah only watched.

Week after week, all summer long, he stood and she obliged. Her power grew each time, until she believed she held command over Jonah, which she could wield by manipulating when she bathed, or what flesh she exposed.

Week after week, summer after summer, until she was a woman, and one day found Jonah standing at water's edge.

Remembering now, she swam underwater, holding her breath until the pressure forced her lungs to crave air. Again she felt Jonah's powerful arms, heard cries that disappeared into silent trees. She relived his taking her and after the whole story unfolded she gasped to the surface and saw the Hardgrave house on the knoll above the lake, and knew the fight ahead would determine her fate. She would never run again.

After Hal climbed to the wagon, barely pretending difficulty with his back, and Rose clambered aboard on her fourth attempt, and Angus leaped to the back, crawled on top of a lashed chair— Grace had prepared a meal for Hannah and Elizabeth, then wandered the land.

She'd seen Jonah McClellan and another man pass before the fields and disappear into the woods where Ian was shot. With pistol in pocket, she'd visited Hawkins Bonter, oil on his hands, at McClellan's barn.

Bonter related Jonah's nuptial plans. He'd secured a wife in Pittsburgh and the day before, Bonter had seen the ring he'd soon claim her with. Jonah was on edge about it, wanted it to go smooth. He had another piece of business that didn't go right, and anxious over the marriage, lashed out at the jeweler.

••

"He had other business. Was there to pick up a pocket knife, but the jeweler botched the engraving. How in sam hell you botch J.A.M—"

Jonah had plunged the shiny new pocket knife into the jeweler's countertop with such force he snapped the blade.

In hip-deep water Grace ground the soap into the rag and crushed the rag to her skin. She rubbed her elbows, and dipped below the surface to scrub her ankles and legs; she scraped her flesh clean; she soaped the rag again and pressed it to her hips, and the line of bone that circled her lower torso, her stomach, her breast. She dipped and under water, ground the rough cloth to her face and neck. She stood and scrubbed her arms, her fingers.

Five months after Jonah took her, she panicked. Her belly was growing round and though her parents were dead—her father from cancer and her mother, it was politely said, from grief—her older brother and his new wife would surely spot the growth and recognize it. And since home at that point was a location with rules associated—rules she had broken—she went to Jonah McClellan. That very day he transported her to a cathouse in Clarion until she gave birth.

Grace emerged from the water, looked to her girls at the crest of the orchard hill, and she splashed each foot, one by one, to remove the mud. She stood in the grass, pure as she would ever be, and turned.

Under the walnut stood Jonah McClellan, transfixed.


Grace donned her boots. Jonah watched her dress, but hadn't moved from under the walnut tree. From her pocket she withdrew the knife she'd found in the field. Kneeling, she opened it and submerged only the blade in lake water, and rubbed the dried blood free with her fingernail.

••

Jonah stepped toward her, only ten feet away. His hand rested on his hip sidearm. She looked up and his face belied neither surprise nor expectation. He appeared tired, but of such immense strength his tiredness would not matter. She tilted the knife blade into the last evening sunrays and read the engraving.

"Your hair's wet," he said.

Grace lifted the rifle, stepped toward him a pace and stopped. "You must have suffered, losing Henry alone."

Jonah shifted toward the walnut.

"Tell me about Henry," Grace said. She stepped closer to Jonah.

"He was a good boy, I suppose. You should have stuck around. Maybe got to know him."

"I wish I had. But it was you I couldn't bear to be near."

"How things change." Jonah walked sideways now, inviting her along. They passed under the walnut canopy.

"A lot has happened, Jonah. But I want you to know that you and I are on the same side."

"That so?" Jonah stopped beside the trunk.

"That's right. Who ever killed Henry is going to die."

Jonah smiled. "You know I got married today. So we can't be on the same side too much." Jonah extracted his pipe and examined the bowl. He blew in it, and stooped to the ground and lifted a twig. He snapped the end in a manner to create a long point, and scraped the tobacco bowl.

Grace pitched the open knife to him. "This might do a better job." Before Jonah could react, the knife bounced from his chest.

"You recognize it, I'm sure."

Bending at his knees, Jonah retrieved the knife.

"You know I've had that knife for days," Grace said, "but it wasn't until a few hours ago I realized what I'd been missing."

"I'll humor you." He folded the knife and slipped it into his pocket, then opened his tobacco pouch.

●●

312 | SOMETIMES BONE

"I found the knife next to where you put Henry, all straight, arms crossed at his belly, ready for a coffin."

Jonah packed tobacco into his pipe and lit it. He leaned backward to the tree, so tall his head was a foot and a half above the rotted hollow.

"It was the burn marks I couldn't figure," Grace said. "Then I remembered the day you planted Henry in me, after you held that very knife to my neck—"

"Different knife. Lost it years ago."

"After you held a knife to my throat and had your way, you used it to clean your pipe. Now you don't have a knife, and the one I just gave you has carbon all up inside."

Jonah left his pipe in his mouth and crossed his arms. He inhaled smoke.

"And of course, your initials are engraved on the blade."

"Henry was a runt."

"You wanted everyone to think it was Hal, so you could steal this land. This... tree."

"The tree? I don't give a fuck about a tree."

"You killed Henry."

Jonah shrugged.

Something clicked behind Jonah. His eyebrows twitched. He placed his open hand to the tree and furrowed his brow. Opened his mouth.

A blast shook the walnut. Orange flashed from within the rotted hollow. Jonah's face was gone and his body was a monolith; brain and bone stung Grace's face and pattered the leaves above. Blood fountained from Jonah's neck.

Grace watched a frozen eternity before the headless body crumpled. She stepped aside to clear its path.

Angus Hardgrave peered from the hollow of the walnut on Devil's Elbow. He slapped his arm. "Fucker."

••

Grace brought her sleeve against her face. She blinked. The grit in her eye was Jonah. She felt calm, as if all the evil she had ever fled or faced was gone. She looked at Jonah's crumpled form, shards of skull like so many pieces of shattered plate.

All that remained for her was to live. To move forward. To protect her girls.

Angus climbed out of the tree. "You mad at me?"

"Where is your father?"

"Probly half to Clarion by now."

"He know you're here?"

"Saw me slip off. Didn't say a word."

"And Rose?"

"She knows by now."

Grace looked at Jonah: a mass of headless flesh; a slick of pooling black blood. Then she looked at the walnut tree, from trunk to canopy, where twilight sky broke through black leaves.

"Angus, I want you to run to the house and come back here with a saw, an axe, and a lantern."

Angus ran.

Grace thought of how Jonah's demeanor had eased upon passing within the sphere of the walnut. How suddenly his face had changed when he placed his hand on the tree bark.

She thought of how Angus didn't carry the Hardgrave form in face or temper; how Rose was once smitten with her neighbor.

She thought about the walnut tree, the stories. And how Angus climbed out after killing a man.

Rebirthed.

She thought about that.

## THE END ...

••

# What's next in the Hardgrave saga?

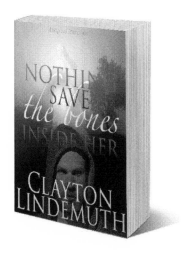

**"It's hard to turn the other cheek with a rifle barrel in your mouth."**

*In 1957 rural Pennsylvania, Angus Hardgrave works an oil rig, fights dogs, distills Walnut Whiskey... and murders wives, friends, anybody. The presence in the walnut tree on a spur called Devil's Elbow instructs Angus what to do, and following the visions has led Angus to a simple country bounty...*

*But Angus wants more.*

*Alone when her father dies, eighteen-year-old Emeline Margulies believes she hears the voice of God tell her to escape the clutches of a violent Korean War vet by marrying Angus Hardgrave—a man rumored to have pitiable luck with wives.*

*She finds herself trapped between a stalking rapist and a serial killer. As each decision leads her closer to destruction, Emeline must choose between following the faith that got her into trouble... Or the moxie, resolve, and evil within that promise to get her out.*

*Praise for Nothing Save the Bones inside Her from readers like You*

★★★★★     *This may very well be the perfect novel for me. It has everything I love about fiction. Within the first couple pages I was instantly transported into a world I will never inhabit, and among people I may never meet. The narrative is rhythmic. Lindemuth never slips you any ten-penny words, but your mind is still blown. The pacing, the suspense, the language... This will do you solid.*

★★★★★     *I could not put the book down until I finished it. I enjoy nothing more than a good page turner. the story was dark yet compelling and it had a satisfying conclusion. I kept picturing it as an award winning movie and wondering who would play the parts of these characters.*

★★★★★     *This is not the genra I typically read. It was recommended to me and once I started I didn't put it down until I couldn't keep my eyes open, then I couldn't wait to finish it the next day. Such a good book that I downloaded another Clayton Lindemuth book to read next. This is a well written and must read suspense.*

••

# ABOUT THE AUTHOR

Clayton Lindemuth writes noir because that's where he lives. He runs ultra-marathons. Reads economics. Eternally misses Arizona. Clayton is the author of TREAD, Solomon Bull, Cold Quiet Country, Nothing Save the Bones Inside Her, My Brother's Destroyer, and other volumes not yet released. He lives in Missouri with his wife Julie and his puppydog Faith, also known as "Princess Wigglebums" and "Stinky Princess."

Made in the USA
Coppell, TX
24 October 2019